THE ONCE AND FUTURE
PRESIDENTS

ISBN: **1978090730**

ISBN-13: **978-1978090736**

Library of Congress Control Number: **2017916403**

CreateSpace Independent Publishing Platform: **North Charleston, SC**

For Frisco, Natalie, Jack, and Gemma

PROLOGUE

I have to kill George Washington.

Any movement will do it.

My feet are pushed hard against the steeply angled rooftop; my fingertips crammed into small cracks between the stones. It's barely enough to hold me for these last few moments. I just have to let go and George Washington—the fifty-seventh president of the United Zones of America, dies.

My heart—*his* heart, is beating hard; it doesn't want to stop. Not here. Not like this.

The skyline of the Washington Metrozone stretches out far below, its glittering lights like a sparkling sea taunting me to jump. I can feel the cold night-wind blowing hard against my face, carrying faint sounds; whispers from the city far below, and something else— a high-pitched hum from the small dark cloud gathering in the sky above me.

One by one, tiny black spheres start to drop out of the cloud, circling the top of the monument until they find me; security drones, like dozens of shiny eyeballs. I guess the entire nation will get to watch their brand-new president fall to his death, live-on-air.

I don't want this. I want to live. I'm sixteen years old and there's so much I haven't done. The thing is, I don't have a choice. This is the only way to stop the endless cycle of lies and suffering; the only way to stop Secretary Cain. George Washington ends here, tonight. He has to. Which means...*I have to*.

I'm shaking so much I slip closer to the edge. One hand loses its grip. One foot kicks in thin air. There are voices coming from the window above. Seconds now.

For a brief moment I wonder if I have the courage to do this. But then something else takes over—something deeper. I think of her. I picture her in front of me; smiling, the wind stirring her hair, her bright eyes focused on mine. I hear her soft voice in my head pushing out the fear.

It'll be OK.

Slowly, carefully I lift up my free hand, middle-finger raised, and facing the dark cloud of drones, I give my best screw-you smile.

My fingers silently let go. I lift the soles of my shoes off the stone beneath me, and that easily, I fall.

Part 1
The Candidates

Chapter 1

Six Months Earlier

If he'd known he would never see his home again, Arthur Ryan might have looked back one last time.

But as the school bus pulled away, he didn't give the crumbling old farmhouse a second glance. As usual, he was daydreaming. His eyes fixed on the skyline of the Metrozone that seemed to float in the hazy distance, rising above the heat of the desolate fields of the Outside.

As he settled into his favorite seat at the back of the bus, Arthur pushed the sweat out of his eyes. He was imagining all those rich Zoner kids, walking to school from their city apartments. Maybe they were stopping off for an ice-cold drink right now at one of the cafés in the shady tree-lined streets. Or perhaps they were taking a morning swim in their private swimming pools.

He pulled out his notebook and started doodling to pass the time, trying to hold his hand steady as the old bus rattled along the potholed road. Before long, the other seats began filling up with the usual stragglers.

Even though Arthur despised the way the Zoners treated the Outsiders at school, sometimes he couldn't blame them. He had to admit they were a pretty rough-looking bunch. Sunburned, dust covered, ungroomed, and wearing government-issue clothes. There were no luxuries like hairdressers and clothes stores out here. Arthur knew he looked like an Outsider. His straggly, sun-streaked brown hair was down to his shoulders and constantly fell in front of his face. His blue-gray eyes were hidden behind his despised thick-framed glasses. They did nothing for his vision, but he had learned, the hard way, to keep them on. Otherwise Uncle would be sent for to straighten him out. Something Arthur avoided at all costs.

He was always hungry and painfully thin. His foster parents rationed out small controlled portions of whatever they were eating, which were not nearly enough for a teenage boy. By bedtime, his stomach would be grumbling, and he suspected that his grades were bad because he spent his time in class dreaming about food. The only thing that he had going for him was height. He had sprouted up a few years before and hadn't stopped until he had even overtaken some of the well-fed, plump Zoner jocks.

As the bus approached the Metrozone, the red fields of dust gave way to the crumbling buildings of the Transition. Rusted shells of cars, all useless now, littered the streets. Occasional figures, hurried by—Outsiders foraging for supplies, bandannas sheltering their faces from the heat and dust.

At the last stop before the wall, Arthur snapped out of his thoughts. He pushed his notebook aside and sat up, watching the door intently. The girl who got on was every bit an Outsider too. She was above-average height and lanky with a mass of frizzy dark-brown hair. Although she was average looking, she moved with a grace and self-possession that could turn heads. Arthur's heart started beating so hard he was sure people could hear it. Ever since she had moved

4

here six months ago, she had become the best part of Arthur's day—of his world. She moved down the bus and swung easily into the seat next to him.

"I have something you want." She grinned cheekily at him, then reached into her dusty jacket and pulled out a muffin.

"Oh yes! Bay, you are the best."

"Can't argue with that."

He ducked below the seat in front and wolfed the muffin down. Bay watched him, smiling. Her eyes were soft blue today, not the intense green they sometimes turned when she was mad about something. She pulled an old notebook out of her bag. They sat quietly for a few minutes, passing their notebooks back and forth, scribbling secret notes, and drawing little sketches for each other. This was their morning routine and something that Arthur looked forward to more than anything else in the day.

He used to keep all the notes in a precious pile under his bed at the farm, but then Uncle found them during one of his random room searches. Uncle wanted to know who was writing the notes, but Arthur didn't tell him about Bay. He paid for it with a beating that put him in bed for a week. Since then, he had been careful to destroy the notes.

The bus was approaching the West Gate. As the shadow of the wall fell across them, the automated virtual television, or VT, sprung to life. An immaculately dressed woman appeared at the front of the bus, flickering occasionally. Arthur recognized her instantly. Hope Juvenal, the familiar host of *The Democracy Games*, the nightly reality VT show that had transfixed the nation. Arthur's foster parents didn't have a VT, but he had picked up bits and pieces of the latest *Democracy Games* gossip from the obsessed kids at school.

"This is Hope Juvenal, reporting live from Camp David."

The VT camera zoomed into close-up. Hope's overly made-up

face loomed eerily over the aisle.

"Today, in a dramatic turn of events, the first presidential primary has turned deadly. An incident during filming has left three people dead and several more injured. No news yet on the identities of the dead, but it is known that two of the candidates were in the building..."

Holograms of two handsome young men appeared where Hope had been standing seconds before. The tallest had reddish-brown hair and an athletic build. He had a confident, slightly jockish look about him and carried himself with an authority that made him look older than he was. The other was just slightly shorter with blond hair and a boyish expression. He had a wolfish grin that gave him an irresistible mix of charming and naughty. Their names floated in the air around them, but Arthur didn't need to read them to know who they were. They were two of the most famous people in the entire UZA.

George Washington and John F. Kennedy.

More than a decade before Arthur was born, at the dark time of the raising of the walls, scientists successfully developed the technology to clone almost anyone from as little as a sliver of bone. Suddenly, the possibility of bringing back people who had been long dead became a reality, and the Resurrection Innovation Program, or RIP, was born. The divided nation needed leadership, and it needed hope. The entire country soon watched, transfixed, as a new Abraham Lincoln was "born."

Since then, the RIP had continued the resurrections. Each year, two new "heroes" were created. They were raised to be the leaders; every detail of their lives was televised, analyzed, and talked over, from their first tooth coming in to their first kiss. As they came of age, they were expected to do their duty and run for president of the United Zones of America, competing in dangerous and challenging primaries designed to test their presidential worth. Their one chance to prove themselves before the nation they were born to save.

All of this was screened nightly in *The Democracy Games*.

The spinning holograms were now floating above a three-dimensional map of Camp David. Hope Juvenal spoke excitedly. "There are unconfirmed reports of an explosion…"

Arthur looked away. He wasn't interested in politics.

He turned to Bay, but she was staring intently at the news report. She looked a little paler than moments before, and he could swear she was holding her breath. Arthur was surprised. In the six months he had known her, Bay had never shown much interest in the news. He wondered if she had a crush on one of the candidates and felt a small flash of jealousy. He shot a nasty look at the two handsome holograms.

The bus had moved into the gate and was being screened by several security drones. Blue walls of light scanned up and down the bus. Arthur looked out at the security police milling around the gate. There seemed to be more than usual. They always looked faintly sinister to him, probably because of their anonymous black military-style uniforms and faceless dust masks. Though it could also have had something to do with the arsenal of weapons they each had strapped to them. Not taking any chances with those pesky Outsiders.

Arthur looked up at the towering wall that loomed over them. The walls had been around since long before Arthur was born, raised at a desperate time in the nation's past. The country's resources had dwindled to almost nothing, and starvation and violent crime threatened the future of the already desperate nation. On the brink of a civil rebellion, the government had built fifty Metrozones across the country, giant urban areas to protect the good citizens of the newly formed United Zones of America. The rest of the country, the Outside, had been left to fall into ruin.

Despite what the walls represented, Arthur was always impressed by the sheer scale and often wondered if the other Metrozone walls were as imposing. Maybe one day he would see them. But even as the thought crossed his mind, he pushed it out of his head. Outsiders like him didn't get to travel.

The bus pulled forward and turned into the school entry tunnel. The news report had finished, and Bay was now looking outside the bus with the same look of intensity. She was looking at the elaborate graffiti that covered the tunnel walls. To Arthur, it was the usual artful mix of spray-painted tags and occasional pro-rebel messages. Giant red As would always appear overnight, a subversive nod to the leader of the rebel gangs, known only as Abel. By the ride home from school, the As would be gone, painted over daily by the security police. Bay always studied the graffiti silently on the way in, and he'd learned not to interrupt. But today she seemed different, agitated. Something was wrong.

"Is everything—"

She shot him a look that stopped him from finishing his sentence.

The bus approached the school's underground entry and pulled up in front of Westgate High School. Arthur hurriedly started digging around for his things and throwing them in his backpack.

Suddenly he was surprised to feel Bay's hand on his. He looked at her and saw a look in her eyes he hadn't seen before. Maybe fear? She moved close to him, her wild hair brushed his cheek, and for a second he actually hoped she was going to kiss him. His heart jumped. But instead, she whispered urgently.

"Arthur, no matter what happens now. Remember who you are."

"Bay, wha…?"

He felt something pushed into his hand, and then she pulled

back. For just a second, her eyes locked on his, now very green and definitely frightened. Then she grabbed her things and was gone. Arthur looked in his hand. It was a snapped-off piece from the emblem at the front of an old car. Three small stars inside part of an oval. Outsiders collected them from the wrecked vehicles dumped all over the Outside like secret trophies.

His heart was beating hard. Something was wrong. Was Bay in some kind of trouble?

He slipped the emblem into his pocket and hurried off the bus after her.

He saw the back of her head disappear in the crowd of kids in front of them. Arthur sprinted forward to follow, but the security police were in particularly aggressive form this morning, and he felt a sharp sting on the back of his neck from one of their disciplinary lasers.

"Walk," a voice warned him over the speakers.

There were two school entrances, one for Outsiders and one for Zoners. Arthur joined the slow line by the Outsider entrance. Outsiders had additional screening, including daily blood scans and rigorous pat downs, so there was always a long wait. He glanced enviously at the clean, relaxed Zoners strolling right in, wishing he could join them and catch up with Bay.

When he finally got inside, Arthur sprinted to the lockers, but Bay had already left. He quickly scrawled "OK?" on a piece of paper and slipped it through her locker vent. She would know it was from him. He felt faintly nauseous as he headed to class. He had never seen her like this. She was usually so relaxed and easygoing. Something must be really wrong.

About ten minutes into the class, a shrill alarm bell rang out. Principal Wright's unnaturally cheerful voice sounded out loudly.

"Good morning, Westgaters. This is Principal Wright with an

important message. I am sorry to have to announce that there has been a serious violation of our school community rules. Serious enough to necessitate the attention of the authorities." The principal paused, allowing this last bit of information to sink in. A shocked silence had fallen over the class. Zoners and Outsiders alike looked around at one another, fear written on their faces.

The principal carried on, his bright tone at odds with his ominous message.

"Teachers are to escort their students to the multiuse hall immediately. A punishment will commence in ten minutes."

Kids were instantly crying. There was a feeling of hysteria as they all started looking for friends, hoping for reassurance. Whenever the students were summoned to the multiuse hall for a punishment, the fear was palpable. Someone was about to be called up in front of the whole school and disciplined in a cruel and humiliating way.

Arthur had seen kids pulled up for all the usual antisocial behaviors, like using illegal substances on school property, or graffitiing the tunnel walls. The severity of the punishment depended on the crime and ranged from watching as their belongings were burned to having their heads shaved. But the punishment everyone feared the most was a disappearance. The disappeared kids were never seen at school again, and rumor had it they never returned home. They were just gone for good, as if they had never existed. No one went in knowing for sure who was going to be pulled up. Students racked their consciences, trying to figure out if it might be their turn.

The teachers struggled to maintain order as they directed the terrified students along the corridors toward the multiuse hall. As they approached the doors, the panic finally died down, replaced with a fearful silence. The Zoner kids were kneeling in rows on one side of the vast hall. The Outsiders were being shepherded to the other.

Black-clad security police marched people into place.

Arthur knelt down in a long line of terrified Outsiders and bowed his head to the floor, hands behind his back, in the position they were required to assume. He stared hard at the polished wood floor. There were quiet sobs from kids all around him. He risked looking sideways along his row, keeping his head down. About twenty kids down, he finally saw Bay. Her face was pale, her shoulders shaking almost imperceptibly.

Usually Arthur wasn't too worried. His worst crime was failing tests, something he did regularly thanks to his appalling spelling. This time, however, was different. This time he was truly afraid for Bay. Something was wrong. Was this punishment something to do with her? Had she done something? Why was she so afraid?

A few minutes passed as the last few students were silently lined up and made to kneel. Arthur studied the floor, feeling his heart thumping hard in his chest.

At last Principal Wright's voice broke the tense silence. "Westgaters. I am sorry indeed that circumstances have brought us here. But as you know, violation of our community's rules cannot and will not be tolerated. One of you has failed this school. One of you has failed your fellow students. One of you has failed me." He shook his head and paused dramatically. "Commence."

The doors banged open as five men in black suits, Secret Service badges clipped to their lapels, marched into the hall. Arthur kept his head down and focused hard on the sound of their footsteps. There was no question; they were heading toward the Outsider rows. Arthur could almost feel the Zoners slump with relief.

He risked another sideways glance at Bay. She looked over at him, tears running down her face. Arthur felt sick to his stomach with fear. *Please, not Bay*, he thought desperately. Anyone but her.

The Secret Service agents turned into their row, walking briskly in their direction.

Arthur could hardly breathe. This couldn't be happening.

The agents were nearly at Bay. She had turned her head down to face the floor as they came close.

He couldn't let this happen. He wouldn't let them take her. He didn't know what he would do, but he would do something. His hands were shaking with adrenalin.

The agents walked up to where Bay was kneeling, but they didn't stop.

Arthur breathed out, his breath ragged. They weren't here for her. He almost laughed with relief, until he glanced across at her. She was looking at him again, just as afraid, and something else too. She looked sad. She was looking intently at him, as though she was trying to memorize his face. For a moment he was confused. Then it dawned on him.

They were coming for him.

The agents were almost upon him. He quickly turned to face the floor, studying the joints in the wood, feeling oddly calm. Bay had known it was going to happen, but he had no idea how or why. His mind raced. What had he done?

The agents' black boots stopped in front of him. He was getting pulled up. He couldn't believe this was happening. He hadn't done anything wrong. He felt the kids next to him almost imperceptibly recoil from him.

"Arthur Ryan." One of the agents stepped forward, stopping just inches in front of him. Arthur stared down at a pair of overpolished black shoes with a distinctive red stripe around the soles. For a second, he blinked in confusion. He recognized those shoes, but it couldn't be possible. They belonged to the one person he feared more than any other, the only constant in a life filled with regular changes. The one relative he could claim, who had followed him like a dark shadow wherever he went, was now standing in front of him.

Arthur looked up in shock. For the first time he could remember, Uncle was smiling.

The other agents moved forward, and rough hands grabbed him, pulling Arthur up to his feet. He was dragged forward through the rows of kneeling kids. The sobbing had stopped, and a wave of relief washed over the students. It was just some quiet Outsider kid. No one who mattered.

Arthur struggled to make sense of Principal Wright's words. "For stealing, illegal transportation of contraband beyond the wall, illegal fencing of stolen property…"

The Secret Service agents didn't stop at the podium as usual, turning instead to the exit doors. Arthur felt a cold shock of fear. This couldn't be happening. Faces started looking up, curiosity overcoming fear. Whatever this kid had done must have been really bad. He wasn't getting the usual whipping or facing a humiliation. He was getting the ultimate punishment. He wouldn't be going home today or ever.

He was being disappeared.

Chapter 2

Dead man walking.

The phrase was stuck in Arthur's head.

He was standing in blistering heat on the tarmac of an airstrip. A handful of Secret Service agents were spread around, looking uncomfortably hot and bothered in their stiff black suits. They were all staring into the far distance at a small silver object shimmering just above the horizon, swooping silently toward them.

A numbness had settled over Arthur, since they had left the Punishment. His brain didn't seem to be processing what was happening to him. It felt as though he was watching someone else, some other poor bastard, being dragged out of school, handcuffed, and forced into an unmarked black unit. Even now, standing here, he couldn't believe that this was real. It couldn't be.

"You have no idea what's going on, do you?" Uncle was using his quiet, sober voice, which made Arthur more nervous than ever.

Uncle was at his most dangerous when he was sober.

"No, sir," Arthur mumbled as inoffensively as possible. He had always found it best to say as little as possible around Uncle. It seemed to provoke him less.

Uncle started laughing. It was such an unusual sound that Arthur dared to shoot a quick look at him.

For the first time in years, Uncle's face was clean-shaven and scrubbed, his blond hair neatly cut short. His once boyish features, buried beneath the bloated skin of a seasoned alcoholic, looked unusually pale without the usual crust of stubble, sweat, and red dust. Harsh lines had etched a permanently cruel look into his face, but today there was something else in his expression. A spark of excitement.

He was enjoying this.

Arthur shifted nervously. The hot metal handcuffs behind his back rattled awkwardly. Uncle had dressed for the occasion. He must have known the Punishment was going to happen today.

The silver object approached fast, hovering low as it swooped in for a landing, clouds of red dust swirling in its wake. As it settled on the tarmac, Arthur got his first clear view of the state-of-the-art Solarplane. It's sleek, mirrorlike contours reflected its surroundings, camouflaging the plane. It would have been almost invisible if it hadn't been for the large official-looking words printed along its sides. UNITED ZONES OF AMERICA. Government.

A sharp jolt of fear cut through the numbness. It was a government plane. What on earth did the government want with him? Is this what happened to all the disappeared kids?

The Secret Service agents moved into a protective formation around the plane as its door slid open and a slender ramp unfurled to the ground. Uncle pushed Arthur forward, and the two of them walked toward the plane.

Dead man flying, Arthur thought darkly.

At the door, they were greeted by a smartly dressed woman in a vintage air steward uniform. She smiled a friendly, professional smile and said, "Welcome to *Air Force One*."

Big trouble.

Uncle pushed Arthur in front of him along a beige carpeted corridor that would have looked more at home in an old building than on a state-of-the-art Solarplane.

As they passed an open door, Arthur glanced curiously inside a room that looked for all the world like an old-fashioned living room with cozy leather armchairs and bookshelves. A young woman was standing by the window, her back to him, her fingertips resting delicately on the glass.

Arthur stumbled to a halt, momentarily transfixed.

He had never seen anyone like her before. She was tiny, almost birdlike, but held herself gracefully, like a ballerina. He couldn't take his eyes off her soft skin and her pale-blue simple shift dress that fell delicately down her back and across her hips. She looked breakable, perfect—like an exquisite statue made of glass.

Girls weren't made like this in the Outside.

"Keep moving," Uncle said gruffly, shoving him hard in the back.

Arthur was caught off balance and fell forward. He tried to catch himself, but his hands were still cuffed behind his back, and he smacked onto the floor, face-planting hard on the carpet, his glasses flying off.

"Get up, idiot." Uncle kicked him.

Arthur was struggling awkwardly to get up, when he felt a hand reach under his arm and gently help pull him to his knees.

He looked up, embarrassed to see the young woman kneeling in front of him, her hand resting on his arm.

Arthur felt like someone had stolen the breath out of him. He had never seen anyone so beautiful in his entire life. It was as though she was crafted out of stone, her smooth skin and delicate features almost disappearing next to her enormous, soulful blue eyes. Her white-blond hair was immaculately swept up into some kind of french knot, with just a perfect single wisp falling across her pale cheek, dancing lightly as she reached across him and picked up his glasses.

Her eyes briefly flickered to Arthur's as she gently reached up and put his glasses on him, her fingertips brushing his cheek.

"You might want to disinfect that hand." Uncle grabbed Arthur and roughly jerked him to his feet.

Wordlessly the girl stepped back, her eyes lingering on Arthur for a moment longer before she turned away, back to the window.

Two doors down, they entered a dark, windowless room. It was almost empty apart from a chair in the center of the floor next to a tray stocked with ominous-looking metal implements.

Two smartly suited men broke off their intense conversation and turned to look at them as they entered. The shorter man with an elaborately shaped goatee made a low whistling sound as he looked at Arthur. He smoothed a manicured hand over his slick dark hair and then muttered in a resigned tone, "Well, OK. I guess you work with what you get."

He half laughed and then walked up to Arthur.

"Ty Carrolton, and this is Van." He gestured toward the other man. Van was tall and immaculately groomed, with his black hair carefully styled into a disconcerting wedge-shaped haircut. He was studying Arthur appraisingly. Arthur tried not to stare at his hair.

"It's really quite extraordinary," Van said. "He's so…different and yet the same."

"Be careful, Van. The secretary said not to tell him anything," Ty cut in, a warning tone in his voice.

"The secretary is here?" Uncle's voice interrupted the moment.

For the first time, Ty and Van seemed to notice he was standing in the room. They didn't appear impressed by him in the way Outsiders usually were. "I want to talk to him now."

"And you are?"

"Agent Robert Connors. Secret Service, Division One. I want to talk to the secretary, right now." Uncle spoke authoritatively. Arthur was somehow surprised to hear that Uncle had a real name. Though he wondered if Uncle was making up the bit about the Secret Service to make himself sound more impressive. He certainly didn't think they employed washed-up alcoholics.

Obviously Ty and Van weren't impressed, either.

"There's a private room through there," Ty replied firmly but dismissively, indicating a door farther down the corridor. "Freshen yourself up a bit. Wash off some of that Outsider sweat. Then if the secretary wants you, I'm sure he'll send for you." Ty and Van exchanged an unimpressed look.

"Now, we have business with this young man. Alone."

Arthur could sense the red anger rising up Uncle's neck to his face. He wouldn't want to be Ty right now.

But after a tense pause, to Arthur's great surprise, Uncle turned and walked to the door as instructed, pausing just long enough to give him a look filled with the usual mix of contempt and disgust.

"For the record, kid. I'm not your goddamn uncle." He spat the words out, before slamming out the door.

Arthur's jaw dropped. He starred after Uncle…or maybe not Uncle. Why would he say that? All Arthur's life, he was the one constant. A constant misery and pain in the backside, but constant all the same. The one and only family Arthur had. Arthur shook his head, trying to clear his thoughts. Uncle was probably just messing with him. He must have been.

"The secretary wants us to get you prepped. We'll start with this mop." Ty broke into Arthur's thoughts, flicking a finger disdainfully at his long hair. "Maybe a bit of disinfectant in the shower," he added, wrinkling his nose. Ty was the first person Arthur had met who smelled of flowers.

The room was dark and dominated by a distracting VT screen floating in one corner. Hope Juvenal's overly made-up face, the size of a beach ball, was animated as she spoke. She seemed unnaturally excited—whatever had happened at the first primary was making exciting news on *The Democracy Games* today.

"*Outside Camp David Medical Facility. Washington's condition is still unconfirmed; however, we do know that a neurosurgeon arrived two hours ago to treat the young presidential candidate's critical head injury...*"

"Enough of that!" Ty jumped at the VT screen, waving wildly in the air until it disappeared. "Plenty of time for that later." He gave Van a meaningful look. Then, turning to Arthur, he pointed to the lone chair in the middle of the room, the tray with various scissors and combs next to it. Arthur wasn't used to having haircuts, and for a moment he thought they must be some sort of torture implements.

Van pulled out the seat and nudged Arthur forward.

As he sat, a man wearing an apron entered and started fussing around him. He began clipping away vigorously at Arthur's hair, great handfuls of it falling to the floor.

As he watched it piling up on the floor, Arthur sat still and tried to tell himself it didn't matter. It was just hair. Maybe this was some kind of preprison ritual. Ridding the prisoner of his identity before throwing him into the system for good. Never to be seen again. He gulped.

"Hungry?" Van slipped a tray of cheese and fresh fruits in front of him.

Arthur hadn't eaten anything fresh since his sixteenth birthday a few months before, and he just blinked at the tray in disbelief for a few moments.

"Go ahead, eat. Oh look at the little poppet. He doesn't know what to do with himself," Van said to Ty.

Arthur didn't need to be told twice. He took a bite of apple. It tasted so good he considered savoring it, but he was so hungry he couldn't resist gulping it down.

He couldn't understand why they were being kind to him, feeding the convicted felon. Until it occurred to him that maybe this was his last meal. He paused for a brief moment as nerves threatened to stifle his appetite. But then his stomach got the better of him, and he decided it would be better to die full of glorious, delectable fresh fruit. Like a fattened turkey at Thanksgiving.

It wasn't long before they were done. Arthur's hair was short, and his much-loathed glasses had been thrown away. Van showed Arthur a side room with an enormous shower and instructed him to undress and wash.

Arthur had never had a shower before. Water was too valuable to waste in the Outside. He stood awkwardly, unsure what to do. Van seemed amused by his confusion and not unkindly showed him how to operate the controls. Then Van left him to it.

His thoughts washed away in seconds as he stepped into the hot steaming water, and he felt almost happy for a few blissful, worry-free minutes.

When he finally stepped out, he could feel the plane rocking slightly. They had taken off while he was showering. A folded pile of dark-blue clothes lay on the chair where his old government-issue jeans had been.

As he pulled them on, he felt something hard in his pocket. He pulled out the star emblem Bay had given him. Someone must have taken it out of his old jeans and put it in his new pants. He was oddly touched. His fingers stroked it; for a moment he could imagine Bay standing beside him. He thought of the last thing she said to him.

"Remember who you are."

He brushed the steam off the mirror and looked at himself. His new clothes still hung loosely off his lanky frame. But other than that, he looked different, almost unrecognizable. His short hair looked darker, a sort of reddish brown now that all the blond streaks had been cut off. His eyes, usually hidden beneath his glasses and a curtain of dirty hair, looked brilliantly blue in his unnaturally clean face.

He was surprised at how he looked. Almost like a Zoner. His reflection was smarter, more respectable and better looking, undoubtedly. But at the same time, not him. He had liked hiding behind his messy, long hair. He had looked like he felt. Like an Outsider.

But what was he complaining about? He was still alive for now, and he had gotten to eat a whole plate of fresh food. Arthur turned away from his reflection and opened the door.

Van and Ty stared at him until he felt himself blushing.

"Amazing," Ty whispered. "It's really him. Who would have thought?"

"Mmm-mmm. We are good," Van added. "Too scrawny of course. Didn't anyone ever feed you, honey?" They both laughed, pleased with themselves.

"Come on. I think it's time to see the secretary." Ty raised his eyebrows in nervous anticipation.

They headed back along the corridor to the front of the plane, stopping in front of a door with a number of security scanners. Ty pushed his thumb against a screen, and the door opened after a short pause. A short, squat man with a red crew cut and crisp black suit looked out at them.

"Hello, Evan. Could you let the secretary know we are here?" Ty could barely contain his excitement at being brought before the obviously important secretary.

"Jus' him." Evan nodded toward Arthur.

Ty and Van looked crushed not to be invited into the inner sanctum and stood wordlessly as the man allowed Arthur inside, shutting the door behind him.

They were standing in a small waiting room, a glowing red door looming ominously to one side.

"Wait here," Evan instructed him brusquely, taking up a position by the door.

As Arthur stood awkwardly waiting, a nauseating sense of dread threatened to overwhelm him.

He knew what he was afraid of. He had seen the public executions televised almost weekly by the government, shown live across the nation's schools and public places. The victims were usually Outsiders; rebels or rebel sympathizers, with the occasional hardened criminal. He had never seen a kid publicly executed before, but maybe he was going to be the first.

Was that what awaited him through this glowing red door? Cleaned and primed so he would look respectable on VT as he died, everyone watching. Bay watching.

In a panic, Arthur turned to the stocky, redheaded man.

"Please, sir. I don't understand why I'm here." His voice was shaky. "I don't know what I did…"

It was futile. He kicked himself for saying anything. Evan just looked at him impassively.

Arthur turned his face away. His eyes were burning. He could feel tears rising up inside him and tried desperately to swallow them down. Whatever happened next, he had to hold it together. He didn't want to cry in front of any of them. He wouldn't give them the satisfaction.

"Jus' breathe, kid."

Arthur looked up in surprise. Evan was watching him, his expression not unkind.

Arthur nodded gratefully, taking a deep breath. The red door suddenly turned green and slid open. As Arthur turned to face whatever future awaited him, he repeated the words to himself—just breathe, just breathe.

It was advice he intended to follow.

Arthur gasped.

He was in the nose of the plane. Windows wrapped around the front of the room with a sweeping, spectacular view of the sky, clouds, and the red, dusty earth stretching out beneath them. It was a view he couldn't have imagined in his wildest dreams, and he was briefly lost in awe, his fears melting away as he looked down on his entire world.

"Beautiful, isn't it?"

Standing by the window at the far end of its sweeping expanse was a man.

He must have been in his midforties, standing with an easy, relaxed manner. There was nothing remarkable about him—average height, average weight, sandy-blond hair. But still, Arthur had the feeling that he knew him from somewhere. He had seen his face before.

The man gestured toward the brilliant red desert far below, curls of dust devils spiraling sublimely skyward.

"A dying world, the very earth that sustains us, burning away beneath our feet. The red dust stifling us, starving us. Deadly, but beautiful. Undeniably beautiful. One of nature's little ironies."

He gave Arthur an easy smile, then turned and walked over to an ornate sideboard, pouring two drinks with ice and lemon. He walked over to Arthur and held out one of the glasses. Arthur took it nervously. His hand holding the glass was shaking so badly that the ice clinked loudly against the glass.

"Do excuse me. I am being rude. Introductions are in order. Arthur Ryan, I am Paul Cain."

The penny dropped.

Instantly Arthur knew why the man had been so familiar. He was standing next to one of the most powerful and infamous men in the nation. Secretary Paul Cain—the brilliant science prodigy turned politician who had masterminded the RIP, personally resurrected each and every one of the candidates and brought about the entire *Democracy Games*.

"You're Secretary Cain? *The secretary of state?*"

The man nodded, a flash of amusement crossing his face.

What could the secretary of state want with him? Did all the disappeared kids get treated to a one-on-one with Paul Cain?

Questions raced through Arthur's mind, but he kept quiet and looked down at his glass. One thing he had learned in life—Outsiders have better odds of survival if they keep their mouths shut.

Secretary Cain shuffled expectantly. He was watching Arthur closely.

"So now you know who I am. The real question today is…do you know who you are?"

Arthur was too nervous to speak. He didn't know what he was expected to say. The answer was obvious. He was Arthur Ryan. Outsider, nobody, and now a disappeared criminal.

"OK, let's start with your name. Do you know how you got your name, Arthur?"

Arthur was taken aback by the question. He liked his old-fashioned name, despite being teased about it relentlessly at school, but he had no idea where it came from. If he had ever had parents to name him, nobody had told him.

"No, sir."

"I chose your name for you, when you were a baby."

Secretary Cain looked at Arthur's baffled expression and laughed.

"It has a special meaning. I named you after a legend about the English king—Arthur. According to myth, Arthur was a great king; when he died, his body was sent to the Isle of Avalon. There he was to rest, asleep until England's hour of need, when he would rise again, England's once and future king." Cain looked like he was enjoying himself immensely.

Arthur's mind was racing. Why had Secretary Cain named *him*? He was nobody. It didn't make any sense.

"You…you named me?"

"Oh, I did a lot more than name you, Arthur. I made you."

Arthur's feet felt wobbly. He clung on hard to the glass in his hand so he wouldn't drop it. Secretary Cain had *made* him?

"Oh, I know it must be a lot to take in. Just this morning you were boring little Arthur Ryan, Outsider, on your way about your average, everyday business. Now…all this." He made a sweeping motion around him with his hand. "It must be a little overwhelming. But the thing is, Arthur, today everything changed. Not just for you. For a lot of people. Today is *our* hour of need."

Secretary Cain walked back to the window. He looked out across the shifting red world stretching below his feet and took a long sip of his drink.

"The candidates—Kennedy, King, Tubman…they are America's very own King Arthurs. They are men and women who have stood up to the worst adversity, horrific war and fear, and have defeated them. Now they are back to lead us out of this new darkness and into the light. They carry the hopes of the entire nation on their shoulders. They are our once and future presidents, you could say.

"But life is a funny thing sometimes, Arthur. There are always bad people who try to destroy hope, who thrive in chaos. Today the Red Rebels brutally assaulted our very way of life. They attacked the first primary and tried to murder our greatest candidate, right before the eyes of the nation. If they are seen to succeed, the damage done to our future is so much more than the cost of one life. It undermines our entire country. Frankly, I can't allow that to happen."

Secretary Cain turned to face Arthur.

He waved his hand in the air and a hologram appeared in the air, the familiar face of a handsome young man floating between them. Arthur noticed it was the same stock footage that had been playing on the school bus that morning. George Washington. At sixteen he was the youngest candidate ever to run for president and wildly popular. His three-dimensional image slowly rotated before them.

All the pieces were falling into place. The attack on the primary…George Washington's head injury…the Red Rebels.

Arthur swallowed, finally finding his words.

"He's dead? George Washington's dead? The Red Rebels…killed him?"

"You're catching up, Arthur. Good."

It was unheard of. The Red Rebels were known to be a bunch of chaotic troublemakers who skulked around the edges of the Outside, carrying out petty crimes to piss off the authorities. If people knew they were capable of pulling off a coordinated attack like this—of assassinating a candidate during a live screening of the presidential primary—then everything would change. People would have to take them seriously. The Red Rebels would be a force to be reckoned with.

Secretary Cain turned and walked over to Arthur, stopping just inches in front of him, as if for effect.

"I'm not a risk taker, Arthur. I am a planner. And I will not let the Rebels win. A long time ago I put certain measures in place to protect against just such an eventuality. Now I am activating those measures. We are switching...to plan B." A smile curled around the corners of his mouth.

"Plan B...?" Arthur's throat felt dry.

He looked at the hologram floating in the air.

It took a moment, but it was probably the piercing blue eyes that did it. It felt like a jolt of recognition or déjà vu. Then several seconds passed before Arthur made the connection between the young man he was looking at and the face he had seen staring back at him in the mirror in the airplane bathroom.

Even then, he couldn't quite believe it. It was as if a better-looking, more well-built, confident version of himself was floating in front of him.

Was it possible?

Suddenly Secretary Cain's words fell into place. Arthur Ryan, the once and future president, the spare George Washington. Plan B.

Arthur was shaking so badly he dropped the glass. It shattered noisily, ice and shards of glass flying across the floor.

"That's not poss...You mean...am I...?"

"Yes, Arthur, you have been asleep all these years in your own Avalon, tucked away where no one would suspect your true identity, where you could live a quiet, normal life, until such time as you were called on to do your duty. That time has come. Your country needs George Washington, and now the honor falls on you. They can never know what the Rebels destroyed today. They can never know the truth."

Secretary Cain stepped forward until he was inches in front of

Arthur. His eyes burned into the younger man.

"As of this day, Arthur Ryan does not exist. As of this day, you will be the man you were made to be—the man I made you to be."

He reached up and put his hand firmly on Arthur's shoulder. "As of this day, you will be…George Washington."

Chapter 3

It was dark by the time they arrived at their destination. Arthur had transferred from *Air Force One* to a smaller plane and finally to an unmarked black unit, all the while hiding under a gray hoodie pulled low over his face. Ty, Van and Evan had accompanied him, briefing him incessantly the whole time. Arthur had tuned in and out of what they were saying and could sense they were starting to think he was a bit slow on the uptake. But he couldn't help it. More than anything he wanted to be alone, pull a sheet over his head, and just think.

Arthur Ryan had never been real. His whole life, everything he had ever known, was fake, just a role he was given to keep his true identity secret. His constantly changing foster parents had been allocated by the government in shifts to watch over him, never staying anywhere for long, always moving before he could make connections, friends, people who might start to wonder.

He had even had his own personal secret service detail watching over him his entire life—Uncle.

When he thought of Uncle, Arthur almost laughed. All those

years he had thought the guy hated him, and now he knew why. Sixteen years babysitting a nobody in the middle of nowhere. Secret Service agent Robert Connors must have seriously annoyed Secretary Cain to get stuck with a dead-end assignment like Arthur. No surprise he resented the kid who had been the cause of his fall from grace. No surprise he had taken out his frustration on him every chance he could.

After passing through several high-security gates, Arthur saw a large house appear out of the darkness. It looked grand, but not ostentatious; something about the generous spacing and symmetry of the facade gave it a peaceful, homely look.

"Welcome home," said Ty. "This is Mount Vernon, a re-creation of George Washington's home, only with all the latest amenities of course."

The unit stopped in front of Mount Vernon, and Arthur stepped out. Warm light spilled from the generous windows.

"I get to stay here?" he asked incredulously.

"Get to stay here? It's your home now, George. You own it."

Arthur was pretty sure his jaw hit the floor. Ty laughed.

"Tyberius Carrolton! So glad you find this situation amusing. Where is that god-awful Van—lurking in the unit, no doubt." Arthur turned quickly at the sound of the sharp voice. In the doorway was a redheaded woman in her late forties, seated in an old-fashioned wheelchair.

"I'll take this from here. Go! Get! Shoo," she said to Ty, sharply.

"Bye for now, George." Ty scampered off toward the unit. Arthur had half a mind to take off after him, but before he could move, the woman spoke sharply to him.

"In." She spun on one wheel and disappeared inside. Arthur and Evan obediently followed, stepping into the wood-lined entry. A staircase climbed off to his right, with two doors on either side and a large door leading out of the back of the house. The woman had disappeared into the first door to the right. Arthur stood for a moment, unsure what to do, then decided to follow, Evan following close behind. He walked through a fancy green room with a grand dining table and followed her through a small hall into a large study. A fire crackled in a fireplace set into the wood-paneled wall, giving a warm flickering glow to the room. Another wall in front was lined with old-fashioned bookshelves.

"Evan Healy, you may leave us now," she commanded the squat Secret Service man. He hovered, looking unsure. He obviously had been assigned to watch Arthur's every move and didn't seem keen on leaving.

The woman looked shrewdly at Evan.

"Do I look dangerous? I said leave us. You are not the only one with a job to do here." She waved a hand in Arthur's general direction. Evan didn't need to be told twice. He hustled out of the room, looking relieved to get away.

The woman had wheeled behind a large desk. Without looking at him, she turned and poured herself a glass of red wine from a half-empty decanter. She drank the glass down in one go. Then she finally sighed deeply and looked at him with a tired expression.

"I doubt anyone has bothered to explain why you are here." She didn't give Arthur a chance to respond, continuing brusquely. "It was my job to teach your predecessor about his namesake, our first president, George Washington. Now it seems I am to teach you how to be like your predecessor." She leaned forward in her chair and looked at him angrily. "But before we start, let me get something straight. We were never friends. You disliked me, and I loathed you. You were an embarrassment to the name you carried. But I am the best teacher there is, so we tolerated each other. Your predecessor understood that; if you do too, then we can proceed with the…job at hand." Again she waved her hand disdainfully in his general direction.

Arthur nodded his agreement with her, not quite sure what he was agreeing to. While she was talking, he had noticed a fruit bowl on a small stand by the window and was finding it difficult to think about anything else. His eyes wandered to a particularly juicy red apple. *Focus*, he told himself. But focusing was never Arthur's strong suit.

The woman seemed satisfied with his response and launched into the first of what would be many lectures. She explained that they had been granted a month, generous under the circumstances, to get him ready to replace the real George. He was going to have to learn mannerisms, study up on key personal information, and go through vocal training. At the same time, he would be physically trained to bulk up his unimpressive build. When the month ended, if Arthur was convincing enough, the press and public would be told that he had recovered from a severe head trauma, and he would return to compete in the remaining two primaries. Intermittent memory loss would be the excuse for any major mistakes he might make.

"Is that all perfectly clear, George?" she asked him, impatient for bed. She drummed her fingers on the desk to hurry him along.

Now that the shock of the day was wearing off, questions started pouring into Arthur's mind. How long would he have to pretend to be George? What had happened to the real George? What would become of him, Arthur Ryan, when all this was over? Would they put him on a diet, dig out his glasses, and send him to another foster home? Would he see Bay again?

He looked at the sweet fruit. A wave of physical exhaustion washed over him, and he wobbled slightly. He knew the woman wanted him to say that everything was clear, and they could all just go to bed, but something felt wrong inside, and he just couldn't say it. He wasn't George Washington, no matter what anyone told him. He was Arthur Ryan, a nobody from nowhere. He gave the fruit bowl one last longing look and turned to face the woman.

"My name's not George. It's Arthur," he said quietly. He felt tears of tired emotion stinging his eyes. "Sorry," he added out of habit.

The woman studied him for a moment, and then her expression softened just a touch.

"Well then, Arthur, allow me to introduce myself. I am Susanna Cain, but you can call me Professor." She held out the apple he had been eyeing. Arthur took it and thrust it into his pocket quickly in case she changed her mind. Suddenly something occurred to him.

"Cain? As in Secretary Cain?"

"Paul is my brother," she said quietly. Arthur could see a resemblance in their looks, the fair hair and dusting of freckles across the bridge of the nose. But that was where the similarities ended. The professor had none of Cain's easygoing charm. In fact, she reminded Arthur more of the cactus weed that grew rampantly over the Outside, prickly and aggressive.

She had gone quiet and was looking thoughtfully at the fire. The warm crackling of the flames was making it hard for Arthur to keep his eyes open. More than anything he wanted to go to bed, eat his apple under the covers, and sleep. It occurred to him he might wake up back in the Outside and that all of this would just have been a crazy dream.

The professor seemed to read his thoughts. She rang a bell on her desk, and Evan soon walked in.

"Evan, please show Mr. Washington his rooms." She turned to Arthur. "We will reconvene after breakfast in the morning. I will expect you at eight." And with that, she spun her chair around and wheeled out of the room.

Arthur's rooms turned out to be a luxurious suite on the second floor.

Evan left without a word, leaving Arthur truly alone for the first time all day. He didn't hesitate for a second. He pulled out the apple and ate it in a few bites, core and all, then flopped onto the enormous four-poster fully clothed. His hand reached into his pocket, and he pulled out the star emblem, his fingertips gently stroking the surface.

It seemed a lifetime ago when Bay had given it to him.

At the thought of Bay, he felt tears sting the back of his eyes. She must be a world away by now in her small, dusty home in the Outside. He wondered what she was feeling, if she was thinking about him too. Did she think he was dead? Arthur swallowed hard, trying not to let his emotions get the better of him.

Maybe that would be for the best. After all, no matter what happened next, he knew Arthur Ryan wouldn't be going home again.

By eight o'clock the following morning, he was standing in the professor's study with a head full of questions.

He had woken early to the delicate sound of birdsong. It had taken him a few minutes to recognize the unfamiliar sound.

The only birds in the Outside were vultures, and they didn't sing.

He looked around at the unfamiliar room, disoriented for a moment, as he remembered where he was. The unmistakable smell of bacon and eggs had wafted to him, and he noticed a cart had been set up in the corner of the room with an immense spread of delectable breakfast foods laid out. There were four different kinds of waffles, breads, sweet breads, bacon, eggs, coffee, and a bowl of sliced fresh fruit. He practically fell out of bed in his hurry to get to it.

After half an hour of contented eating, he felt like his stomach would burst. The clock on the mantelpiece said it was only seven thirty, so decided to walk off his bellyache. He walked out to the stairs he had come up the night before, noticing an open door to the left. Carefully, he peeked inside.

The bedroom was unoccupied but had a number of women's things spread around: a hairbrush, some delicate pale-blue heels, and some makeup on the dresser. He thought it might belong to the professor, but the shoes were so petite and fine, he couldn't imagine her wearing them. Besides, he doubted she would make the trip upstairs to bed every night in her wheelchair.

His curiosity getting the better of him, Arthur started exploring. The house was a rabbit warren of rooms and corridors and back staircases. Anyone else might have gotten lost, but Arthur had a good sense of direction and soon had a sense of the layout.

He moved carefully—quietly, unsure if he was allowed to be here, but too curious to stop himself.

Behind one door he found a small back staircase up to a large garret filled with dusty boxes. A small ladder led up to a cupola completely surrounded with windows that had sweeping views over green meadows. He could see everything for miles around. Deep-green forests and hazy, cloud-topped mountains, even a lake sparkling in the bright sunlight. It was the most beautiful landscape he had ever seen; he'd spent his entire life in dusty red deserts.

As Arthur looked around, taking in the view, his heart was pumping so hard that he felt like he couldn't breathe. How was it even possible places like this still existed?

A chiming sound brought him back to reality. Clambering reluctantly down, he promised himself he would be back, soon and often. A vintage grandfather clock in the attic bedroom was chiming eight. Not wanting to get off to a worse start with the professor than he already had, Arthur scampered down the way he had come and raced into the study.

When the professor arrived, she was businesslike and immediately launched in to a schedule of training activities. She didn't seem melancholy like the previous night, and Arthur suspected that might have had something to do with the newly full decanter of red wine on her desk. As she talked, he noticed her eyes kept glancing over toward the wine, and he felt pretty sure that if he hadn't been there, she would have poured her first glass already.

"Now let's see how good your general knowledge is," the professor said and directed him to sit at a writing desk by the window.

She put a small disc on the desk in front of him and waved her hand over it. A virtual screen appeared with a floating blue hand. Arthur had used cd's comp-discs before to take national tests at school, and he knew what to do. He put his hand into the floating blue one and waited for it to flash green. Eve, the universal operating system, spoke to him calmly.

"Welcome back, George. I have been screening the news and am glad you are recovering from your accident. What can I help you with today?"

The professor cut in, "This is Susanna Cain. Activate test module—George Washington, past and present iterations, please." Instantly a multiple-choice quiz started flashing questions at Arthur. They were all about President Washington and George.

Arthur instantly panicked and went into shutdown mode, the way he always did in school tests. He was feeling unnerved by the professor, who was watching him closely, so he opted for random answers poked on the virtual screen in a deliberately careless manner. Better just not to try than to humiliate himself in front of her.

After several minutes, the professor sighed loudly.

"Eve," she directed the operating system. "Show learning modes."

"Of course, Professor," a smooth woman's voice said as several icons appeared. The professor tapped one and then sat back in her wheelchair, looking just a little bit smug.

Arthur turned back to the quiz. The words had been replaced with images and colored icons. He touched one and a voice explained the question. He touched another and the multiple-choice answers appeared in a branch diagram, each described by the voice. He could reorder the icons throughout the virtual screen's 3-D space and link them with just a swipe of his hand. Arthur had never seen a test like this. For the first time in years, he became so engrossed that he was almost sad when he finished. Almost.

"That was so…cool," he said. "How did you do that?"

"It's just dyslexia mode, Arthur. Did no one figure out that you're dyslexic?"

Arthur shook his head.

The professor looked at him thoughtfully. "School must have been quite challenging for you?"

"Yeah, you could say that," Arthur said, thinking of the hours he had spent trying and failing to keep up in class. "So does that mean the other Georges…they were dyslexic too?"

"My goodness. I have an original example of Washington's writing that will show you just how appalling he was at spelling."

"Could I see it?" Arthur suddenly felt the urge to look at the real Washington's own words. Maybe he would recognize something of himself in the first president's writing or turn of phrase. Maybe he would feel some kind of connection. Something that might help him understand the legend, which he was supposed to live up to.

The professor looked completely delighted to be asked to share her prized possession. She wheeled out happily.

While she was gone, Arthur wandered over to one of the windows. He looked out across the green lawn and saw a lone figure standing, her back to the house.

Arthur's heart skipped a beat.

Even without seeing her face, he could tell she was the blond girl from the plane; petite and exquisitely dressed in a pale-blue skirt and jacket that skimmed perfectly over her slender curves. As if she knew she was being watched, she turned and started walking toward the house.

As she came closer, she glanced up enticingly for just a moment at the window where Arthur was standing and then headed to the front of the house. Arthur ran his hands self-consciously through his newly short hair and for the first time realized he was still wearing the clothes he had slept in. He hoped she hadn't seen him.

"Her."

The professor had returned, and her tone indicated she was not swayed by the glory of the beautiful nymph who had just passed out of sight.

"Well, I can see she already has you under her spell. Watch that one, Arthur. She's not good news."

"Who is that?"

"Your girlfriend, Claire Jackson. Don't you watch the news? Your adoring and loyal, long-term girlfriend, not to mention media darling. Waiting patiently by your bedside as you recuperate."

Arthur couldn't stop a smile from slipping out. His girlfriend. Obviously he wasn't stupid, and he knew that meant she was George's girlfriend. But if he was to play George, surely…His mind raced for a few blissful seconds.

Unfortunately, Arthur had to snap out of his reverie. He had a full day of training ahead of him. The professor drilled him relentlessly and impatiently on the history and policies of both George Washingtons. He watched footage of his predecessor and practiced copying his accent and mannerisms. He got to eat a huge lunch alone in the green dining room, constantly looking around and listening for the woman in blue. He noticed that the professor never seemed to eat and wondered if she was taking in her calories from the wine decanter she had cracked open midmorning.

After lunch, Evan, who turned out to be a dour Scotch ex-Navy SEAL, took him outside for training. This consisted of an entire afternoon of physical torture, including running, push-ups, obstacle courses, and all manner of weight training. Arthur struggled not to lose his glorious lunch many times over. And when it was done, it was all he could do to drag his leaden legs up the stairs and crawl into bed.

Dinner was to be served at seven. After a fitful half-hour nap and a brief shower, Arthur sprinted downstairs in his sweatpants, ready for more food. He swung into the green room and froze like a deer in headlights. She was there, seated at the round table next to the professor. Claire, the glorious nymph, was even more breathtaking close-up. They were both wearing fancy evening dress, sitting in a frosty silence, waiting for him. Claire turned to him, her soulful eyes coolly appraising him. He suddenly felt like he was twelve again, awkward and gawky. He swallowed nervously and wondered if everyone heard his Adam's apple bobbing up and down.

"Arthur, meet Claire. Claire, this ish'ur replacement boyfriend. Oh wha' shall we call this un, eh? How 'bout George the third? Georgy Porgy?" the professor slurred, obviously enjoying herself. Arthur could tell her filters were down for the night after a long day of steady drinking.

Claire stood and gracefully moved toward Arthur. She stood for a long moment in front of him, looking intently into his eyes as if she was trying to recognize him.

An image of the last time they had met flashed into Arthur's mind— lying handcuffed on the floor in *Air Force One* in all his Outsider glory; dust, stink, sweat. Arthur flushed with embarrassment. He dropped his eyes to the floor.

"I believe we have already met," she said softly, her small, lily-white hand reached out toward his rough, sun-damaged one, and she gently slipped her hand into his.

His skin buzzed. She felt like a flower.

Claire shook his hand, then slowly untangling her fingers, she turned and sat back down in her chair.

"Ser'ously, Arthur. Dress more appropriately for dinner. Shu're not on a farm now," the professor slurred.

She seemed oblivious to what was going on around her and throughout the meal, she prattled on as though she was in her own little world. Arthur and Claire ate in near silence, only breaking the quiet long enough to ask for food to be passed. At first Arthur felt too self-conscious to tuck in. He was sure his manners left a lot to be desired. But temptation won out, and soon he was piling his plate high and scooping forkfuls happily into his mouth. He'd take a quick swill of water before loading up his next fork load. The sound of laughter broke his focus. He looked up.

The professor was watching him, cackling with mirth. Claire was staring down at her untouched plate.

"D'ya thin' you can do it, eh, Claire? Convin'sh the whole world you're 'n love with this heathen? Ha! Gonna hold his hand an' kiss him? Wipe his sweaty brow? Wat'sh it doesn't rub off'en you. My goodness. Red dust makes'ush a mess with lavender. S'going to be amusing. Sooo amusing."

Arthur could feel his face turn red with shame. He hung his head over his loaded plate, wishing he wasn't such a pig.

Claire stood suddenly. She looked coldly at the professor and then turned to leave. At the door she paused, seeming to think for a moment. Finally she spoke.

"Good night," she said, looking at Arthur kindly. He muttered a half-baked good night, but she had already left.

The professor wasn't laughing anymore.

They sat through the rest of dinner and dessert in silence. She kept refilling her glass over and over, barely touching her food. By the time the meal was finished, she was too uncoordinated to even hold her wine glass and knocked it onto the floor where it smashed. Arthur stood up, desperate for this to be over. But before he could leave, she started wheeling herself away from the table, knocking it hard as she turned toward the hallway. She banged against the door frame and seemed to be struggling to maneuver herself out, her drunken movements futilely flailing her wheelchair against the wood.

Arthur paused for just a moment, then walked over to her. Without a word, he pulled her wheelchair back and freed it from the frame. Then he steered her over to the hall. She nodded toward a closed door and fumbled in a side pocket for the key. Arthur took it, unlocked the door, and wheeled her into the dark bedroom.

This wasn't the first time Arthur had had to help someone to bed, tuck them in, and lay them on their side so they wouldn't choke on their own vomit. At all the different foster homes he had lived in, Arthur had come to know people in all stages of life. He had seen depression and addiction and the ugly face of both—abuse. He knew that good, kind people could be brought to their knees by life's twists and turns. Above all else, he knew not to judge anyone.

When the professor was comfortable, Arthur turned to leave. He paused for just a moment. Then knowing she was probably too drunk to hear, he whispered, "What did George…what did I do to make you hate me so much?"

A gentle sobbing made him realize she had heard him. As he walked quietly to the door, an old framed photo on a dresser momentarily caught Arthur's attention. He froze in shock. It didn't make any sense.

There were three youthful men and one red-haired woman in the photograph, standing arm in arm by a green lake. They were all in swimsuits and laughing. The first man was obviously Cain; he hadn't changed much and had the same easygoing, relaxed manner he had had when Arthur met him. Next to Cain was a tall, lean man with dark hair. His face was turned down and his features partially hidden, but there was still something oddly familiar about him.

The woman, who was obviously the professor, was standing— no wheelchair in sight, smiling up at the blond man next to her. He was looking back lovingly at her. With a jolt, Arthur recognized a younger, handsomer version of a face he knew all too well.

It was Special Agent Robert Connors. Uncle.

Chapter 4

The next few weeks followed a pretty similar routine: studying with the professor in the morning, working out with Evan in the afternoon, and a formal dinner with Claire in the evening. Arthur had developed a newfound love of running now that he was becoming stronger. He found he could sneak out early in the morning and run out in the cool dawn, down to the forest and lake. There he would often slow to a walk or stop and sit on a stump and just breathe in the glorious moist air and smells of the luscious green land.

After an enormous breakfast, he would make his way to the study. At first there was a stilted awkwardness with the professor. She obviously remembered some of what had passed that night, and Arthur could tell it weighed on her. But over time, they managed to find other things to think and talk about. She was obviously deeply passionate about all things to do with President Washington, and their mornings spent exploring the past became a great source of pleasure to both of them. Arthur often felt in awe of the man he was meant to be. He couldn't see any similarities other than the obvious physical ones, but that didn't worry him. He just enjoyed the time spent getting to know the great leader. He would even borrow old paper books and journals whenever he could and bring them up to the cupola at night to read when everyone else was in bed.

Afternoons had transformed from a kind of torture into a part of the day that Arthur enjoyed. Evan had adapted their boot camp workouts when he discovered Arthur's love for physical labor. They stopped swinging weights around and started working around Mount Vernon and the surrounding lands. They put up fences and mended roofs, cut up fallen trees for firewood, and were even working on building a small barn from the foundation up. Both men worked and sweated hard in peaceful silence, feeling deep satisfaction by the end of their hours together. Arthur's body was transforming. He could see muscles he never knew he had and felt energized and strong. In fact, between the exercise and the food, he was starting to look less like dorky Arthur Ryan and more like athletic George.

The part of the day Arthur loved the most was dinner. At first it had been just him and Claire. The professor had not joined them after the first night. They never spoke much, but he felt a fuzz of anticipation every time she walked into the dining room. She sometimes seemed almost otherworldly to him. Something perfect and yet breakable. He would eat his food self-consciously, trying not to make any sound that might be offensive, all the while sneaking sideways glances at her. People weren't made like her in the Outside.

After a week, Arthur managed to convince the professor to return to dining with them. She had been reluctant at first, but he had convinced her under the pretense of finishing a particularly amusing discussion about President Washington's eating habits. Soon after, Arthur persuaded Evan to join them too, after a late finish putting up fence posts. Soon it became normal for the four of them to dine together every night. As the weeks passed, these dinners became the highlight of his days. Arthur wasn't sure if it was the candlelight, the wholesome meals, or the rich red wine that made them lower their guards. Whatever it was, they all started to relax into the evening with a kind of oddball feeling of companionship.

The professor, who was drinking a lot less, had quite a charming side to her. She combined sophisticated small talk with a kind of raucous dirty humor and soon managed to bring the dour Scot, Evan, out of his shell. Evan and she were the life of the party, while Claire and Arthur played quieter, more observant roles. Arthur was often on the receiving end of the jokes, as his good-natured cluelessness made him fall for every trick, to the amusement of the others. Claire seemed to take in everything, her eyes sparkling, occasionally smiling or laughing out loud. Sometimes Arthur caught her looking at him, though he couldn't read her expression.

As the weeks passed, Arthur felt healthier and happier than he could ever remember. The warm flush of friendship hung over his days building, learning, and exploring the house and forest. He would look up at Mount Vernon sometimes in the evening light and feel a pull in his chest. For the first time in his life, he felt like he was home.

At night he dreamed about the Outside. On a few rare Sundays, when his foster parents went away, Arthur risked sneaking away from the farm and rode his old bike for miles into the deserted outskirts of the city to meet Bay. Carefully watching out for signs of the Red Rebels or street gangs, he would head to the once vibrant headquarters of a large advertising company, now a crumbling, ruined tower. He would climb carefully up the precarious concrete stairway to the highest floor of the old office building. Then he would crawl along a hidden air-conditioning duct under a collapsed roof slab to reach "the castle," Bay's secret hideaway.

Bay had filled the space with her treasures, bits and pieces of junk, like the prized car emblems that she had collected in the ruins. One entire wall was missing, leaving a spectacular view over the ruined city, broken pieces of glass bottles dangling from strings across the opening, a crude homemade decoration. As the evening sun slowly crept toward the skyline, Arthur and Bay would sit together on their concrete sofa in the warm wind looking across their damaged world, the light sparkling off the shards of glass dancing all around them.

Every night now, Arthur found himself dreaming about Bay and the castle. At first the dreams were happy, like faded memories, but as the nights went on, they became more jumbled. Bay became Claire and then turned back into Bay again. In one dream she stopped speaking to him, as though he was invisible. Then another night, she spoke incessantly, making no sense. Long dark shadows started creeping in too, draining the warmth and light from their hideaway. Even the glass bottles started to look jagged and dangerous like teeth waiting to bite down.

Arthur would wake in his four-poster, a dark knot of anxiety in the pit of his stomach. He would look around at his sunny room and try to remind himself that he was home. But his feelings of happiness were slowly becoming overshadowed by a cold fear that this would all end, that at any moment it could all be taken away from him. For the first time in his life, Arthur knew he had something to lose.

That moment came one evening at the end of the fourth week. Arthur and Evan were walking in from the fields, joking competitively about who had chopped the most firewood, when they saw a black unmarked unit in the driveway. For a moment they both stood still, looking equally disappointed, then Evan snapped into professional mode.

"C'mon, son," he said kindly. "Playtime's over." They walked across the driveway, just as the unit's front doors opened and Ty stepped out, followed by Van. Uncle and three people wearing white smocks climbed out of the back and middle doors, carrying a variety of suitcases and boxes. Arthur recognized the hairdresser from *Air Force One*.

"Oh my! Van, you have to see this. Un-be-effing-lievable!" Ty walked directly up to Arthur, pushing him around so he could get a good look from all sides. "We have a candidate. Fantastic job." He grabbed Evan's hand and shook it.

Arthur felt a wave of embarrassment. A month ago, he might not have minded being treated like a piece of meat. It seemed to be part of his Outsider life. But here, at Mount Vernon, his home, it felt wrong.

To make matters worse, Uncle walked up to him and stared hard into his face. Arthur tried to hold his gaze, but the years of fear had worn him down. He swallowed hard and looked down.

"Looks the same to me," Uncle said menacingly. Then he gave a derogatory laugh and walked toward the house. The group headed inside. Immediately they took over the two bedrooms on the left side of the house, pushing furniture aside and setting up their boxes, which seemed to be filled with all sorts of digital devices and tools.

Van told Arthur to sit in a chair in the middle of the room, and the team started working frantically on him. His hair was styled. His skin was zapped with some kind of device to soften sun damage. He was tweaked, plucked, and scanned, with Van calling out measurements, which were recorded on a comp-disc. Uncle sat upright in the corner, watching the whole parade with a look of equal parts boredom and disgust.

All the while, Ty asked him questions about George, recording his facial responses and voice. Arthur's large virtual floating head was projected disconcertingly in the center of the room in front of him.

People kept walking through it as they bustled back and forth. Every time the head answered a question, red lines and statistics popped up across his face.

"Eight percent muscle mass deficiency. Eleven percent tonal inflection variance. Two percent compensatory radial movement." When the percentages went over 15 percent a small alert would buzz, and the offending statistic would flash blue.

Arthur did what he was told quietly, wishing for it to end. He felt like a lab rat trapped in an experiment, but kept telling himself it would be over soon. They'd let him go, and he could head up to his room and hide out. After all, there was no pain involved; he had been through worse things. He kept repeating that to himself, over and over, and it seemed to be working until he noticed Claire standing in the doorway, watching.

Instantly about ten alerts buzzed, Arthur's giant floating head was covered in flashing blue.

"Twenty-eight percent deviation. Fifty-two percent deviation. Forty-four percent deviation…"

"Oh, hello, well now that is interesting," Ty mused. "Claire Jackson. Ty Carrolton, and this is Van. Big fan. Huge. Adore your work." Ty sidled over to Claire and pumped her hand vigorously. Arthur wished the floor would open up, and he could sink into it. It was more than he could stand to have Claire see him like this. Every ounce of pride he had left was decimated, and his humiliation was written on his giant hovering face for everyone to see. This was worse than physical pain, he decided.

"I came to let you know, dinner is served," she said impassively and turned and walked to the dining room. Instantly the whole party dropped what they were doing and followed, muttering about what a hard day they'd had and how much of an appetite they had worked up. Arthur pulled off the bits of tape and wires still attached to various bits of him. He stood up slowly and walked to the door, checking behind to make sure his floating head wasn't following.

He paused in the hallway. Loud noises of talking and eating were coming from the dining room. His dining room. He guessed the evenings with just the four of them were over now and felt their loss bitterly. Someone else seemed to feel the same. He saw the professor in her doorway, looking like she would rather be anywhere else tonight. She must have noticed Arthur's expression, as she wheeled up next to him.

"Strength and honor, as the Romans used to say before going to battle." She smiled encouragingly at Arthur. As they turned to go in to the dining room, the professor froze. At first Arthur thought she must have gotten something caught in a wheel, she stopped so abruptly. But then a shadow fell across them both.

"Robert," the professor said to Uncle. Her tone was oddly stilted. Uncle had the strangest expression on his face, one Arthur had never seen before. Maybe fear?

"Susanna." Uncle's voice was choked with emotion. He looked like he was almost about to cry. Arthur stared at him in surprise. It was weird to see Uncle let his guard down like this. He remembered the photograph in the professor's room. The expression of love the young woman and man had, as they looked at each other. So Uncle was human then after all. Arthur started toward the dining room, not wanting to interrupt the moment, but a glance at the professor's face made him stop. She looked broken, and he felt protective of her around Uncle.

"You look…good," Uncle stammered.

"You look like an old drunk," the professor responded, but her tone wasn't unkind.

"Yeah. Well, you too." Despite the tension, they both almost smiled.

"Arthur, let me introduce you to the man who put me in this wheelchair, fifteen years ago," she said, her self-control returning. Arthur just blinked in surprise. No question how Uncle had done it. There were times Arthur had wondered if he would ever walk again after a particularly rough lesson.

"We know each other," Arthur said quietly. "Right, Uncle?"

It was the professor's turn to look surprised. He had mentioned his uncle to her a few times, and even though he had never talked about the beatings, he was pretty sure she had guessed. She stared hard at Arthur for a moment and then looked up at Uncle. He seemed to shrink under her glare.

"Still up to your old games then Robert?" She said, a shadow of disgust crossing her features. She shook her head as though pushing away dark thoughts.

"Let's eat."

The three of them moved awkwardly into the dining room, moving to opposite corners as soon as the opportunity presented itself.

After dinner, it was announced, that Arthur had been deemed to be a "good enough" George. He was to return to Camp David and the candidate primary training the very next day. Apparently Secretary Cain was in a hurry to continue with the primaries, after such a long delay. The second primary was scheduled to start in one week's time. Everyone was obviously very excited; after all, this was what they were all here for. Everyone except Arthur.

The professor had briefed Arthur on what to expect in the primary training. For one week before each primary, the candidates would be brought together for a week of intense training, all of which was to be recorded and viewed in the nightly edition of *The Democracy Games*. The purpose was said to be mental and physical preparation for the upcoming primary, but often it seemed more like an opportunity for viewers to compare the candidates and watch them interact in a series of entertaining challenges.

Someone flicked on the VT in the corner, and everyone turned to see a breaking news update from *The Democracy Games*. Hope Juvenal was in front of a large, rustic building.

"We are standing outside Laurel Lodge, where our sources tell us candidate George Washington is expected to return to the primary training any time now. It has been a month since the entire nation was shocked by George's accident, during the first primary. Since that day, rumors have been circulating about his condition. Earlier today we managed to get an exclusive interview with the Washington campaign's public relations manager, Ty Carrolton."

Everyone broke out into a cheer as Ty appeared in midair. The real Ty, looking delighted at the attention, jumped in front of his image and took a bow.

Hope was interviewing the floating Ty. *"Can you give us any information about George's current condition?"*

"He's great. I mean, it was touch and go for a while there. Brain injuries can be difficult to predict with the initial swelling, and George has experienced some retrograde amnesia as a result of his traumatic head injury. But the good news is his memory loss is short-term, confined to events occurring in the last few months."

"Ooh don't you sound almost smart," someone shouted.

"After the initial recovery and plenty of rest, I can now confirm that there is no permanent brain damage. He has been given the all clear. Our boy is back!"

"That certainly is the news we have all been waiting to hear." Hope's lips curled slightly upward in what looked like a crease-free attempt at a smile. *"But we have to ask you, Ty, the big question everyone is asking. What about George and Claire? Shortly before the accident, there were rumors he was going to propose. Has this ruined things for the young lovers?"* Hope's heavily shaped brows pushed themselves into a look of mock concern.

"Well, Hope, we can only 'hope' for the best." Virtual Ty winked at

the audience. The real Ty guffawed with delight. *"But seriously, Hope. You will just have to watch The Democracy Games this week like everyone else and judge for yourself."*

"Thank you, Ty Carrolton," said Hope, suddenly vanishing as someone swiped the VT off. Instantly the room buzzed into action. Coffee and cookies were brought in, while the conversation centered on logistics. Arthur tried to listen to everything that was being planned for him, but soon realized he had the least to contribute to the discussion. He just needed to show up. As soon as he could, he excused himself, saying he needed a good night's sleep so he could be in top form for his first day on the job, as presidential candidate George Washington.

As he walked up the stairs to his bedroom, he noticed he wasn't the only one to sneak away. The door to Claire's room was slightly ajar. Arthur couldn't resist peeking in.

Claire was standing with her back to him wearing a simple white nightdress, silhouetted against the soft lamplight. As he watched, she casually unclipped her perfect hair, letting waves of white gold fall across her bare shoulders. Arthur blushed, feeling mortified to be spying on her, and was about to tiptoe away as quietly as he could, when he noticed her back. Harsh red lines of old scars crossed the pale skin in a cruel pattern. Arthur felt a wave of shock and anger. Who could have done this to her? How could anyone have hurt someone so defenseless?

He stood frozen to the spot, unsure what to do, when he felt her eyes upon him. She had half turned, her arms covering herself, and was looking at him with an expression of shame. For a long moment they just stood, staring at each other, neither sure what to do or say. Finally Arthur walked forward into the room.

He stopped a few feet away from her. His hands fumbled to untuck his shirt at the waist, and he pulled it up to reveal a long crudely stitched red scar across his abdomen.

"Fell onto a fence," he said. He left out the part where Uncle had drunkenly shoved him off a porch, causing him to land on the metal railings. Claire's expression softened.

"Walked into a door," she said, nodding toward her back. He laughed. She smiled gratefully at him.

"Yeah, we should probably be more careful," he added, turning and heading to the door.

"Arthur." Her voice stopped him. He looked over at her. She had dropped her arms and was facing him, her expression somehow softer than he had seen before. She seemed to be struggling to find the right words. Finally she spoke.

"You're different…Thank you."

He nodded, feeling confused. As he walked to his room, he made a mental note not to peek through her door again. Unless he was invited.

At dawn Arthur was downstairs in the hallway, waiting for the unit that was going to take him, as George, out into the spotlight. He was wearing the dark-blue training uniform he had been fitted for the night before. The sweatpants and jacket were made of some fabric that Arthur had never seen before and were soft and seamless.

As he stood in the half light, his heart racing, a wave of self-doubt washed over him. Was he good enough to convince people he was George? He knew he looked and sounded like him, but what would happen if he messed up and said something to give away who he really was? He would let everybody down, the professor, Evan, Claire, even Secretary Cain. He heard the door to the professor's room quietly open. She wheeled over to him, still in her silk pajamas, her face soft with sleepiness.

"I wanted to say good luck, Arthur," she said, looking

affectionately at him.

"What if I…I mess up? Do something stupid? What if everyone guesses I'm not George, and they find out they've been tricked?"

The professor looked at him kindly. "Arthur, people believe what they want to believe. And right now, they want to believe that their hero has returned. You will be fine." They heard the sound of a unit driving up outside. Arthur turned toward the door, but before he could leave, the professor reached out and touched his sleeve.

"Arthur, whatever happens now, I want you to remember something. Don't let them take away who you are inside. I have seen more of President Washington in you, than I ever saw in your predecessor. Never forget who you really are, Arthur Ryan."

The last person to tell him that was Bay. He swallowed down a wave of emotion, his hand reaching in his jacket pocket to touch the broken star emblem. The door opened, and Evan stuck his head in.

"Hey, kid. I get to be your Secret Service detail." Evan grinned wolfishly.

Arthur felt a wave of relief. This would be a lot easier with a friend by his side. He gave the professor a last look and walked out.

Chapter 5

Arthur felt the familiar cool mist of the dawn air when he stepped from the unit at Camp David. But there was none of the peace he had enjoyed on his morning runs. A crowd of about twenty people waited for his long-anticipated arrival. They had press corps badges and looked like they had been camping out in sleeping bags all night, waiting for him. Several of them had remote eye recording lenses clipped over their glasses. Some had camera drones hovering near their shoulders. Most of them looked cold, bad tempered, and determined to get what they had sacrificed a good night's sleep for.

"George, tell us where you've been."

"Are you and Claire still together?"

"Show us your scar."

Arthur did what he had been told to do. He smiled and waved his hand, then walked through to the entrance of Laurel Lodge, Evan clearing a path. He could hear the furious cries from the press corps who obviously felt robbed of their scoop. Arthur stepped inside the relative quiet of the lodge and realized his hands were shaking. He did not like being the center of attention one bit. He had spent his entire childhood avoiding people and keeping his head down; now he realized he would be recognized and hounded wherever he went. Apart from Mount Vernon of course. He would be safe there. The inside of the lodge had a dated unpretentiousness that gave it a cozy retreat-like feel. The wall-to-wall carpeting, wood paneling, and vaulted ceilings had a slightly musty smell, a combination of wood smoke and damp. Evan briefly indicated the direction of conference rooms, a dining room, and a presidential office, lastly opening the door into a large room he called the rec room.

"Candidates only—even cameras are not allowed. Good luck, kiddo," he said as Arthur stepped into the room, closing the door behind him. Arthur looked around. There was a huge two-story brick fireplace in one corner, with a VT in front of it. Sofas and armchairs were scattered throughout the room, mixed in with all kinds of vintage games. One corner had table tennis, pool, and foosball tables. There were board games and books in another corner, including chess and Monopoly. Arthur recognized some of the old arcade games lined up along another wall like pinball and Pac-Man. There was even a virtual Pokémon dancing around the room waiting to be caught.

"Awesome!" Arthur whispered happily to himself.

"You think?" said a woman's voice, snapping him out of his thoughts. There were four people he hadn't even noticed seated near the fireplace. He knew exactly who they were. Growing up, he had watched these people on news feeds and entertainment shows. They were probably four of the most famous people in the UZA, five if you included him. The last four weeks he had taken intensive courses on the behind-the-headlines versions of them. Now Arthur had no small task. He had to walk up to these celebrities and act as if he knew them. He knew they had been primed to expect him to be different. They had been told his memory loss for the entire last six months of primary training was pretty severe. But would that be enough to fool them?

Reluctantly, he walked over to them.

The woman who had spoken stood up. She was tiny. A lot smaller than she looked on VT, but her presence made up for it. Harriet Tubman. She tossed back her head; a mass of black curly hair fell across her shoulder.

"The prodigal clone returns." She gave Arthur a cheeky grin, her dark brown eyes crinkling with amusement.

"Hi, Harriet…er Harry," Arthur muttered, using the nickname the candidates had given her. He looked around at the group. On VT they looked normal, but in real life they were all stunningly good-looking. Well-fed, healthy, beautiful people, radiating empowered self-confidence. Arthur couldn't have felt less like them, but realized with a jolt of surprise, that on the outside at least, he probably looked the same.

"Welcome back to the funhouse, George," said a low resonant voice. A short but strong-looking man stood up and walked over to him. He flashed him a blinding smile and shook his hand firmly.

"Martin, hi," Arthur muttered. He couldn't believe he had just shaken hands with Martin Luther King Jr. For a second, he was tempted to ask for his autograph. Martin had always been his favorite candidate. He was the underdog, along with Harry. A lot of people believed that they didn't have a legitimate right to lead, as they had technically never been presidents. Of course no one complained about Benjamin Franklin's right to be there.

Martin's intense brown eyes were studying Arthur intently.

Arthur felt a wave of panic. Did Martin know already? Could he tell he was an imposter? He swallowed nervously. He tried to remind himself of what the professor had said—people believe what they want to believe, and they want to believe George is alive.

"You really forgot everything?" Martin asked him.

"It's, er, it's hazy. You know."

"Is it a frontal lobe injury? I've been reading about traumatic brain injuries leading to memory loss. Very interesting! I have a stack of questions for you." An affable voice cut in, talking animatedly and fast. Benjamin Franklin stood up. He was barrel-chested and a little on the heavy side, with a large head and a mass of brown wavy hair. He smiled a warm, intelligent smile, and Arthur instantly took a liking to him.

"Ben," he said, grinning tentatively at him.

Only one candidate didn't welcome him. John F. Kennedy hadn't moved from his armchair, his handsome boyish face turned toward the VT in the corner.

"Hey, John Boy. Gonna welcome the conquering hero?" Harry called out to him. She walked up to Arthur and whispered, none too quietly, "He's just jealous. Doesn't like the competition. I think he was actually happy when you got hurt." Kennedy resolutely ignored her and kept watching the VT.

"So, how much exactly do you recall? Is there a specific timeline to the memory loss?" Ben seemed genuinely delighted to have the chance to ask his questions. He had obviously been studying George's condition in depth.

"It's kind of hazy, you know," Arthur repeated himself. He had been prepped extensively on his "condition" and felt confident he could answer anything Ben could throw at him. He could feel Martin's eyes watching him.

Suddenly a large clock on the mantelpiece chimed loudly.

"Ding dong, the wicked witch is not dead," Kennedy muttered under his breath, glancing in Arthur's direction. All the candidates automatically started moving, gathering identical jackets and water bottles, and heading to the door.

"Going to whump your butt today, King." Harry swiped her towel at Martin as she passed him, smiling naughtily at him. Martin grinned at her.

"You can try, Minty." He jogged up behind her, and they headed out the door. Arthur was not the smartest where it came to relationships, but even he could tell those two were together. He wondered how the professor had missed that bit of information in her briefings. Kennedy swiped the VT off and walked past Arthur, bumping him with his shoulder as he passed. When he got to the door, he slammed the lights off and walked out, leaving Arthur and Ben in the dark.

"Don't mind him," Ben said, fumbling in the dark for his water bottle. "He just really wants to be president."

"You don't?" Arthur asked.

"Of course, sure, who wouldn't? If you want the party line." Ben's dark outline paused. "You really don't remember, do you? Wait. I know. It's hazy." Ben started moving toward the door, bumping into pieces of furniture as he went. "Come on, George. You don't want to be late for training. Cameras start rolling oh seven hundred." Arthur grabbed his water bottle and sprinted after him, feeling immensely relieved that the first meeting with the candidates was over. *So far so good*, he thought happily as he headed after Ben.

The candidates were lined up across the concrete of training court one. The recommissioned tennis court was filled with a physically daunting obstacle course, a cloud of camera drones buzzing all around them. Each candidate had a personal camera drone that hovered close to his or her shoulder. Arthur had to resist the urge to swat it away.

The footage from that day's training would be edited and

broadcast in an hour-long VT show that would be viewed by millions that evening in Metrozones across the UZA. *The Democracy Games* had been the most popular, most viewed entertainment show since it started airing years ago. People would tune in obsessively to get a fix of their saviors' daily lives. Arthur had seen enough episodes to know that tonight he would be appearing on the primary watch segment. There would be a frenzy of interest in primary training week. The weeklong tests of physical, moral and intellectual character were all designed and edited to create drama and entertainment. There would be tears, heartfelt moments of bonding, and plenty of showing off. Of course tonight might even be a George Washington special. It wasn't every day that a candidate returned from a life-threatening injury.

Arthur looked at the obstacle course with towering climbing walls and ropes and wondered if he might be getting another life-threatening injury in the near future. Mikelmas "the Mik" Thomas strode onto the court in front of the candidates. The thickset ex-army trainer was a popular fixture in *The Democracy Games*, known for his colorful cussing and verbal abuse of candidates.

"Right, you lily-livered, pieces of sheep excrement. Good breakfast I hope, because you're going to be seeing it again shortly," he bellowed in an impossibly loud voice. "You know the drill, unless you've conveniently forgotten it," he added, glancing at Arthur. "Three minutes, complete the course, or you'll be frickin' repeating until your puny little legs drop off and you cry like a baby."

He strode over to Arthur.

"What the frick happened to you, Washington? Take a cozy little vacation? You look like something the cat dragged in. Don't expect special treatment here boy, vacation's over." He glared at Arthur for a moment and then strode purposefully over to the sideline. "Course record two twenty-seven, Washington. You got a shot at this, Kennedy," he added.

Kennedy nodded, focused.

"Three, two, one…Go!"

The candidates sprinted forward, Arthur starting a heartbeat after them. They vaulted over a series of low walls and then scrambled up a steeply reclined rock wall about thirty feet into the air. Arthur paused at the top, breathing hard. The only way forward was to zip-line down a cable to a small round landing pad. The zip line handle was a T-shaped bar in midair, about five feet in front of the wall. To reach it, he would have to jump. Arthur looked down, hoping to see a safety net but there was just concrete. He glanced over at the other candidates. Kennedy and Harry were already zip-lining down ahead of him. Martin was assessing the distance. He glanced over at Arthur and winked, then sprinted forward and leaped into the air, catching solidly on to the handle and swinging down.

Ben was calmly undressing. He pulled off his shirt, looped it over the cable and tied it to one arm. "Better safe than sorry!" he called over to Arthur. Then he stepped off the wall and glided slowly down to the handle, which he pushed into his self-made safety harness, and sedately drifted down.

Arthur knew George would have jumped. George was an outstanding athlete, and he probably would have finished the course by now. He knew he should jump too. But he just didn't trust that he could catch that little bar. He glanced at the long fall to the concrete below, his knees feeling wobbly. The problem was he wasn't George. Whichever way Arthur looked at it, there was no guarantee that he could do this, just because George could.

"Sorry, Professor," he whispered, pulling off his shirt and trying to throw it over the cable like Ben. He threw too hard and the shirt flipped over the cable and dropped off the edge of the wall. Arthur stood shirtless, wondering what to do next.

The other candidates were long gone. Arthur stood at the first major obstacle, frozen, his mind racing through the alternatives. He could jump like George and probably fall to his death. He could go back down the wall, but Arthur wasn't a quitter. As far as he could see it, there was only one safe way forward. Arthur blushed red at the thought of what he was about to do, but decided it was better to be humiliated in the eyes of the world than die painfully or quit. Reluctantly he pulled his sweatpants off, aware that about five camera drones had instantly zeroed in on him. They weren't going to miss this. George Washington, flying through the air in his presidential underpants.

This time he was careful to hold on to the other end of the pants when he flipped them over the cable. It worked. He had a harness of sorts. He quickly wrapped a pant leg around each hand and stepped tentatively off the wall.

The harness didn't slide.

He was dangling in midair, halfway between the wall and the T-bar. He tried swinging his weight forward to budge the pants, but as he did so, he heard an ominous ripping sound. Every time he swung forward he sunk lower as the pants tore. He looked up to see there was just a small shred of fabric left holding him up. What a way to die, he thought. Dangling in your underpants in front of millions of viewers. He almost laughed at the ludicrousness of his situation, but before he could, the pants ripped through, and he plunged toward the concrete.

Arthur saw the ground rush up to meet him and then, just as he was about to be dashed onto the concrete floor, it passed through him. He bounced into a giant safety net under a floating virtual concrete plane.

Of course, he thought, mad at himself for being so stupid. They wouldn't really kill George off after everything they had done to bring him back to life. What was he thinking?

Drones swarmed around him as he bounced up and down. He knew his face was red with mortification, though he couldn't tell what he was most embarrassed about; being in his underwear or the fact he hadn't realized there had to be a safety net. He was silently cussing himself in his head when the Mik's face popped up over the edge of the net.

"Washington. You have to be the single most dumb ass piece of dog spit I have ever had the frickin' misfortune to train. Stop bouncing around like a ninny and get back to the line. You are going to be doing this over until you puke."

The Mik was true to his word. The rest of the candidates headed out to work on other training modules, but Arthur stayed, running the course over and over without breaking for lunch. All the while, the Mik stood by, shouting, berating and heckling him. By dusk, Arthur could barely move and felt sick as a dog, but he could complete the course in less than three minutes.

Finally, he staggered into the rec room long after dark, sore and exhausted. The others were sitting by the fire, watching the VT. They all looked up as he entered, even Kennedy, with a smug grin on his face.

"Oh man. That was priceless." Martin laughed.

A virtual replay of Arthur falling in his underpants was repeating over and over on the VT. As mortified as he felt, Arthur was too tired to look. It probably would have been less embarrassing if he had fallen to his death.

"The thing is," Ben piped up from his favorite red winged armchair, "you really needed to consider friction. The shirts are tacton, which has a low coefficient of friction. Fuzzy cotylon blend sweatpants, not so good. Not good at all. Not to mention low tensile strength—not the best choice for swinging on." Ben didn't look like he was trying to be unkind. He actually seemed to be relishing the scientific analysis of Arthur's demise.

"Not helping, Ben." Harry walked over to Arthur with a plate of food. "Saved this for you when you didn't make the mess hall." Arthur was touched by the gesture, but knew he couldn't touch food yet, not without risking vomiting it up again for the tenth time that day. All the same, he thanked Harry and sat stiffly in a free chair, wondering if he'd have the strength to get up again.

The episode of *The Democracy Games* had ended, and the CBN nightly news was on. Arthur's antics had made it to the headline news, with an in-depth expert analysis of George's erratic behavior. An athletic George was shown gracefully leaping onto the zip line like a panther, followed by a movie of Arthur's stumbling epic fail. The analysts came to the conclusion that George was now experiencing crippling fear as a result of his traumatic injury. *How about George is actually a different person?* Arthur thought angrily.

He glanced up and caught Martin's eye. He was watching him quietly. Arthur blushed, wondering if Martin had somehow guessed what he was thinking.

The clock chimed loudly. "Bedtime, losers," Harry called out as she bounced out of her chair and headed to the door. "Same time tomorrow."

Arthur stood painfully, simultaneously delighted at the thought of heading to bed and dismayed that this was just the first day. Tomorrow he would have to face this all over again.

Evan was waiting outside to drive him to Aspen Lodge where he would be sleeping during training. He must have seen the footage from the day, but thankfully, he didn't mention it. Though when he left Arthur at the door to his room, he did pat him on the back and say with only the hint of a smile, "It'll get easier, kiddo."

The following morning, as Arthur walked through the entrance to Laurel Lodge, he noticed a plain-looking sliding door to one side, almost hidden behind a screen of potted plants. The metal surface was crossed with a distinctive pattern of scorch marks and dents that reminded Arthur of the gun damage that covered many walls in rough parts of the Outside. It looked like an elevator door, complete with call button and an indicator light. But that didn't make any sense. Laurel Lodge was a rustic single-story cabin. Where would an elevator go? His curiosity got the better of him, and he walked over to the door and pushed the button, but nothing happened. Then he noticed a scanner lock panel below the button. He swiped his hand across the panel. It flashed red, and CLEARANCE DENIED appeared on the screen. Obviously George wasn't important enough to use the elevator.

"Wrong way." Martin's unmistakable low voice distracted Arthur. He must have entered just behind him. Arthur had no idea how long he had been standing there watching him.

"I was just, er, just thought I'd…" Arthur couldn't finish the sentence. He wasn't sure if his curiosity would give him away. Martin looked at him for a few long seconds, then turned and headed in the direction of the rec room.

"Come on. You'll have enough troubles today without adding to them," he said over his shoulder.

The others were already in the rec room. Martin and Harry headed straight to a corner by the pool table, looking like they wanted some private time. Kennedy was talking to a pretty woman with dark hair and almond-shaped brown eyes on a hand-size virtual screen. He sounded almost pleasant with her, unlike the abrupt tone he used with the candidates. Ben was hunched over a writing desk, swatting away with his plump fingers at a comp-disc. Unlike yesterday, no one seemed remotely interested in Arthur's arrival.

Arthur guessed this was business as usual and was relieved not to be attracting any more attention. If he could just keep it that way.

Training time with the Mik was on a repurposed golf course and involved a lot of running. The candidates had to race around a marked course, collecting flags at intervals along the way. Every so often they would run through some kind of interference, like a river or thick mud.

Occasionally something nasty would surprise them, like a vicious pack of dogs leaping out of the bushes, or an angry bear chasing them. This time around, Arthur knew that the dangers weren't real, no matter how they looked. Though he would still jump every time something popped up, and he might have screamed one time when a particularly nasty virtual snake flew out of a tree toward him.

Once again, he rolled in last, after the other candidates had moved on to the next training task. The Mik made him run the course at least a dozen times, but this time he made it in time for a late lunch.

In the afternoon he even got to try out one of the character training tasks, involving sitting in a simulator and facing a series of virtual scenarios. Each scenario had a different historical period and represented a real challenge that past leaders had faced. There were options to supplement his knowledge of the situation by selecting informed sources, but there was also a critical timed element. Decisions had to be made before it was too late. At the end, the results of his decisions were analyzed, and Arthur received grades for several presidential qualities, including moral leadership, ethics, and effective coordination.

These scenarios would have been quite fun, only Arthur didn't trust his instincts. He was constantly battling a state of confusion about what George would do, what President Washington would have done and lastly what Arthur Ryan would do. He would often feel paralyzed with self-doubt and failed every scenario for being too slow.

Once again, he rolled into the rec room stiff, sore, and exhausted several hours after the others had finished. Ben had saved a sandwich for him. At least today he still had an appetite. That was progress. He ate the sandwich watching the VT's daily replay.

"*What a difference a month makes. Once neck* and *neck for the title, now Kennedy has swept away the competition, breaking several training records, while Washington is struggling to stay the course,*" said an ever-chirpy Hope Juvenal. Replays showed Kennedy storming ahead, sweeping through mud and snakes gracefully. A heavily edited replay of Arthur's low points followed, including his snake-induced scream and when he caused World War IV in the simulator.

Arthur felt the small amount of confidence he had built up, trickle away. He looked like a fool. Kennedy was enjoying himself. He kept laughing out loud at Arthur's replay.

"Unbelievable. You are such a loser," Kennedy muttered in Arthur's general direction. Arthur was surprised that Kennedy was actually talking to him. He usually just glared.

"Sorry?" he asked for want of anything better to say.

"See any other losers in the room?" Kennedy really didn't like him.

"I see one," said Harry. She moved in front of the VT, so the images danced in the air around her, and put her hands out to playfully stroke virtual Kennedy's hair.

This seemed to infuriate Kennedy. "He's making a joke out of all of us, Tubman. Can't you see it? This is serious. We are here to save our country, and he is making us all look like fools."

"At least he doesn't seem more concerned with how he looks on VT than the real world. Seems to me you are more interested in winning the election than saving the country...Mr. President."

Harry had to be the coolest person Arthur had ever met. She never seemed flustered or raised her voice, and she certainly wasn't afraid of Kennedy. She placed her hands on her hips and raised her chin challengingly.

Kennedy jumped to his feet, towering over her. "Get used to saying it, Tubman," he growled.

"Children, play nice." Martin's voice cut through the tension. "George is just providing some much-needed light relief." Martin walked up behind Arthur and slapped him on the shoulder. "I for one like this new, recuperating George. He's a lot more fun." He slapped his shoulders again, hard; for a moment, Arthur actually felt like he might fall over.

"This is not a game," Kennedy said sharply. There was obviously no love lost between these two.

"Never said it was," Martin replied, the humor draining out of his voice. He looked at Harry, and they seemed to share a moment.

"Bedtime, children," said Harry. "You gonna walk me to my door, King?" She smiled warmly at him, and they both turned and gathered their things, heading for bed. Kennedy paused long enough for them to leave, before walking out, once again managing to bump shoulders with Arthur on his way. Arthur sighed tiredly and was about to head out too, when he heard a small cough. He had forgotten Ben was sitting at a writing desk in the corner.

"Night, Ben," he said.

Ben smiled at him. His warm, friendly expression made Arthur feel better instantly.

"Good night, George. Sleep well. To quote myself, 'Early to bed, early to rise, makes a man healthy, wealthy, and wise.'" He smiled happily. Arthur smiled back.

"So why aren't you going to bed?"

"Oh, I'm already healthy, wealthy, and wise. I prefer to spend my evenings becoming wiser." He nodded toward the comp-disc screen he was working on. Arthur glanced at what appeared to be some kind of technical documents with 3-D scans of brains rotating in the air. The title hovered in the air: "Patterns of Traumatic Memory Loss and Recovery."

Arthur gulped. If Ben was researching George's injury, he was bound to figure out that he was a fake. Maybe he had already. Arthur looked searchingly at Ben's face, but all he saw was Ben's open and friendly expression.

"You, however, could do with the sleep. From what I understand, best fix for brain damage is rest. That and virtual, electrocognitive therapy, but I'm sure you've tried that." Ben turned back to his compact disc, reaching up his hand and spinning the brain dizzyingly.

"Yeah, of course. OK then. Good night," Arthur mumbled awkwardly.

There was no point in worrying about it...tonight. Ben knew what he knew, and Arthur couldn't change that. He walked out of the rec room, past the elevator, and headed outside to where Evan was waiting with his ride back to Aspen Lodge.

CHAPTER 6

The rest of the week followed a similar routine. Hours of intense physical training in the morning, followed by mental training simulations in the afternoon. Arthur stumbled through everything that was thrown at him, consistently failing and finishing hours after the other candidates. His brief encounters with the other candidates in the rec room were fast becoming his least favorite part of the day, which was saying something. There was always an atmosphere tinged with nastiness and fraught with the risk that he would accidentally reveal who he really was.

The only bright spot was Ben. He always seemed happy to see Arthur and often made him feel better after another rough day of humiliation. They didn't speak much, but Arthur enjoyed his company immensely, feeling an easiness around him. More and more, they gravitated toward each other, and Arthur couldn't help but feel as though, in a different lifetime, they would have been best friends.

The daily VT edits and newscasts were speculating that George wasn't recovering from his injuries and that maybe there was permanent brain damage. Constant comparisons were played over and over, showing George's before and Arthur's after attempts at different training tasks. Live, interactive polls were now floating at the corner of the screen, whenever *The Democracy Games* was on, asking if Washington should pull out or stay in the race. The results had started around the 50 percent mark, evenly split between his supporters and opponents, but his support was dropping daily. Arthur couldn't blame them. He would vote to pull himself out. It was obvious to him, and it seemed to most other people, that he was no longer presidential material.

By the end of the week, Arthur's already lacking confidence had sunk to an all-time low. The second primary would take place at the weekend, and he knew that it would make the training look like child's play. Each primary was designed to test a different presidential trait and push the candidates to their limits. The first primary was the test of leadership, the second was the test of intelligence, and the third was the test of courage. The brutally challenging primaries were designed to filter out the weakest candidate, with the loser forced out of the presidential race for good. For the candidates, who had spent their entire lives training to lead the nation, this was the ultimate test. Arthur could sense the tension rising among them all as the weekend drew closer.

There was no question who the weakest candidate was this time, and Arthur had started lying awake at night worrying about what would happen to him when he lost and was kicked out of the race.

Failed candidates were always a problem. They had no place in society. The first few candidates had been given roles in the government, but had proved wildly unpopular. They were tainted by their failure, and there was always an aura of fear around them wherever they went. People seemed happy to have clones as great, distant leaders, but no one wanted to sit next to them at dinner. They were unnatural, inhuman, and dangerously powerful. People were scared of them.

Eventually a solution was found. Martha's Vineyard, the island favored by many ex-presidents as a vacation spot, had been transformed into a "retirement" community for the ex-candidates. They were taken there immediately upon being voted off and lived out their days in what was meant to be an idyllic life of service to the nation, in remote isolation. Out of the way, often forgotten, but supposedly happy. Though Arthur wondered how happy they could be in enforced isolation.

Now, Arthur realized, imprisonment at Martha's Vineyard would be the best he could hope for. It didn't seem possible that Cain would return Arthur Ryan to the Outside. His physical transformation into George had been so successful, a bad haircut and glasses wouldn't hide his identity anymore, and he knew that Cain couldn't risk people finding out who he really was. Whatever they decided to do with him, his chances of a normal life were over. Arthur Ryan would have to be kept out of sight for good. He was a dangerous secret.

At dawn on the final day, Arthur sat on the edge of his bunk, tempted to just stay there and let them come and find him. He felt sick at the thought of another day of abject failure and humiliation. But whatever else he was, Arthur knew he was not a quitter.

As he reluctantly stood up, his star emblem clattered noisily out of his jacket pocket and bounced across the floor. He reached to pick it up, and as he did, he thought of Bay's last words to him. "Remember who you are." For a moment he could almost imagine her standing in front of him, her intelligent eyes shining green as she looked at him. He missed his friend so much it felt like a physical ache.

With a flash of shock, Arthur realized she was probably watching him on *The Democracy Games*. Did she know him? Would she see through all the superficial changes and recognize her old friend?

Arthur looked down at the star emblem and, and a smile slowly crept over his face. He jumped up, grabbed a marker from a small desk and his training shirt, and carefully drew the stars and segment of a crescent from the emblem onto his shirt pocket. After he showered and dressed, he threw his sweater over his shirt to hide the markings. When he took the sweater off during training, the stars would be clearly visible. Maybe, just maybe, Bay would see it and know he was still alive.

The final day of training was just as rough as Arthur had expected. When he finally got away, he walked dejectedly into the rec room. He had tried his best, and there was no question he was improving. But it was too little too late. The training was over, and tomorrow he would be knocked out of the primary. It was over for him. No point in pretending. He slumped into his favorite fuzzy red armchair.

"Arthur?" He leaped out of the chair, surprised to hear his real name. Claire was standing in front of him. She was dressed in a figure-hugging, midnight-blue dress, her hair swept up in a perfect chignon. For a moment he wondered if he was fantasizing.

"Claire, what…?" Arthur mumbled.

"It's the primary party night. Don't you ever watch VT?" she added, smiling at his confused expression. "All the others left hours ago to get dressed. I've been waiting here, for you." She looked at him coyly.

"Party? What for?"

"To celebrate the end of training, of course. The candidates always get a night to relax and be social, before each primary. You deserve it, Arthur. I know it hasn't been an easy week for you."

"I guess you do watch the VT." Arthur looked down, embarrassed. He didn't know why it mattered to him, but the thought of Claire watching the underpants incident mortified him to his core. Claire just smiled.

"I had Evan pick up your dinner jacket in case you were running late. You can shower through there." She nodded at the door to the bathroom suite.

Obediently, Arthur showered, carefully feeling his way around the many bruises and sprains he had collected during the Mik's torturous sessions. Slowly he dressed in the immaculate black dinner jacket. He knew nothing about fashion, but he could tell from the feel of the crisp, cool fabric that this suit was something special. He paused briefly and took in his reflection. He looked striking. Strong and handsome, maybe even presidential. Everything he was not. He turned away and walked back into the rec room.

Claire was waiting for him by the bathroom door. When she turned to look at him, her mouth dropped open in surprise. It was the first time Arthur had seen her flustered. Her eyes looked searchingly at him for a brief second, and then she pulled herself together, her self-control restored.

"You look good. You look like George. Just like him." She reached up, her fingertips softly touching his face. For one brief moment they stood unmoving, then all too soon she pulled her hand away. Arthur's skin tingled where her fingertips had been.

Claire broke the moment. "Arthur, tonight's being recorded. Be careful what you say, OK?" Arthur nodded, and together they turned and headed to the door.

The party was in Aspen Lodge. The whole place had been transformed with hanging lights and candles and looked every bit like a romantic cabin in the woods. Doors unfolded to a back deck with dozens of floating fairy lights gently circling and dancing in the air. Gentle music played softly on the evening air. The candidates were already there, lying on enormous, brightly colored cushions that surrounded a crackling bonfire that kept changing color. Everything looked so coordinated, Arthur felt like they were in an advertisement. There were people he didn't know there too. Kennedy's girlfriend, Lucella Kohli, was sitting behind him, stroking his hair. Arthur recognized her as the lovely, dark-haired woman who been talking to Kennedy on his tablet. Kennedy looked menacingly up at Arthur and Claire. Arthur had to admire his tenacity, holding a grudge against George, even now when he was so obviously not a threat.

Martin and Harry were with partners too. For a moment Arthur was taken aback. It was so obvious that Martin and Harry were in love; they were hardly ever apart and couldn't keep their hands off each other. Why would they be with other people?

Then he realized for the first time that they never showed their affection outside the camera-free rec room. Tonight was all for the cameras, not for the candidates. It was a performance, light entertainment to reward the viewers for sticking with them through a week of training.

As if on cue, Claire's arm gently slid around his waist. This time, he didn't feel anything.

Only Ben wasn't with anyone. He was happily working his way through a spread of desserts set out at the far end of the deck. Arthur felt a wave of affection for him and wanted to head over, but he felt Claire guide him firmly to the cushions next to Kennedy. She certainly seemed to know what she was doing.

Sparkling flutes of a gold liquid were served and as he sipped tentatively, Arthur started to feel a deep warm glow inside. By his second glass, he was starting to feel almost happy, the picture-perfect setting starting to take on a comforting warmth he hadn't noticed before.

The conversation was going on around him, but he was barely listening. Claire seemed to be charmingly holding up his end, affectionately cuddling with him as she casually joked and talked with the others.

He was just wondering if he could take a little nap without being noticed, when he became aware that the conversation had stopped. He looked around at the beautiful, perfect faces, all looking expectantly at him. Claire nudged him gently.

"What do you think, George? Do you remember any of the first primary?" Her expression gave nothing away.

"Um. Fire and er, pain," Arthur said.

"I think we all remember that," Martin said with a laugh. "Especially you, John." He nodded toward Kennedy. "You were right there when George got hit in the head, weren't you?"

Kennedy glared at him. "Yes. You know I was. It's no secret. And if I had been just a few steps ahead of where I was, I would probably be dead now."

"I'm glad you were safe, John," said Claire sweetly. "I wouldn't wish for anyone to go through what we have been through." Her head dropped a little, and she leaned in toward George's shoulder, with a vulnerable little shudder. Arthur almost choked on his drink. She was faking it, but if he hadn't known better, he would have believed the long-suffering girlfriend act. Bravely standing by her man through thick or thin.

Another flute appeared in his hand, and he downed it in one go. Hoping for the warm glow to wash away the bitter feeling that was growing inside.

"Well, we are glad you're back too." Harry's no-nonsense voice changed the mood. "Best in class or worst in class. You are always interesting, George. Things are a lot more fun when you are around."

"Thanks, Harry. I think." Arthur smiled. At least he could take that away from this whole experience. He was entertaining. "Right, because that's what a president needs to be. Amusing. What is wrong with you people?" Kennedy snapped angrily. The golden flutes seemed to be having the opposite effect on him. He was getting more and more agitated.

"Better that than a president who can't handle his liquor without having a tantrum," Harry taunted him. She really seemed to enjoy pushing his buttons.

Martin cut in. "How's law school, Claire?" Arthur realized that Claire had never talked about what she did, and he had never asked.

"I took a deferment so I could spend more time with George, while he was recuperating. It was touch and go for a while, and I just couldn't bear to be away from him." She smiled self-deprecatingly. "But after the primary I am looking forward to returning. George is so strong now. He doesn't need me holding his hand and worrying about him all day long."

For the first time Arthur noticed the effect Claire seemed to have on people. Everyone watched her when she spoke, nodding his or her agreement and support. She seemed to have a power over people. When she spoke in her quiet way, people fell under her spell. Arthur knew he was no exception.

"I'm sorry. It must have been a tough time for you. Watching the man you love suffer," said Harry, quietly. "I don't think I could bear it if something happened to the man I love." Her boyfriend, a tall, handsome young man, reached over and put his arm around her shoulder. But Arthur knew who she was really talking about.

"He's here now. That's all the matters." Claire turned her face up to look into Arthur's eyes. Suddenly she reached her hand up behind his head and pulled him down to her, kissing him passionately on the lips.

The buzz was back.

Arthur had never been kissed before, and the sweet softness of her lips enveloped him. It was the single most perfect moment of his life, and he wished it could last forever. But Claire pulled away.

"Get a room!" Martin laughed.

The conversation moved on. As the flutes were drained, the mood lightened. The music became livelier and people started moving into the house to dance. Claire went inside to join them, leaving Arthur outside alone. He stood, wobbling a little. He couldn't stop thinking about the kiss. He desperately wanted to believe the kiss had meant something to Claire too. But he knew that she wasn't his. She had never been his. She loved the other George, the real one. Arthur desperately needed to think straight, away from the music and floating lights and cameras. He needed space.

There was a gate off the deck, leading down a dark set of stairs. Arthur headed down. At the bottom was a wide patio with a dark pool sparkling quietly in the moonlight. Arthur breathed in the quiet, letting the noise of the gently lapping water calm him. Suddenly a voice behind him made him jump.

"Washington. You think I don't know what's going on? You think I can't see that this is all an act?" Kennedy's dark outline appeared from the shadows behind him.

Arthur's heart started racing. How much did he know?

"This whole memory-loss act might fool everyone else, but I see right through you. I was there. I saw everything. Or did you forget that?" Kennedy walked menacingly toward him. Arthur took a few steps back until his feet felt the edge of the pool. "You can try for the sympathy vote and act the fool. But it won't change anything. You can't beat me, Washington. You're going to lose. I am going to humiliate you in front of the whole nation. I am going to be president, and Claire is going to be my first lady. You can't stop me."

He moved forward, just a foot from Arthur's face.

"Why do you hate me so much?" Arthur said quietly.

"Forgot that too?" Kennedy said with barely contained anger. Suddenly he swung his right fist hard at Arthur who was caught by surprise. The blow snapped Arthur's head back and knocked him off his feet. For a few seconds he was in the air, and then he crashed into the water.

He came up gasping for air. His arms flailed in the water. He heard the gate bang shut. Kennedy had gone, leaving him alone. His wet clothes started weighing down on him, pulling him under the water.

Arthur had never learned to swim. He had never even been in a swimming pool before. They didn't exist in the Outside. He beat his arms desperately, but every movement he made seemed to sink him. He struggled to pull off his jacket, but he was choking gasping, sinking lower under the surface. He saw the side of the pool, mere feet away, but he was helpless to reach it. He breathed in mouthfuls of water, black spots appearing in front of his eyes.

This was it. He was going to drown, and there was nothing he could do. The black spots swamped his vision, and he stopped struggling, slipping toward darkness.

Suddenly powerful arms pulled him up. He broke through into the air, but couldn't breathe or move. Moments later he was lying on his back on the ground, with no idea how he got there. Something hard was hitting his chest. He gasped but there was no air, no way to breathe. He was rolled onto his side, his back hit hard.

"Breathe, damn you. Come on!"

The next thing he knew he was retching, coughing up water. In between bouts, he sucked in air. His chest hurt so badly he moaned.

But he was alive.

"Man. You scared me." For the first time Arthur noticed his rescuer. Martin sat down on the ground next to him. "Take your time. Breathe slowly. You'll be OK."

Coughing and shaking violently, Arthur rolled slowly onto his back. He suddenly felt icy cold.

"Th…thanks," he tried to say.

"Yeah. All right." Martin reached out and patted Arthur's shoulder. "Look, man, I have no idea how you got yourself into that pool. But I do know one thing. George Washington is the best swimmer I know." Martin paused, looking thoughtfully over the surface of the now peaceful water.

Arthur struggled up to sitting, still shaking with cold and shock. He looked at Martin.

"Martin…"

Martin held up his hand to stop him.

"I don't know how, and I don't know why. But I do know one thing for sure. You aren't George Washington." He turned to face Arthur. "So, are you going to tell me? Who the hell are you?"

Part 2
The Primaries

CHAPTER 7

The first thing Arthur noticed were beads of sweat rolling down his face and onto his neck. After a few more moments, he became aware of the stifling heat around him. His breathing felt labored as he struggled to suck in the hot, heavy air. It was a familiar feeling from his mornings in the Outside, and when he finally blinked his eyes open, he half expected to see his bedroom at the farm.

A glaring white light made him squint. It looked like he was inside some kind of underground bunker or prison cell with whitewashed concrete walls, empty apart from a basic metal cot and an old table and chair.

Arthur tried to sit up, but a wave of dizziness made him lean against the wall for support. He closed his eyes and sat still for a long moment, trying to make some sense of his surroundings. The last thing he remembered was going to bed at Mount Vernon, the night before the second primary.

Why was he here?

This had to be part of the test. The other candidates were

probably waking up right now in other similar rooms. He shook off the feeling of disorientation and told himself to focus. The dizziness had passed, and he tentatively opened his eyes, taking in his surroundings.

As his eyes slowly adjusted to the glaring light, he noticed some incongruous-looking high-tech devices, located around the room, standing out against the concrete walls. The heavy steel door had a square panel in the center, a four-by-four grid of sixteen squares in bright colors—red, blue, green, and yellow—each color lighting up in a weird, seemingly random sequence of flashes. Two flat speakers were built into the whitewashed ceiling with camera drones hovering almost silently in each corner. The most ominous looking device, however, was set at eye level in the center of the wall opposite the cot. It looked like some kind of monitor with a digital readout that clearly stated the oxygen level was 16 percent. As Arthur watched, the number ticked down to 15 percent.

Arthur stood up, wobbling a little. So this was his first test, escape before he ran out of air. He almost laughed. He'd had plenty of experience surviving high temperatures, and the feeling of being trapped in a dangerous place was pretty much a way of life for him growing up. So he didn't panic; instead, he started slowly toward the door, keeping his movements to a minimum to conserve air.

The square panel on the door was vastly more sophisticated than any lock that Arthur had seen before. He tried the door first, pushing hard, but as expected, it didn't budge an inch. He randomly pushed a few of the colored squares, each lighting up as he did. When he hit the fourth square, the ceiling speakers emitted a loud beep followed by Eve's voice announcing calmly, "Clearance denied."

He tried again, with the same result.

The next time he tried an order—he went with rainbow. Why

not? Red, yellow, green, and blue.

Instantly an unbearably shrill alarm ripped through the hot air, making him grab at his ears. Eve's voice spoke again.

"Violation three." An ominous hissing sound accompanied her words.

Arthur felt his chest tighten. The air was getting noticeably thinner. He looked over to the oxygen monitor as the number dropped suddenly. It was 14 percent oxygen. He fought back a feeling of panic, making himself lean against the door and breathe calmly and slowly.

OK. So now he knew the rules. This was some kind of code. A puzzle. He had a limited number of attempts before setting off some kind of tortuous penalty. He could have expected no less; it was the second primary after all—the test of intelligence. He sat down on the cot and watched the lights.

They were flashing fast in combinations from one to four colors. About ten or so, then a pause and a new sequence started.

Arthur inwardly groaned. Sequences. He hated them. He always struggled to hold things in his head, especially in the right order. *Maybe dyslexics aren't meant to be president*, he thought grudgingly. He looked around for something to write with, eventually coming up with a small rusty screw that must have come lose from the cot. Scrunching down on the floor, he pushed the sweat out of his eyes and started writing:

YYG—RRG—BRB—BY—RG—RGB—GG—B—RBY

It made no sense. He couldn't see any patterns. He tried again, writing down another sequence.

YGB—YY—B—GBY—BB—YR—YGB—BG—RRRB—GR

Maybe it was simple. He could be overthinking it. There was a single blue in both so he tried blue first. But then he was stuck.

Eventually he had to try something, so he went with his first instinct. One blue, two—mostly greens, three—mostly reds, four (he took a deep breath)—mostly reds.

"Clearance denied."

He had to try something. The air was cloyingly hot, and his chest was hurting from the burning air. He did the best he could, coming up with two new half-baked codes.

Woot woot. "Violation three." Woot woot. The hissing sound.

Arthur braced himself for the sharp reduction in air, but it didn't come. The hissing was louder this time. He looked around quickly. Steam was rising from the floor around him. Water was pouring out holes that had appeared in the corners. As the first wave rushed over him, Arthur yelped and jumped onto the cot.

The water was cold—no, not just cold. Bitterly freezing, like liquid ice. It burned his hot skin.

Think, he told himself. He couldn't risk the door again. He had no idea what the code might be, and couldn't get another violation trying to figure it out. What would it be this time? Fire?

Reluctantly he put his feet in the icy water, gasping. It was already up to his ankles. He waded over to the door and started reaching his fingers around the solid metal door frame, feeling for weaknesses. For several minutes he studied every part of the door, slowly and methodically, finding nothing. This thing was built to withstand a bomb blast. There was no way he was going to break through it.

He was starting to shiver, his feet were numb, the water up to his calves. The oxygen monitor had dropped to an ominous 13 percent.

For just a moment he wondered about the other candidates. They had probably all escaped already and were sitting in the rec room, drinking cool drinks, watching Arthur struggling—failing, live on *The Democracy Games*. He imagined Kennedy looking happy, a rare smile on his smug face.

He wasn't done yet.

Staying close to the wall for support, he moved into the room. For what seemed like an eternity, he examined everything, moving the furniture, running his hand over the walls, looking for anything that could possibly help him escape. But there was nothing. The oxygen monitor ticked down to 12 percent.

Feeling light-headed, Arthur slumped to his knees. The shock of the water rushing over him felt like someone had punched him hard in the chest. His heart was pounding violently. He knew he didn't have much time before he passed out, or ran out of air…or drowned.

It didn't make sense, he told himself. Something about the room bothered him, but he couldn't think clearly enough to put a finger on it. He splashed water on his face, trying to wake himself up. He pulled himself onto the cot, out of the water. Again he told himself to think, but his thoughts were starting to get muddled.

He closed his eyes, trying to distract himself from the feeling of tightness in his chest. No worse than a high-pollution day in the Outside he told himself, remembering the stifling, oppressive heat. His thoughts drifted to the castle. He imagined the hot wind blowing over the city and up into his hideaway, rustling his sweaty regulation clothes, making the hanging glass decorations clink together like dusty wind chimes. Why did he keep thinking about the castle now? Arthur's disoriented thoughts kept coming back to it. Something about the castle. He needed to think.

He pulled himself up to standing, trying to shake off the dangerous lethargy that was stealing up on him. He pushed his forehead against the cool concrete wall and ordered himself to stay calm. He was struggling to form coherent thoughts. The oxygen monitor was at 11 percent. The water had reached the top of the cot. It wouldn't be long now. He felt like a great weight was sitting on his chest as he struggled to breathe.

Again, the castle popped into his thoughts. He pictured the rough piece of concrete he used for a sofa, the collection of car emblems displayed on a broken window frame.

Something he needed to remember.

Crawling down the hot metal ventilation duct, his hands wrapped in cloth so they wouldn't burn, hoping that when he finally got inside, Bay would already be there waiting.

That was it.

He knew what his addled mind was trying to tell him.

There was no ventilation in the room. If the room had been built just for the primary, it might not have had vents, but the aged concrete walls gave away that the room wasn't new. So if it wasn't new, there had to have been some kind of ventilation that had been covered up for the test. Arthur looked closely at the ceiling, the glaring brightness causing him to squint. Nothing, just the two large light fixtures. Then it occurred to him. It was too bright. A room this size didn't need two lights.

He grabbed the table and pulled it under the lights, climbing on top. For a moment he paused, kneeling on the table, as a wave of nausea hit him. The table shook under his weight.

Shaking, he stood up, wobbling precariously. This was not a good thing to do while feeling dizzy, but he had no choice. The air near the ceiling was so hot it felt like his lungs were on fire. He reached his fingers along the edges of first one, then the other light. The plaster holding the second light in place was soft and damp. This light was new. He'd found it!

He pushed his fingertips into the plaster, scraping away at it until he got a hold under the edge of the light frame. Then, taking a long deep breath, he pulled as hard as he could.

The light fixture fell out of the ceiling, knocking Arthur off the table. He crashed into the icy water, hitting the edge of the cot hard. For a few moments he must have blacked out from the shock of the cold. But slowly, as he came to his senses, shivering violently, he looked up and smiled. The light fixture, sparking wildly was dangling from a wire from the ceiling leaving a large black hole.

He was getting out of here.

A little fresh air filtered into the room. Arthur gasped it in happily, instantly reviving. He couldn't wait to get out of this unbearable cell. After several more deep breaths, he clambered back up onto the table and pulled himself into the ventilation duct. Two of the camera drones dived in after him.

It was a tight fit, but he was so sweaty he could drag himself along using his hands to pull him forward. The air in the duct wasn't good, and it was even hotter up here than the room had been, but there was more oxygen at least and the dizziness subsided. He shuffled forward in complete darkness; his shoulders tight against the duct, trying not to let a feeling of claustrophobia panic him.

The professor had once told him about President Washington's fear of being buried alive, and he wondered if the modern version was fear of being trapped in a ventilation duct forever. Worse ways to go, he tried to tell himself, but started shuffling along a little faster.

Suddenly one of his hands slipped onto a jagged edge, cutting into his palm. He yelped at the sharp pain, pulling his hand back quickly. He could feel something warm and wet dripping from the cut. He pulled his sleeve over his other hand and tentatively reached forward. The duct was blocked by what felt like another light fitting. He had made it to another cell. He was getting out of here.

After several minutes of scraping at the edges of the light, Arthur had loosened it enough to push through the ceiling. It smashed to the floor below and Arthur swung forward through the hole, grateful to be out of the duct.

The room was identical to the one Arthur had just escaped from and felt equally hot and stuffy. The water was several feet deep, thick steam curling around the room.

For a moment Arthur cursed. This was no better than before. He might as well have just stayed and hoped to be rescued before asphyxiating.

But then, through a small break in the clouds of steam he saw someone.

Ben was slumped on the floor by the door. His head had fallen forward on his chest, and his face was underwater.

"No!" Arthur leaped forward, grabbing Ben and dragging him up out of the water, over to the cot.

He gently lifted Ben's head to check his breathing, but couldn't feel anything.

"Oh God. Ben. Please. Please don't do this."

He propped him up against the wall, turning his face up toward the air flowing in through the hole in the roof.

"Ben…please."

He felt a movement. Ben was alive. He was waking up. The fresh air from the ventilation duct seemed to be helping him, and he murmured slightly.

"Ben," Arthur said softly. He patted his friend's round cheek gently. "Ben, wake up. It's me…George."

Ben's eyes opened and slowly focused on Arthur's face.

"Hey, buddy. Come on. Wake up." Arthur grinned at him.

"Oh. Hi, George." Ben smiled weakly back, looking around slowly, gathering his senses. He paused when he saw the hole in the ceiling.

"Did you come from there?"

"Yeah." Arthur laughed. He felt a little giddy with relief. It was so good to see Ben that right now, he didn't care what happened next. He sat down next to him and pushed his sleeve up to examine the cut on his hand. As he did so, the crude tattoo he had given himself with a marker the night before was revealed clearly in the bright light. An oval with three stars, drawn hastily on his inner forearm. His message to Bay.

The cut was pretty jagged, but even though there was a fair amount of blood, it wasn't deep. He pulled his sleeve over it. His thoughts briefly flashing to Bay again. Wondering if she had gotten his message. Wondering if somehow, somewhere, she recognized him.

The water was up to their waists by now. Both of them were shivering.

"I thought I was escaping, but looks like we are both stuck now." Arthur almost laughed at the precariousness of their situation.

"Maybe not." Ben was regaining his strength by the minute. "You see. It's all quite simple really. Basic, and I mean basic, numeric cypher. I had it, George. Did you see it?" Ben pointed at the panel on the door, the water lapping just inches below it. Three colors were glowing steadily. Ben had entered the first three colors of a code, and it was waiting for the last color in the last column.

"You figured it out? Ben, you know the code?" George asked incredulously.

"Yes, of course. It was simple. Red has three letters so it is number three, blue is four, and so on and so forth. The sequences are just numbers. Add them together and every sequence comes to the same total—5463."

"Green, blue, yellow…red?"

"Exactly!"

"Ben, you are absolutely brilliant." Arthur started laughing. He looked at his friend's pudgy flushed face. "You, my friend, should be president."

"Well, thanks...but I really think you are overstating. It really wasn't that hard."

"Yeah, right." Arthur grinned, making a mental note not to mention his own poor attempt at the code.

"I just had to push the last color...but I guess I must have passed out."

A sharp crackle and painful flash of electric shock made them both jump. The water had reached the panel on the door. Electricity fizzled dangerously as the water lapped the bottom of the colors.

Any second now, the water would engulf the panel, and they would both be electrocuted.

Without hesitating, Arthur put his foot on the cot, propelling himself out of the water and onto the table, wobbling precariously. He had to push the last button—3...red. He couldn't risk wading over. Any waves would spill over onto the panel and short-circuit it, frying them both.

"Don't move," he called back to Ben.

"I had no intention of moving," Ben replied, his voice nervous as he became aware of their new predicament.

The water was so close, and Arthur realized he had to do this now. He had to push that last color.

If he missed, then he would fall into the water and be instantly electrocuted.

One shot.

He grabbed the dangling light and swung himself forward, his foot outstretched, his toe kicking out, aiming for the last color. The red square.

At the last second he released the light, praying that his aim was good.

His foot smacked into the panel, and he crashed down into the water. His entire body burned with shock, and for several seconds he thought he had failed, until the icy chill of the water registered on his nerves. It wasn't electricity. Had he done it?

He pulled himself up. The water level was dropping fast. He heard a whooping noise that at first sounded like the alarm, but then he realized it was coming from Ben.

"Now who's the genius? That was awesome, George! You did it! You did it!"

The door was open, the water flowing out. Glorious fresh air flooding in.

"No. *We* did it, Ben. We did it together."

He couldn't restrain himself. Arthur jumped to his feet, letting out a whoop of joy.

"Oh yeah! That's how it's done!" He fist-pumped the thin air, then turned and high-fived Ben, who wasn't expecting it and almost fell sideways. They were both grinning from ear to ear like a pair of kids in a candy store.

"Shall we?" Ben said. He stood up and bowed, grandly swinging his hand toward the door.

"Together," said Arthur. They looked at each other and nodded. Then, side by side, they pulled the door open and stepped out into a stark white corridor filled with cool, fresh air.

Chapter 8

Half an hour later, Arthur, Ben, and the other candidates were sitting primed and primped in an exquisitely fancy lounge area with the largest VT Arthur had ever seen floating in the center of the room. They had been rehydrated, stitched up, and made up to look customarily gorgeous, ready for their prime-time screen debut on *The Democracy Games—Post-Primary Special.*

Nobody looking around at this room full of beautiful young people would have guessed that they had just been through a fight for their lives.

A weird muffled roar like the sound of ocean waves rising and falling was coming from a door to the side. Ty bustled through the door and as it opened, the roar became unbearably loud. It was the sound of a massive crowd, cheering and shouting.

"No way," Arthur said.

Harry laughed outright. "That's your adoring public out there, Washington. You got nothing to be afraid of from them. It's the backstage crew you need to keep your eye on." She stood up and walked behind Van provocatively as she said this. Van glared at her and pulled himself to his feet, every inch of his tall frame dominating Harry. But as always, it didn't seem to have any effect on her. Nothing intimidated Harry.

Arthur glanced nervously at the other candidates' faces. They'd all survived. That was good, considering how close he and Ben had come to frying.

Kennedy also seemed to be trying to figure out the competition. He had a smug smile on his face that was belied by the nervous expression in his eyes as he glanced at Martin and Harry. He looked confident but hungry for more, and Arthur could only guess that he had done fine, but fine wasn't good enough. Kennedy wanted and out-and-out victory. He wanted to win.

Martin was sitting quietly, his head down. His manner gave nothing away.

As Arthur watched him, Martin seeming to sense he was being watched and glanced up, catching Arthur's eye.

Arthur blushed, feeling embarrassed to be caught staring. This was the first time he had seen Martin since the incident at the pool. He felt his heart racing as he looked at him nervously.

Martin knew everything. He knew who Arthur really was, where he came from, everything. It was in Martin's power to destroy him. He just had to say one word, and George would cease to be. But he had sworn to keep Arthur's secret safe, for now, on the condition that Arthur didn't tell anyone that he knew. He had given no explanation or discussion. As soon as Arthur had agreed, he had walked away, ending the conversation abruptly, forcing Arthur to trust him with his life, whether he liked it or not.

Martin's face was impassive as their eyes met, and this time Arthur looked down. He didn't want to face this right now. He just wanted a break. A rest.

Abruptly, the roar of the crowd subsided, replaced by the powerful swelling theme of *The Democracy Games*. The primary VT special had started. The five candidates suddenly appeared in the center of the room, larger than life, slowly rotating through the air as a pulsating beat of music played. Their names appeared over them, WASHINGTON…KENNEDY…KING…It was dramatic and a little exhilarating.

Arthur looked at his handsome, ghostlike self, spinning slowly, heroically before him. He couldn't help finding it a little ridiculous and glanced over at the other candidates for moral support. Kennedy seemed to be drinking the Kool-Aid. He watched himself hungrily, wanting a piece of that floating image. Harry didn't seem remotely bothered, taking a seat provocatively next to Van to watch the show. Martin was staring intently at the floor again, unreadable as always.

Hope Juvenal was the anchor for the special edition show. Her enormous, smiling virtual head replaced the spinning candidates, looming huge and clown-like in the center of the room. Arthur felt himself recoil. Something about Hope creeped him out. She was too made up, too perfect.

Hope was giving her standard spiel, explaining how each candidate's scores had been tallied. It was based on three things: time, technical performance, and the popular vote (voted for by the nation and always the unpredictable wild card). Five points for a first place win. Just one point for the loser. The three scores were added for each candidate's final score.

Ominously Hope ended by describing how the loser would be eliminated from the presidential race for good, implying that his or her life's purpose, to lead the nation, would come to a premature end. Arthur knew he had more at stake than that. Failure for him would be dangerous to Secretary Cain. He would be an unwanted spare with a big secret. He quickly replayed the primary in his mind, wondering desperately if he had done enough to make it through to the finals.

The moment had come. The spinning candidates were back, the results were being announced. Suddenly Harry's virtual self was alone, surrounded by fake fireworks and crashing swells of music. Harry was ushered quickly through the door to the stage. She didn't seem too surprised and smiled graciously, waving to the audience. A replay of her escape was playing.

Harry had suspected that the candidates might be drugged and had secretly avoided eating and drinking at dinner the night before the primary. When the Secret Service had come for her in the middle of the night, she had faked unconsciousness and calmly watched as the color code to her cell was entered on the panel. She had missed the last two colors, her view blocked by one of the agents, but had enough to work out the missing colors before she had run out of time. It had taken precisely three minutes for her to escape her cell.

Harry's scores flashed dramatically across the sky above the amphitheater. First place for time and performance. Fifth place for the popular vote. A tally of eleven points.

"Wha...?" Arthur was shocked. Her performance had been nothing short of brilliant. She had put him to shame, but her popular score was abysmal. "It doesn't make any sense. She was amazing."

"She is amazing," Martin said quietly. "But she will never be popular." Arthur was too upset about the vote to realize that this was the first time Martin had spoken to him since he had found out who he really was.

"But she's the best candidate. I mean she wins most training sessions and challenges. She should be president. Easily, hands down. Why can't people see that? Why didn't they vote for her?"

"Because she doesn't look like you," Martin said angrily. "Grow up...George. You want to be president, but you don't even know the country you live in." He stood up and slammed the coffee table so hard it fell over. Arthur felt ashamed of himself. He did know. He did understand. As an Outsider, he had faced discrimination all his life. But Martin was right. All it had taken was a good haircut and a change of clothes, and he had crossed over to the other side of the wall. Now he looked right.

"I'm sorry," he said quietly.

Martin's body language softened, and he sat back down on the sofa.

"I don't know, George. Maybe you do know. Maybe you know better than I do. It's not like I've ever been outside of a Metrozone." Martin stopped himself, careful not to say too much.

While they were talking, they hadn't even noticed that Kennedy had been called up. The replay of his escape was being shown on the VT. Arthur watched distractedly, still fuming over Harry's scores. A half-dressed Kennedy was pacing around his cell, his sweaty six-pack rippling to great roars of approval from the audience. He had pulled his shirt off and used it as a net to catch the camera drones, smashing each one with his shoe. Then, unseen, he had wrapped the oxygen monitor with his shirt, opening it only long enough to breathe out onto the monitor. Soon the monitor was showing alarmingly low levels of oxygen; medical personnel rushed to the room, allowing Kennedy to escape.

Arthur grudgingly had to admit it was quite effective. Not as efficient as Harry, but vastly more sophisticated than his own brute-force, eleventh-hour escape.

Obviously he wasn't the only one impressed. Hope was fawning all over Kennedy on the VT, and he seemed equally pleased with himself. His scores were announced to great fanfare. Second place on time and performance, first in the popular vote. A total of thirteen points. He was in the lead. He'd like that, Arthur thought grumpily.

Martin was next.

He walked out onto the stage, leaving just Arthur and Ben behind to watch the replay. Martin had figured out the air vent, just like Arthur. He had also scratched himself up, gotten heat stroke, half-frozen in the icy water, and escaped looking generally hot and bothered, but he had done it with a lot more finesse than Arthur and in half the time. The adjacent cell he'd dropped in on had been Harry's empty one, so he had been able to just walk out. His scores were announced. Third place for time, performance, and popularity. Nine points. He came in after Harry.

As Hope interviewed him, Arthur looked over at Ben.

Ben's soft, gentle face was uncharacteristically pale. He was sitting rigidly in his chair, looking forward, watching the performance playing out in the air in front of him. But his eyes were unfocused, as though he was deep in thought, his fingers tapping animatedly on his knees. Arthur guessed he was calculating the variables, running through the different ways this could play out.

Well, the odds weren't good for either of them. Arthur looked down at the ground, swallowing a rising feeling of panic. He didn't have to do the math to know that one of them wouldn't be going home.

"Ladies and Gentlemen...I give you George Washington and Benjamin Franklin."

Arthur started at the sound of his name being called. The two losers were being summoned to the stage together. Ben met his eyes, and they briefly held each other's gaze, their faces tense. Then Ben nodded and gave a small, tight smile. Arthur smiled back, weakly, as the two young men stood and, side by side, walked onto the stage.

It was showtime.

The audience went wild. Arthur looked around shocked at the immense crowd looming out of the darkness before him. The roar was terrifying, unlike anything he had heard before, and for a moment, he froze on the spot.

Hope was sitting center stage next to two brightly spotlighted interview chairs. Her voice announced them enthusiastically.

"Welcome…George Washington…and Benjamin Franklin."

The other candidates were seated along one side of the stage in front of immense, floating images of themselves. On the far side, stylish, long sofas were filled with family and friends of the candidates. Surprised, Arthur noticed Claire and the professor seated on the last sofa. Even though they were far away, he thought Claire gave him an almost imperceptible smile. He smiled back, feeling a rush of warmth. They were there for him. His friends and family.

Arthur reluctantly followed Ben across the stage, heading for the interview chairs, feeling like a criminal taking his place in the dock.

A narrator with an unfeasibly low voice was talking in the background.

"Two young men. Two candidates. Tonight they stand before you. Tonight…for one of them, the journey ends. A sad farewell to one of our heroes. Who will it be? We will be right back after the break."

As Arthur took his seat, he realized that this was the first time he had seen Hope Juvenal in the flesh. She looked just as creepily immaculate as on the VT. What he hadn't expected was the fact that she was floating a few inches above the floor. Of course, it all made sense, Arthur thought in surprise. Hope wasn't real. That's why she looked so unnaturally perfect. She was generated by the universal operating system.

She was Eve.

Heavily edited replays of their escapes were playing in the air over their heads. The editing made the whole primary into quite a nail-biting piece of drama, a race against time. The crowd roared its approval, cheering as George climbed into the air duct, gasping as he cut his hand, oohing and aahing as George and Ben finally escaped the cell, side by side.

It was all pure showmanship. Pure theater.

Every so often, the replays were interspersed with footage of the candidates and a round of questions from Hope. "How do you feel?" "If there was one thing you would like to say to your fans?" "Are the rumors true?"

Arthur felt like a deer in headlights. The crowd was overwhelming. He hated attention at the best of times, but this was pure hell. He swallowed a lot and bumbled awkwardly through some banal responses, often giving one-word answers. Hope switched focus to Ben, who had the experience and good humor to respond more fully, and after several painful minutes the interview was over.

Time was up. The crowd went quiet. Hope stood (floated) and turned to face the audience, an intense expression on her face.

"And now, Ladies and Gentlemen, people of the UZA. It is time. Time to say goodbye to one of these, brave young heroes. Forever."

The front few rows of the audience's faces were lit by the reflected glow from the stage lights. They were silent now, their faces racked by nervous anticipation.

Arthur remembered the kids at school, the crazed fanaticism that The Democracy Games inspired. They entire nation had watched the candidates grow from infancy, remote illusory figures who had peopled their daily lives, like characters from a soap opera. Many had formed strong, obsessive attachments to one or another of them. The candidates were the nation's heroes.

Well, tonight some of them would lose their hero, for good.

It was powerful stuff.

A hovering, spotlighted dais had appeared behind them, columns of brilliant light giving it the appearance of an ethereal gateway. The loser's exit, Arthur thought, glancing nervously at Ben. Step through that gate, and you will never be seen again.

Music swelled, the crowd had fallen silent. It was the moment they had all been waiting for.

Hope led them both toward the ominous dais, indicating that they should each take a spot on either side.

Arthur's heart was beating hard. He glanced over at Claire. Was this it? Would he ever get to see her again?

"Can we have the score for time, please?"

Brilliant graphics filled the sky above their heads like fireworks. Arthur forced himself to look up as the dancing lights formed themselves into numbers. Ben had won the time score. Ben was in fourth place now. Placing George Washington in the remaining position of fifth place. Even though they had left the cell together, a video replay behind them showed that Ben's foot had crossed the threshold inches before Arthur's. Two points to Ben. One for George.

Drum roll, Arthur could imagine the heavy editing that would be playing on the VT. Cut to George's face, cut to Ben's. Cut to excited crowd members, back to both candidates.

Arthur's heart was beating so hard now, he felt as though it would jump out of his chest and roll away. His life, his future, was being decided, and all he could do was watch.

"For performance, ladies and gentlemen…" Hope paused for dramatic effect.

The brilliant lights appeared again, swirling tantalizingly before forming the score. Arthur could see that he had the edge this time. In fourth place, for two points: George Washington. Leaving Benjamin Franklin in fifth place with one point. They were now tied with a total of three points each.

A wave of panic rose up inside Arthur. He was sixteen years old, but if he stepped through that gate, then his life would be over. He didn't care what Martha's Vineyard was like—it would be his prison, his tomb. He felt physically sick.

More dramatic music and pauses.

Arthur looked around desperately. Claire and the professor were watching nervously. The candidates' expressions were unreadable, guarded. Uncle was still standing in the wings, his arms folded across his chest, his eyes not leaving Arthur for a second.

"Finally. The moment we have all been waiting for. One candidate will be leaving tonight. His political dreams over forever. Scores, please."

The music swelled as images of the two final candidates flashed in the air *all around the auditorium. The excitement soared. The lights that would determine their destinies appeared, dancing interminably, tantalizingly around the entire amphitheater. Slowly, painfully slowly, pulling themselves into place, high in the sky.*

It was done.

In fourth place, with two points: Benjamin Franklin. Leaving George Washington in second place. Ben was out, and George had made it to the final primary.

The crowd was going crazy, screaming and cheering, chanting, "Wash-ing-ton! Wash-ing-ton!" over and over. For the first time, Arthur noticed his hands were shaking. He felt numb. A condemned man given a temporary reprieve. A temporary stay of execution.

Quickly he glanced at Ben, who was looking out impassively at the crowd. Arthur's relief evaporated as it hit him. He had been so caught up in his own fate that he hadn't stopped to think about Ben.

The sad notes of the "Retirement Theme" swelled in the air. Heavy, powerful music that brought tears to the nation's eyes, as Ben was escorted to the shimmering arch. As the low voice of the narrator droned on, images of Ben's life swirled across the sky, in the air.

But Arthur saw none of it. He was focused on Ben's face. Ben's quiet, sad face.

This was wrong. So wrong.

Ben did not deserve this. Ben was brilliant and kind. He had the right to have a future. Same as everyone else. Not buried away for convenience, by someone afraid of the power he wielded. The power they had given him.

Ben turned slowly to face the light. The audience roared, his silhouette standing resolute against the pearly gateway.

The music gave way to a sad, melancholy coda. Close-ups of Ben's face faded to black across the sky. It was time. Ben stepped forward, slowly climbing the stairs toward the arch. He reached the top of the dais, pausing inches from the light.

"No!" Arthur sprinted toward Ben, vaulting onto the dais.

He had no plan, no idea what he was doing. He just knew that this wasn't right. He grabbed Ben's arm, pulling him back from the arch. The audience squealed in delight at the surprise entertainment. This was nail-biting drama. No candidate had ever challenged the Retirement. It would be talked about in locker rooms and cafés for weeks.

Ben looked at him in surprise.

"George, what are you doing?"

Arthur couldn't answer that. He was acting on instinct alone, and his instinct was to protect his friend.

"This isn't right. You haven't done anything wrong." Arthur's voice echoed around the amphitheater. "You…you have your whole life ahead. They can't take that away from you. Don't do it. Just don't go through there." Arthur waved his arm wildly at the arch. His fingers sweeping inside the light. His fingers tingled.

No more music. No more mawkish voiceovers. The crowd had fallen quiet in rapt anticipation, not wanting to miss a word. Hope was frozen, twitching slightly as though her programming was being reset.

Everyone was watching the two candidates.

Ben smiled at Arthur, sadly.

"I appreciate the gesture, George. Really. But we both know that's not an option." He was speaking softly, carefully choosing his words, like an adult explaining something to a child. With a tight smile, he turned back to face the arch.

For the first time, Arthur noticed that Uncle had stepped onto the edge of the stage surrounded by Secret Service men. Poised and ready. The Retirement was happening, whether Arthur liked it or not. Ben understood that and somewhere inside, Arthur knew it too. Cain wasn't about to let his Democracy Games get messed up by a rebellious candidate.

So maybe he couldn't stop the Retirement. Maybe Ben was going through that arch tonight, and maybe there was nothing Arthur could do about it. But one thing he could do was stand by his friend. Arthur put his hand on Ben's shoulder and turned to face the arch with him.

"If you go…I go."

The silence was deafening.

The lights were subtly dimming. They were being shut down. Out of the corner of his eye, the black-clad Secret Service agents were moving in, but they would never reach him in time.

Arthur looked into the shimmering lights, his heart racing with fear. This was it. He put one foot forward.

A solitary clapping suddenly rang out across the auditorium, shattering the tense silence.

Arthur turned in the direction of the sound. It was coming from the press section. He peered into the dark, trying to make out the source. It seemed to be a woman. She looked young with long, smooth dark hair, dressed in a smart black suit, like all the press corps. She moved a step forward so that the light from the stage reflected off her face.

Arthur held his breath in surprise. He knew it couldn't be her, but somehow she reminded him of Bay. A smarter, more sophisticated version of his scruffy best friend. He squinted into the dark, trying to focus on her face. Their eyes met briefly across the immense auditorium, and then the young woman almost imperceptibly shook her head. She took a step back and was instantly lost in the dark crowd.

Suddenly a new noise caught Arthur's attention. The crowd had picked up on the young woman's lead, and a wave of clapping was spreading through the audience. The crowd hadn't known what to make of Arthur's unprecedented behavior but must have decided to run with it. After all, if their hero, George Washington, was prepared to risk everything for his friend, it must be the right thing to do. The clapping turned to cheering and stomping, getting louder and louder until it sounded like a hysterical roar.

Arthur felt a flash of hope.

Maybe, just maybe, if the crowd was on their side…was it possible that *they could stop the Retirement? Arthur quickly turned to Ben, to see what he was making of this.*

But Ben wasn't there.

Arthur spun around quickly, to face the arch, dreading what he would see.

Ben's shadowy outline was floating in the arch, shimmering ethereally just beyond reach. It seemed to pause, as though for one last look at the world, before evaporating into a shower of golden sparks, whipping through the air as the arch swirled into a vortex and closed, for good.

Ben was gone.

"No!" Arthur fell to his knees.

The lights in the amphitheater faded to black. The stars appeared twinkling peacefully in the night sky above them, as if none of this had happened. The delighted crowd continued chanting, shouting, wanting more. This had to rate as the best Retirement ever.

The dramatic finale music was wrapping up.

The Democracy Games—Retirement Special was over.

Show's over, folks. Go home. Hope you enjoyed watching teenagers battle for their freedom, for their lives. Great fun, right?

Arthur shook his head, trying to clear his thoughts.

An unwelcome figure pushed in front of him, his heavy outline looming against the night sky.

"You're coming with me, *sir.*" Uncle managed to make the *sir* sound like a dirty word. Two more Secret Service agents moved up next to Uncle.

But as Arthur looked at the jowly, angry face of the older man, he felt something new stirring inside him. Something strong rising through the sadness. He had just been through a tortuous primary, faced Retirement, and watched his friend sacrifice himself. What more could Uncle do to him?

For the first time he could remember, Arthur met Uncle's

bloodshot glare. With his heart thumping wildly, he defiantly stood up. His fists clenched tight. Uncle's eyes widened in surprise. But before Arthur could move, an arm locked around his neck, firmly pulling him backward. He struggled, but the neck grip just tightened, until stars appeared in front of his eyes.

"Dumb freak." Uncle leaned forward, his breath reeking with the stink of stale alcohol. "Think you're something now, do you? Well, I know who you really are. Loser."

More hands gripped Arthur's arms, and before he knew it, he was being dragged off the stage, backward. He half stumbled, half fell down the stairs, Uncle pushing him down the last few steps. A circle of black-suited Secret Service agents quickly surrounded him, and he was forcibly hustled out of the dark amphitheater and into a waiting unit.

Not taking any chances, Uncle climbed in behind him. "Mount Vernon," he barked at the unit console, one hand grabbing Arthur's jacket and forcing him back into the corner of the seat.

As they silently swept away, Arthur noticed a commotion behind the amphitheater. A small fire was flickering wildly at the base of the wall behind the press area, right where he had seen the woman with the dark hair. Security Police had the area surrounded and locked down. Arthur pushed back hard against Uncle's grip, twisting in his seat, trying to get a better look.

There on the wall, lit by the dancing shadows from the flames, he saw something that made his heart skip a beat. A red oval, spray painted crudely, with a large inverted V crossing the bottom. He had seen the red "A" many times in the graffiti on walls in the Outside. A for Abel, the mysterious rebel leader. But this, there was something different.

Three small stars were painted scrappily on one side of the oval.

Arthur's mouth dropped open in surprise. He glanced down at his forearm, the smudged marker still visible against his skin. The crude stars on his arm matched the graffiti exactly.

Turning slowly back in his seat, Arthur's exhaustion finally caught up with him. His mind wandered, filling with images of Ben dissolving into light, the girl with the dark hair, the graffiti. He had to know what was going on. He was a part of something he didn't understand. Something Uncle was determined to keep him away from.

Tonight someone had sent him a message, and he was damned if he would let this go.

Chapter 9

The following morning, Arthur woke to the sound of birds singing and the delectable smell of a wholesome Mount Vernon breakfast. But instead of savoring the moment, he felt a faint sense of nausea, as the events from the night before flooded his mind. He bounded out of bed, his mind racing. An anxious energy burned at him.

Throwing on his running clothes, he quietly tiptoed down the stairs and out the back door. He was careful to avoid running into anyone, staying clear of the doors to the professor's study and Claire's room.

Today, he wanted to be alone.

He ran hard and fast, as if something was chasing him, pushing himself until he couldn't take it any longer, and collapsing breathlessly onto a tree stump deep in the woods. There, in the peaceful green glen, his thoughts finally caught up with him. What was going on? He kept seeing the woman in the press section. It couldn't be Bay. He knew that. But then there was the graffiti on the wall. The oval with three stars. Of course it was a coincidence. It couldn't have anything to do with his car emblem; that wouldn't make any sense. He had nothing to do with Abel and the Red Rebels.

Confusion tore at his thoughts until a noise behind him made him jump.

A small brown rabbit was sitting about ten feet away from him. Its big brown eyes staring nervously at him, ears straight up, alert. For a moment Arthur and the rabbit just stared at each other, feeling like two prey in a world full of predators. Then suddenly a small movement in the bushes made the rabbit hop away.

Arthur looked for the source of the movement, peering closely at the bushes. He stood up and walked over, keeping his eyes on them at all times. He reached out and pulled aside a fern, peering into the shadows. Suddenly a small camera drone swooped out, nearly smacking him in the face. He stepped back in surprise, almost tripping over a branch. The drone hovered in the air above him for a moment. Then slowly, all around, more drones materialized out of branches and leaves. There were at least ten of them, all making their presence known to him.

Arthur's hands were shaking now. He felt anger rising up. Deep, strong anger. At the security police for spying on him, violating his privacy. At himself for being so stupid he thought that he could actually be alone, free even for just a short time. When would he finally get it? When would Arthur Ryan finally wake up to the fact that he was not free? That his life in the Outside, with no opportunities or hope, had been freer than this crazy world he was now a part of. Like it or not.

He instinctively grabbed the branch at his feet and swung it hard at the nearest drone. The drone moved easily out of the way. Arthur threw the stick at another drone, then turned on his heels and ran.

By the time he arrived back at Mount Vernon, the exercise had done little to quell his bad mood. He noticed a Secret Service unit parked in the driveway as he bounded up to the front door. This time he wasn't quiet and didn't care if he ran into anyone. He felt like he was ready to burst with indignation and would have happily let rip at anyone in his path. But the house was eerily quiet. He stomped over to the professor's study, but unusually she wasn't there. Disappointed, he spent the rest of the day in his room, banging things around and doing push-ups and crunches, trying to dissipate some of his pent-up emotions.

By dinnertime, he was starting to feel more cheerful. His confusion and anger at being spied on had passed, and the thought of food and friends warmed him inside. He had missed his Mount Vernon evenings and threw on some respectable clothes, racing downstairs to the green room.

Claire and the professor were already there, but instead of Evan, another man in a dark Secret Service suit was seated with his back to Arthur. Claire and the professor had stony expressions and were both looking down at their plates. The man stood up and turned to face Arthur. It was Uncle, his puffy face pulled into a smug expression. Arthur's happiness evaporated instantly.

"Where…where's Evan?" Arthur said, worried about his friend.

"Patrolling the perimeter. Doing his job for once," Uncle said dismissively. "Secretary Cain personally requested I take over your security detail. Seems he was not too impressed by your televised performance and wants a firmer hand involved in your supervision."

Arthur winced when he said "firmer hand."

Uncle continued.

"Wherever you go, I go from now on. So no more little solo excursions to the woods." Uncle was beaming. He was obviously delighted to have been given this new responsibility and seemed to be taking it as some kind of promotion.

Arthur felt like vomiting. His stomach felt like it had flipped upside down. The one place he had felt safe, was now violated. The one man he feared more than any other sat back in his chair, spread his legs arrogantly, and made himself comfortable, the gesture asserting his dominance over the younger man.

Arthur looked at Claire and the professor. They were both watching him. The professor looked concerned, but Claire's expression was unreadable. He couldn't stand this and needed some space to think.

"I just came to say I'm not hungry. I'm not eating tonight," he mumbled awkwardly. He turned toward the door, but Uncle's low, menacing voice stopped him.

"Yes, you are. You will sit down and eat with us. Nephew."

It was as though nothing had changed.

Arthur was the little, scared kid in the Outside, with Uncle ordering him to the table. If he defied him, Uncle would take a strap to him until he couldn't stand or walk. If he didn't eat everything on his plate, he wouldn't be fed for days as a punishment. If he dared to make eye contact, he would get a hard slap to the head.

Arthur felt his hands shaking. He wanted to tell Uncle to get out of his house and never come back. But it was like something inside had locked up.

A flush of humiliation rose to his cheeks.

He wasn't a little kid anymore, he told himself. He had stood up to Uncle at the Retirement, in the heat of the moment. He could stand up to him again, here in his own home. He was strong now, taller than Uncle. He was George Washington, damn it.

But it didn't help. He couldn't do it.

The years of abuse had left their mark on him, deep inside

where no one could see it.

He knew he was broken, damaged, no good.

"Arthur." Claire's calm, sweet voice cut though his confusion. Arthur jumped at the touch of her small hand in his. She was close to him, pulling him to face her.

Her large eyes were fixed on his, pulling him back from the edge. He felt his anxiety melt away.

"Come and sit by me." She led him to a chair at the farthest end of the table from Uncle and sat down between them.

Then she did something unusual for her.

She started making small talk. She asked questions about everyone's day, the weather, and the food. She was collected and calm and steered the way through dinner. She had quietly stolen the power away from Uncle, and everyone knew it. Uncle had fallen quiet after a while, sensing the change in dynamic. He would have to get his satisfaction some other time.

Arthur focused on Claire. On her voice, her face, on the feeling of her hand that kept reaching out and gently touching his. Seeing her handle Uncle, undermine his brute authority with such gentle grace was a beautiful thing, and he felt an odd mix of respect for her and shame at his own weakness.

They all ate fast, finishing dinner in record time, and quickly headed off separately to their own rooms.

Arthur dashed up the stairs toward his bedroom, lost in dark thoughts. Uncle's unwelcome arrival had felt like the icing on a bitter cake he was being forced to eat. His bad mood from earlier was back in full force, and he was actually looking forward to returning to Camp David in a few days' time, to start training. At least there, with the other candidates, there was no pretense that he was a free man.

He was so consumed with his resentment that he almost tripped over a pair of big feet blocking the top of the stairway. Evan was sitting on the top step, looking the worse for wear.

"Was'h it ya wee piker," Evan slurred, swinging a hand and knocking over a bottle of scotch. Fortunately, the bottle was empty and rolled noisily across the wooden floorboards without breaking.

"Evan!" Arthur was so delighted to see his friend he hugged him, almost immediately backing off and turning the hug into a manly backslapping. "I was worried about you. What happened? Where did Uncle send you?"

"Och, he tried ta ke'p me busy wi' bits an' pieces. But he can'na wa'sh me all a time, big, hairy git." Evan descended into chuckles of laughter, and Arthur couldn't help but join in, even though he hadn't understood a word. Evan's accent became more Scottish the more he drank.

Arthur's bad mood had completely evaporated, and he happily sat down next to the drunken Scot.

"Tha' said, I can'na stay long, afore said git comes a lookin'. I came a gi' you this." He reached into his pocket and fumbled around for a moment, eventually pulling out a small package wrapped in lined white paper.

"You brought me a present?" Arthur almost laughed out loud. Evan didn't strike him as the present-giving sort.

"Och, is no from me, laddie." Evan pulled himself to his feet, pushing down heavily on Arthur's shoulder. When he made it to standing, he paused and wobbled, reaching out his big hand to pat Arthur affectionately on the head.

"Ow," said Arthur, and they both laughed.

"Ahm bein' reassigned ta Washington firs' thing tomorrow," he said, swaying slightly. "See ya round, kiddo. An' you can keep the whiskey."

"Gee, thanks," Arthur said glancing at the empty bottle. They looked at each other warmly. Arthur didn't want to think about when they would see each other again. He pushed the thought from his mind and watched his friend stumble down the stairs, singing some old army drinking song as he went.

Arthur walked into his bedroom, squeezing the small package curiously. It felt like something small, about the size and shape of a lipstick tube. He was about to rip off the paper when he noticed there was writing on the inside of it. He unwrapped it carefully, pulling out a silver tube with a fine line around the middle. Etched into the surface at one end were two small letters.

Arthur held it up to the light to see better—SW. He fiddled with it curiously, realizing that the two halves rotated a quarter turn. He turned them back and forth a few times, but nothing else seemed to happen, so he turned to the paper, smoothing it flat on his desk. The writing was Ben's.

To George Washington,

Thank you, my friend. The courage you showed gave me hope for us all. Please don't worry about me. Retirement is undoubtedly a risk, but in my case, it is a calculated one. After all, I am a man of science, not theater. I believe that this will not be the end and that someday we will meet again. Until that day comes, take care and use this gift wisely.

Your friend,

Benjamin Franklin

Arthur's mind was racing. A "calculated" risk. What did Ben mean?

His mind flashed back to the primary. Ben slumped by the door to his cell, all the colors figured out. He had only one color left to enter, one button to push, and he would have escaped. Suddenly it made sense. Ben had it all ready to go, but he had waited. He had failed on purpose. He had deliberately thrown the primary.

Arthur's mind reeled. Why would anyone choose to be Retired? Was it, like, a suicide? Was Ben saying that he was done with the games, the struggle? But then the note had said that Ben believed they would meet again. That did not sound like someone who was giving up on life.

Arthur realized he was gripping the cylinder hard, a rising tide of frustration building inside him. The one thing he did know was that Ben didn't deserve this. Not any of it. None of them did. They may have been made by Cain, but they were still human, under everything. Still people trying to live their lives. Not lab rats or Cain's playthings. But what could any of them do about it?

Arthur walked over to his bed and slipped the cylinder under his pillow next to Bay's car emblem, pausing for a moment to look at the two objects, lying next to each other. As he stood there, he made a silent promise to Bay and Ben. He would try to fix things, to make things right for them all. He had no idea how or when, or even if he could, but he as he looked at the two small silver objects, he promised to try.

The next few days passed painfully slowly. Claire had left Mount Vernon early the following morning, and Arthur and the professor barely saw each other, both trying to stay out of Uncle's way.

Uncle had practically taken over the house. He had security drones patrolling the hallways and agents stationed at all the exits. He seemed to go out of his way to try to make Arthur feel particularly uncomfortable, following him around, even walking into his room uninvited at random times. He was trying to assert his authority through his usual tactics of bullying and cowing people into submission.

The night before training was due to restart, Arthur found he was actually looking forward to it. Anything was better than being here at Uncle's mercy. He lay awake in the refuge of his sheets for hours, tossing and turning, reliving memories in an ugly mess of dark thoughts, not daring to think about the future, willing himself to sleep.

At three, when he had given up all hope of sleep, a quiet knock at the door made him jump. He had thought everyone else must have been asleep hours ago. He rolled off the bed and walked to the door, opening it a crack, keeping his fingers crossed it wasn't Uncle trying to mess with him one last time.

Claire was standing outside in a casual pair of sweatpants and a vest, her white-blond hair loose and messy, falling across her narrow shoulders. She looked different without her usual perfect hair and makeup; younger and more vulnerable, like the eighteen-year-old girl she was underneath everything.

"Hey. When did you get back?" Arthur asked, glad for the company.

"Just now. I guessed you would be having trouble sleeping too. Want company?" Claire asked, looking up at him questioningly.

"You mean, in my room?" Of course she meant in his room. What was he thinking? Or more to the point, what was she thinking? He swallowed nervously, not wanting to get ahead of himself.

Claire nodded, and Arthur stepped out of the doorway, quickly looking around to make sure his room wasn't too messy. Claire walked straight over and perched lightly on the edge of the bed. She looked like a delicate little bird, her usual self-possession stripped away without her high heels and smart suits. Arthur shifted his weight awkwardly from one foot to the other, not daring to approach the bed. He wasn't going to take any chances on misreading the situation.

"Agent Connors is still here, isn't he?" she said. Arthur just nodded uncomfortably. He really didn't want to think about Uncle right now.

"You know, we're more alike than you realize." She hung her head, pushing her hair back out of her face. "I was wondering if you could see it, if you could tell from looking at me. No one else here would ever know because they're not like us. They can never, ever understand." She looked at him searchingly, trying to see if he understood. But he had no idea what she meant.

"Arthur, I'm an Outsider too."

"You're from the Outside?" Arthur couldn't believe what she had just said. People weren't like her there. They were tough and dangerous. Damaged by life. As he thought it, an image popped into his mind of the scars he had seen on her back. Could it be possible? He walked over to the bed and sat down next to her, a dozen questions racing through his head.

"But…you can't be. Look at you." He gestured at her petite build and soft pale skin, unable to find the words.

"My parents were farmers. We were very poor, I remember days with no food, the farm always failing. But I remember being happy with my mom, dad, and baby sister." Claire paused, looking forlorn. "When I was six, the paravirus hit our town."

Arthur remembered it well. The paravirus was the fear of all

Outsiders. A constantly evolving virus, it thrived in host animals, occasionally changing into a new lethal strain that would ravage the Outsiders. During an outbreak, the zones would be sealed, and the Outsiders left to fend for themselves until a new vaccination was engineered, which could take days or sometimes weeks. Arthur had lived through three outbreaks and remembered well the horrifying fear as people hid in their houses, powerless and afraid. He remembered going back on the school bus after each outbreak and counting the number of now empty seats, trying to remember the faces that had gone for good.

"They didn't make it. I lost my family." Claire's voice had dropped to a whisper.

For a moment Arthur wasn't sure he had heard her correctly, but then the words sank in. He felt a well of pity in his stomach. He had never had a family and had spent his life feeling like he was missing the most important part of him. Having parents, siblings, a family—and then losing them all—must be the worst pain a person could feel.

"Oh, Claire. I'm so sorry," he finally managed to say. He reached across to touch her hand, but she pulled away from him slightly, almost imperceptibly. She didn't want sympathy.

"I had a choice to die or survive." A hard edge had crept into her tone as though protective walls had dropped down inside her. "So I learned to be strong and fend for myself, because from that day on, no one has ever looked after me. I did what I had to do."

Arthur didn't know what to say. His head was full of everything she had told him. He had never guessed for even a second that Claire was hiding such dark secrets, such pain. No wonder she was so protective and private. The thought of a six-year-old, vulnerable little girl, completely alone in the brutal Outside, was nothing short of horrific.

He wanted to gather her up in his arms and hold her, as if he could somehow protect her from the past. He reached for her hand again, and she let him take it this time.

There was a long moment of silence. Both of them lost in their thoughts. Finally, Claire turned to him again.

"Arthur, I loved George, with all my heart. He was a good man, a great man." Arthur felt chastened as if she was warning him off, but then she continued. "But he never knew me. He couldn't. To him, I was perfect, pure. He worshipped me in a way I didn't deserve. He put me on a pedestal, the last place I should be."

Arthur was surprised.

"He didn't know about you? About where you came from?" he asked.

"He wouldn't have understood," Claire said quietly.

Arthur was shocked. For a moment he felt confused. If she had never told George, the man she loved, why was she telling him? Why now?

As if she had read his mind, Claire looked at him.

"But you're different, Arthur. You do understand," she said softly.

Her expression was filled with a new intensity now. She moved closer to him, pushing against him. Arthur swallowed nervously, not daring to move, wondering if he was misreading the situation.

Through the fabric of his shirt he could feel Claire's heart beating calmly as she leaned into his shoulder. His heart was racing wildly, and his stomach felt like he had just dropped ten feet on a roller coaster. He swallowed again loudly, cussing himself for the nervous habit, and hoping she didn't hear him.

"Can I stay? I don't want to be alone," she whispered.

Gently she pulled him toward her, looking into his eyes as somehow they fell back onto the bed, still wrapped together. As they lay there, Arthur's awkwardness started to disappear as something deeper took over. A warm fog blurred his thoughts, and feelings he had never experienced flooded through him. Instinctively he did the one thing that felt right, leaning in and softly, sweetly kissing her. As she kissed him back, it felt as if time stopped, as if it was just the two of them alone in the world.

The only thing he knew in that moment, the only thing that mattered, was that Claire, his Claire, would be staying the night.

Chapter 10

Early the next morning, Arthur was standing, shivering in his shorts by the edge of a forest, wondering dreamily if he looked different now. Everyone must see that he was a changed man. A man, not a kid anymore. He felt so good, he couldn't have cared less about the training exercise they were about to start. He glanced over toward the other candidates. Only four now, with Ben gone. He slipped his hand into his shorts pocket and pulled out the smooth cylinder Ben had given him. He liked the feel of the smooth metal and turned it around with his fingers distractedly, his fingers brushing the letters SW.

Sadness rose up inside him as he thought of his friend, but he pushed the feeling away. Not now, there wasn't room for any bad feelings today.

He couldn't wait for the Mik to quit barking and start the challenge. Arthur had so much energy he felt he would explode if they didn't get going soon.

Every day this week, they would be completing a joint training exercise before returning separately to their own homes for the late afternoon and evening. Arthur suspected the exercises were just to provide daily footage of the candidates. They had to fill *The Democracy Games* with something new, to build the excitement before the final primary in a week's time.

Today's challenge actually looked fun. It was like a giant game of capture the flag with laser tag and virtual soldiers thrown in for good measure. The goal was to locate and make it into the soldiers' virtual camp and procure key intel without getting shot. The candidates would get a five-minute head start on their virtual enemy.

The Mik was still talking, but Arthur tuned out; thoughts of last night wafted into his mind, and he smiled to himself. His reverie was broken abruptly when Kennedy whomped him hard with his shoulder on his way to the starting lineup. The cylinder went flying onto the ground, Arthur quickly bending down to pick it up and slipping it back in his pocket. He glanced around to see if anyone had noticed. Martin was staring right at him, a hard look on his face.

Arthur wasn't sure if he should smile or glare back. Ever since the night at the pool, he had felt awkward around Martin. He was pretty sure that Martin wasn't going to tell anyone who he really was; after all, he would have done it by now if he was going to. But Arthur felt intimidated by him. Martin could destroy Arthur in a second if he wanted to, and they both knew it.

"Just ignore him. He's just jealous," Harry said as she moved past him into her place in the lineup. For a moment Arthur thought she was talking about Martin and looked at her in confusion. Then he realized she was glaring in Kennedy's direction.

"Why would he be jealous of me?" Arthur asked, a little incredulously.

"You don't know? You really are just a pretty face, aren't you, Washington." Harry laughed, but not unkindly. Martin had joined the lineup, and Arthur shuffled forward into position.

"You forgot that you stole his girl? That crack on the head must have given you selective memory."

"His girl?" Claire. Of course, that made perfect sense. George must have seduced the lovely Claire away from Kennedy, and he had never forgiven him for it. No wonder Kennedy hated him. He would have hated him too.

Arthur glanced over toward Kennedy. He was poised to sprint, looking lithe and athletic like a tiger ready to pounce on an unsuspecting prey. Arthur had to admit Kennedy was an impressive candidate. He was the full deal—intelligent, strong, handsome, and determined. If only he could lose the giant chip on his shoulder, he could make a good, possibly great president, maybe even outliving the legacy of the original J. F. Kennedy.

As if noticing Arthur's attention, Kennedy glared over at him and gave an obnoxiously smug grin. He surreptitiously pointed two fingers at him and pulled an imaginary air trigger, then turned back dismissively to face the forest, not wasting his precious focus on losers. Arthur mentally took back all his charitable thoughts, hoping he'd get a chance to shoot him with his laser and wipe that smug expression off his face.

The countdown had begun. The last few seconds ticked away, and they were off, running into the woods, trying to get some distance from each other. Arthur ran for several minutes, finally stopping to catch his breath by a fallen tree. He fiddled with his gun, trying to figure out how to shoot, accidentally hitting a few innocent trees and bushes with flashes of blue electricity.

He hadn't come up with a great strategy other than hide and follow soldiers, so he slowly started creeping through the woods, quietly listening for any sounds that might give him a lead. Soon he dropped to his knees as he spotted a movement in the distance. Two virtual soldiers seemed to be patrolling along the edge of a small gully. As they moved out of view, another more subtle movement caught his attention. Harry stepped out from behind a tree, barely visible in her camouflaged training clothes, her hood pulled over her head. She moved after the soldiers, silently and stealthily through the forest, laser ready. Keeping as far back as he could without losing sight of her, Arthur followed. He watched as she paused at the edge of the gully, squatting down as if listening. The distant sound of fighting came to him through the trees, somewhere off to the left. Harry jumped up, moving quickly toward the noise along the gully's edge. Arthur followed, running after her at a safe distance.

Suddenly, as Arthur sprinted past a large tree, something whammed him hard in the chest. His feet flew out from under him, and he crashed to the ground, landing on his back. He gasped to catch his breath, winded by the impact, when a boot kicked him over the edge of the gully. He tumbled down the grassy slope, dropping his gun as he scrambled for a handhold to slow his fall. The instant he stopped sliding, his assailant was upon him.

It was Martin, looking dangerous and angry. Martin roughly pushed an elbow into Arthur's neck, squeezing hard so Arthur couldn't speak. His hands roughly searched him, finally reaching into his pocket and pulling out the cylinder. As soon as he had it, he jumped off Arthur and stepped back.

Arthur coughed, rubbing his neck and started to sit up, but Martin held up a hand warningly. Camera drones were swooping in on the two of them, capturing the moment. Martin lifted his gun, pointing it directly at Arthur's chest. Arthur readied himself for the blast, and then he noticed something that stopped him. Martin's right hand hung at his side, but his palm was turned forward, giving Arthur, and only Arthur, a clear view of the cylinder. As he watched, Martin flicked the top half with his thumb, holding it in a quarter turn for about a second, then squeezing down on the top. Instantly all of the camera drones dropped out of the sky, crashing dead to the ground.

Arthur's jaw dropped open in surprise. That's what Ben's present was for? He looked back at Martin, who for the first time in weeks, was smiling.

"One of Ben's little toys; he called it the IMP, Intra-Magnetic Pulse," Martin added, tossing the cylinder back to Arthur. Arthur held it in his hand and stared at it, fascinated.

"OK, so…I'm confused," Arthur said, squinting up at Martin.

"You're always confused, man. Seriously. You've made this whole, babe-in-the-woods, naive thing into an art form." Martin lowered his gun and walked over to Arthur, squatting down on the ground next to him. Arthur almost protested, but then it occurred to him that it was probably a fair assessment. He felt like he was always blowing in the wind, trying to catch up with everything going on around him.

"It's not a criticism. I like you," Martin added, inoffensively. "Look, we don't have too long. The IMP only works for a few minutes, and Cain's going to go ballistic when he finds out his eyes and ears are out of commission." As he said this, he reached out and picked up one of the drone cameras, pitching it hard against the nearest tree. It smashed with a satisfying crunch.

Ben's gift finally made sense. Ben had given Arthur a way to escape from constant surveillance, a way to speak freely without Cain's supervision. Arthur smiled and silently thanked Ben.

"Listen, Arthur. I needed to warn you. You *must* be more careful, man. All that business with Ben and the Retirement—directly challenging Cain's authority in front of the entire UZA! And what was with the shirt art, the arm tattoo?" He shook his head, looking for all the world like a despairing parent.

"You mean the car emblem?" Arthur was surprised to even hear it mentioned. It was such an insignificant thing, a small gesture he had made to try to let Bay know he was OK.

"Yes. The Outsider car emblem." Martin was talking slowly like he was explaining something to a small child. "Arthur. In case you haven't noticed, we are a nation at war with itself. You are in Cain's world now, and if he thinks you are a threat, if he thinks you are playing both sides, he will take you down." Martin emphasized the last three words, sending a small chill down Arthur's spine.

"But, I'm not! I'm not a rebel. Why would anyone think I am? That's just crazy." Arthur realized he was shouting.

Martin laughed loudly.

"I know you're not a rebel, Arthur." Martin was grinning at the thought. Arthur tried not to be too offended. "But you have got to be more careful. Maybe you really are just clueless, but that won't stop Cain. If he thinks you might hurt his cause, he will destroy you. Keep to the script. No more unpredictable stuff, all right?"

Arthur looked up at him. A dozen questions raced through his mind.

"Martin, why are you telling me this?"

For the first time, Martin looked serious.

"You've got people worried about you, Arthur. Good people."

"Who? What good people?" Suddenly a thought occurred to Arthur. It made sense, clear as daylight. "Martin, are you…playing both sides? Are you a rebel?"

As soon as he said the words out loud, Arthur regretted it. You can't just go around accusing people of being Red Rebels. Being a rebel, or even a rebel sympathizer, was considered the worst crime on the books. The punishment was public execution.

But Martin just looked at him thoughtfully, until a gentle whirring noise cut in, signaling the awakening of the camera drones.

Martin was on his feet in seconds.

"Another time, my friend. Don't forget what I told you. Be careful, you're playing with fire. Oh, and…sorry," Martin added, giving a faintly uncomfortable smile.

"Sorry?" Arthur said, confused. "For what?"

Martin pointed his gun at Arthur's chest and pulled the trigger without a moment's hesitation. Arthur fell back as the blue, electric shock coursed through him. He wouldn't be going anywhere for a long time.

Through a disoriented fog, he heard Martin's footsteps disappear into the trees, replaced seconds later with a buzzing as a camera drone zeroed in for a close-up on his face. What he wouldn't give to shoot the darn thing out of the sky. Right now though, all he could do was lie back, close his eyes, and wait for this day to be over.

The rest of the week went by quickly. The morning training exercises were becoming a welcome break from the uncomfortable evenings at Mount Vernon. Uncle still followed him everywhere, making his unwelcome presence felt at every opportunity. Arthur had accepted that Mount Vernon was no longer safe. His hours there, under constant surveillance, felt the hardest, as they reminded him of what he had lost. He desperately missed the good old days when it had just been the professor, Evan, and Claire.

Claire was in the Washington Metrozone and wasn't expected back until the night before the final primary. Arthur hadn't spoken to her since they'd spent the night together, and he felt a weird mix of exhilaration and nervousness at the thought of seeing her again. He had no idea where they stood now. Perhaps this the start of something? He really hoped so but didn't want to get his hopes up. It could also have been a one-off. Maybe she regretted it and was avoiding him? After all, he hadn't heard a word from her since she left. Whenever he thought about it, his stomach felt tied up in knots, so he tried to keep busy and distract himself.

At night he'd been having trouble sleeping. Maybe it was because of his chat with Martin, but he kept having intense dreams about Bay and the Outside. The dreams always followed the same story.

He was in the Outside, and Bay was standing in front of him, calling to him, only she had no voice. She was trying to warn him of something, but he just couldn't understand. Then finally something would make him turn around, and he would see a giant wall of red fire, as high as a building, racing toward him. He would start running toward Bay, but it was always too late. The fire would lap at his heels and as it consumed him, Arthur would wake up, dripping in sweat, his heart racing.

One night, after a particularly horrible dream when the flames had turned into wild dogs, Arthur decided to walk off his anxiety rather than lie in bed worrying. He tiptoed down the stairs, hoping that some of the evening snacks were still in the dining room. He was lucky; there was still a delicious spread of fruit and sweets set out just waiting for him. He happily piled up a huge stash in a fold in his shirt and was about to sneak back upstairs, when he heard voices.

There was some kind of argument going on, the voices raised in anger. For a moment Arthur considered staying out of it and sneaking back to his room, but curiosity got the better of him, and he followed the sound. The voices were coming from the professor's study, a man and a woman, sounding alternately furious and anguished. Arthur knew the woman's voice was the professor's, but it took a few more moments to recognize Uncle's rough low accent. The door was open and Arthur peeked through. The two of them were by the window, Uncle pacing furiously in front of the professor, who was sitting in her wheelchair, her face turned away from him.

"How could you even think I would ever forgive you, Robert?" The professor's tone was higher than normal, and she sounded tense. "After what you did to me? You betrayed me. I came back for you. I gave up everything for you, for us. I gave up what I believed in, my freedom…I gave up my daughter." These last words were choked as emotion overwhelmed her ability to speak.

Arthur stood in stunned silence. Her daughter? She had never mentioned a daughter. He suddenly felt ashamed of himself for listening in. This was obviously very private, and he had no place being here. He turned to go, but Uncle's next words stopped him.

"You betrayed me. You said you loved me, but all the while you cheated. You had a child with…that bastard." These last words were growled, menacingly.

"So that's it. After all these years, it still comes down to plain old jealousy. What predictable creatures we humans are." She wheeled over to her table and picked up her glass of wine. "Those times, when the walls were being raised…they were dark, terrible days for all of us. I was lonely and scared. My own brother was having us hunted down like dogs. We didn't know if we would survive the week, and…" she paused. "You weren't there, Robert. You chose my brother and left me…" A sharp crash of glass interrupted her.

Arthur quickly moved back to the door and looked in. Uncle had the professor by the throat; her glass lay shattered on the floor next to her. Arthur recognized the look on Uncle's face. It was the same look he used to have all those times when he lost his temper with Arthur and was usually followed by a beating.

"Don't you dare blame me, you cheating liar!" he roared.

Arthur was frozen on the spot. He was more afraid of this man than anyone on earth. He felt like his five-year-old self, rooted in complete terror, watching helplessly as Uncle's meaty hands gripped the professor's throat. Arthur could hear her gasping for air. She was hitting him with her hands, fighting him with all her strength, but Uncle was too strong. She looked around wildly, desperately, her eyes finding Arthur. For one long second they stared at each other, fear written on both their faces.

Then suddenly, it was as if a spell had broken; for the first time in his life, Arthur's fear receded. He threw open the door and ran into the room, spraying his stashed pastries and fruit across the floor. He didn't pause, tackling Uncle hard and knocking them both to the floor. Arthur was the first to his feet. He stood over Uncle his fists clenched, feeling stronger than he ever had in his life.

Uncle looked up at him in shock, but his expression quickly changed to a mocking smile when he saw who his assailant was.

"Look at the scared, cowardly little mouse. Trying to fight me? You really want to do this, boy? Do you?" Uncle roared the last few words and scrambled to his feet. He stood in front of Arthur, his enormous mass looming threateningly toward him, his body tensed, his fists clenched. He was ready to hurt someone.

Arthur felt his courage ebb away. Fear started creeping in as he faced up to his abuser. He knew he couldn't win the fight. Even though he was stronger now, he wasn't a fighter like Uncle. He would get beaten like all the other times in his life. He would have to take it and hope it would stop before it killed him.

Uncle seemed to sense Arthur's self-doubt and edged menacingly forward.

"Just like I thought. Run away, Mr. President. Leave the grown-ups to talk," he said mockingly.

But Arthur wasn't done quite yet. "This is my house, and you will leave." Arthur spoke with all the authority he could muster.

"I don't take orders from you. I work for Secretary Cain, not some useless, little nobody," Uncle sneered, looking momentarily thrown by the change in tactics.

"Then call Secretary Cain now. I have something to say to him." Arthur had no idea what he would actually say to Cain, but he seemed to have stopped Uncle's destructive momentum for now and had to keep going.

Uncle shifted his weight uncomfortably from one foot to the other, looking flustered. Arthur guessed that Uncle did not have the authority to just call up his boss unannounced, but that he didn't want to reveal his lowly status to Arthur. He could tell he had hit a nerve.

"You can't just call the secretary like that. He wouldn't waste his time on idiots like you. It can take weeks to get an appointment to talk with him. He's a very busy man," Uncle said defensively.

"Good thing I have him on speed dial then," the professor said curtly from behind her desk, moving her hand swiftly over the CD. Her voice sounded hoarse from Uncle's chokehold, and her neck had red finger marks around it. She glared defiantly at Uncle, showing no fear of the man who had just attacked her, then turned slightly to face the wall. Cain had appeared, floating in the air, glowing with an unearthly blue light. He was wearing pajamas, his hair ruffled from sleeping.

"Sister, dearest. What a pleasant surprise to receive your call after…oh at least the better part of a decade." He smiled his customary affable grin as he turned slowly and took in Arthur and Uncle.

"Well, isn't this just the family reunion? Arthur. Robert." He nodded in their general direction, the hologram off by a few degrees.

"Arthur has something to say," said the professor, nodding encouragingly to Arthur.

Arthur froze. He really hadn't thought this far ahead. He scrambled to collect his thoughts, blushing red under the hologram's gaze. A long moment of silence passed, everyone staring expectantly at him, his mind blank.

Then Uncle broke the silence with what sounded like a cross between a snicker and a snort. Although he had probably intended to humiliate Arthur even more, it had the opposite effect, and Arthur focused hard on his jowly red face.

"I want Uncle, er...Agent Connors, to be reassigned somewhere, anywhere else. Sir." Arthur looked nervously at the professor for support. Her expression was guarded and unreadable.

"Well now, I assigned him to you personally, Arthur. He's the best in these situations. Why would I move him?" Secretary Cain spoke in his confident, easygoing manner, but his words were tinged with authority. Arthur had no idea where he found his voice; he usually shied away from confrontation, but he had come this far.

"Because, sir, it's him or me." Arthur swallowed nervously, cursing himself for being so darn shy. He dropped his eyes to the floor and focused on his words. "I'm sorry, sir. But either he goes, or...I won't be George Washington anymore. And I want Evan back to replace him." He added this last part spontaneously.

Secretary Cain put his head back and roared with laughter.

"See this, Susanna?" He turned to his sister. "Give them an inch, they take a mile. Well, Arthur, I will say I'm impressed. The little boy who came on board *Air Force One* has indeed grown up. Though, you haven't really thought this through, have you?"

Arthur couldn't have agreed more. He hadn't thought this through at all.

"You see, what will happen if I decline your offer? Uncle would stay, and you would retire as George Washington. So then, what possible use would I have for you, Arthur? You would be, redundant, to put it kindly. So really, the choice you are offering is this: a life without Uncle, or no life. Is that really a hand you want to play?" Cain had the look Arthur remembered from *Air Force One*. He was enjoying himself, playing God with others' lives, without a care.

Arthur looked at the professor. She was sitting quietly, coldly looking at Cain, her hand gently rubbing her neck. There was no love lost between these two. He knew he had to say something, but he was tired and done with these games. Right now he wanted Uncle out of this house, whatever the consequences.

"I'm sorry, sir, but that's the deal. What's it going to be?" Arthur spoke quietly. His words sounded oddly commanding, as though someone much older and wiser had spoken them. Arthur made a mental note to himself—if you don't care what you say, you sound a lot cooler.

Cain was watching him again, fascinated. As though he had created this person and could now test his creation. Finally he spoke.

"I will reassign Agent Connors to Washington." Uncle made a squeak of protest, but Cain held up his hand and silenced him. "Evan will be assigned to your personal security detail. But in return, I require something from you. Quid pro quo."

"What?" Arthur asked nervously.

"It's quite simple really. When you challenged the Retirement, in front of the entire UZA, you challenged me. Publicly." Cain's face had darkened, his eyes glowered menacingly. Arthur was glad the hologram was a few degrees off; the focus of Cain's intense glare landed on a bookshelf.

"That can *never* happen again. From now on, you will agree to do exactly as I instruct you. You will say what you are told to say and do what you are told to do and only that. Do you understand?"

Arthur understood all too well. Cain was tightening his leash.

"Well. Do we have a deal?"

Arthur hadn't planned what had happened during the Retirement. He hadn't meant to challenge anybody, so it should have been easy to agree to Cain's demand. But something about Cain's manner, the bullish tone and implicit threat maybe, made him pause. Arthur knew bullies. His childhood had been spent running from them.

He didn't feel like running anymore.

Cain's eyes narrowed as he glared at the bookshelf. It was as if his hologram could somehow sense the challenge to his authority.

"Choose your next words *very* carefully, young man. Your future depends on it." Without raising his voice, Cain managed to sound both angry and dangerous.

Arthur felt the hairs on the back of his neck rise. More than anything, he wanted to tell the great Secretary Cain to get lost. To stick his deal, no matter the consequences. But even in the heat of the moment, something pulled him back.

This wasn't just about him.

Arthur's eyes flicked over to the professor. She was watching the exchange, her hand still rubbing her neck, her face taut with worry. Right now he had the power to get Uncle out of her life. He could bring Evan home. Mount Vernon would be safe again for the people he cared about, at least for now. There was no way he could pass that up.

"Yes, sir. We have a deal." Arthur's voice was quiet.

"Good." Cain instantly reverted to his usual self. All geniality and affable charm. "Then all that remains is for me to remind you that if you fail to live up to your end of our bargain, we will have to resort to plan B." Yes, no life. Arthur understood. He nodded wearily.

"Now leave us please, Arthur. Robert, I will expect you in Washington, immediately. I have business with my sister." Summarily dismissed, Arthur and Uncle turned and left. As they walked out the door and into the green room, Uncle smacked into Arthur's shoulder hard, swinging him around by his shirt. He pulled him close enough that Arthur could smell the stale beer on his breath.

"I won't forget this. You may think you're safe, now you're all high and mighty with your important friends. But never forget, I know you, the real, sniveling coward inside. I know how to get to you, Arthur Ryan, and I will."

With one last shove, he was gone.

Arthur stood completely still for a few minutes in the cold dark. He listened to the sound of his own breathing and tried to still his racing heart. He had confronted two powerful men tonight and survived. At least for now. That was something that he could hold on to. Tomorrow, he could worry about the rest, he told himself, holding back a feeling of disquiet. He glanced at the snacks still on the dining room table, but his appetite had completely gone. Giving the food one last regretful look, he headed back to bed.

True to his word, Evan was there the following morning. At breakfast no one mentioned the events of last night or Uncle's sudden reassignment. But Arthur noticed that everyone was being unusually nice. The professor was generally pretty bad tempered in the morning, probably hung over. But today she kept wheeling herself past Arthur, passing him food he really could have reached for himself. She had a colorful scarf tied around her neck to hide the bruises Uncle had given her.

Evan was particularly chatty and made even more jokes than usual at Arthur's expense, which Arthur took to be a Scottish sign of affection.

It was the day before the final primary, so there was no official candidate training. Without Uncle, Arthur was free to do whatever he wanted, so he chose to do nothing and wasted the entire day, hanging around Mount Vernon. It felt so good. By evening Arthur was the most relaxed he had been in a long time. He had successfully managed to avoid thinking about the primary all day, and he headed down to dinner, humming cheerfully to himself.

He could hear the sound of laughter from the dining room. The professor and Evan were already there, serving themselves appetizers. Next to them, sitting quietly, was Claire, smiling at the conversation. She turned when Arthur walked in and looked at him warmly, her eyes sparkling in the candlelight.

Arthur's heart leaped with happiness. He had been desperately hoping he would see her again before the primary; tonight, with Uncle gone, it felt like the good old days. The friends were back together one last time. Claire was back.

As usual, the professor and Evan led the conversation, making small talk and jokes. They were animatedly discussing Mr. Sandwich, an infamous hacker who was creating havoc on *The Democracy Games*. The yellow duck avatar of the mysterious computer rebel was popping up almost daily and seemed to have a grudge against Hope. She had unwittingly conducted an entire interview the night before, wearing nothing but a pair of Superman underpants and a deer stalker hat, much to the professor's amusement.

Arthur listened and laughed, only speaking when prompted. He was trying to lock this moment into his heart, taking in every detail and burning it into his memory. The crackle of the fire, the smell of roast turkey and crispy potatoes, the earthy chuckles when the professor laughed at Evan's naughty jokes. The soft, shimmering rose color of Claire's lips.

No one mentioned the primary.

After dessert, everyone started drifting off to their own beds. But Arthur wanted the night to go on longer. He wasn't ready for this to be over, and he certainly wasn't ready to face tomorrow. He turned to Claire.

"Take a walk with me?"

She smiled, and they stepped out into the warm, evening air. They walked down to the lake, the sound of crickets filling the quiet night, their hands finding each other as they wordlessly headed to the old wooden boat dock. They sat on the very end, floating high above the dark sparkling water. Claire slipped her feet out of her delicate, high-heeled shoes, and the two dangled their legs over the end of the dock, swinging them in the air like two kids, without a care in the world.

It was a long time before either of them spoke.

"Are you afraid?" Claire's voice was soft, almost a whisper.

"About the primary? Yeah." Arthur watched the ripples cross the lake's surface as a warm evening breeze gently ruffled their hair. "Just trying not to think about it, I guess. It's not so bad if I don't think about it."

Claire wasn't smiling. She looked out at the dark, sparkling water.

To Arthur's surprise, her enormous eyes had filled with tears. One rolled softly down her face, leaving a trail that shimmered in the moonlight. He tentatively pushed his hand across the wooden dock next to hers, trying to think of what he should be saying. But he couldn't find the words; he could never find the right words.

Finally Claire turned to him and spoke.

"When George had the accident, I thought it was the worst thing that could ever happen to me. Losing someone you love hurts worse than any physical pain ever could. Do you know?"

Arthur didn't know. He had never had anyone close enough to love. He dropped his head silently and listened.

"But now I know I was wrong," Claire continued quietly. "There is something worse. I could lose both of you." Claire's voice tailed off as she choked back a sob.

Was she saying that she cared for him? No one had ever said

that before. He felt a warm fuzzy feeling in his stomach that grew until he felt soft inside and out. Claire cared about him!

"You won't lose me, Claire. I promise."

But even as he said the words, a cloud fell over his happiness. It was a promise he couldn't keep. Tomorrow he would probably lose the primary, and then the best he could hope for would be lifelong incarceration at Martha's Vineyard. More likely, Cain would get rid of him quietly somewhere, burying his secret with him. The more he looked at it, the more he realized that tonight would almost certainly be his last night with Claire. His heart sunk, his momentary joy gone.

"Arthur, I know you can win the primary. That's not what I am worried about. I believe in you more than you believe in yourself."

"Yeah, of course. Sure I can win." He didn't speak with conviction.

"It's just, there are rumors, in certain circles, in Washington. Rumors about you."

Claire turned to look at him; her enormous eyes seemed to draw him in. Arthur didn't care about rumors, but he could see that she was upset, so he went along with it.

"What rumors?"

"People are saying that…maybe you're not who you're meant to be. Maybe you're not George."

Arthur looked at the ground. He wasn't surprised. He was a lousy actor. Of course someone would start wondering. That's why Cain started the story about his memory loss and head injury, to cover any suspicion.

"Arthur, are the rumors based on something? Does anyone know who you really are? Has anyone guessed?"

"They're just rumors, Claire. Who cares what people say?" But he spoke a little too quickly, his face flushed.

Claire was watching him closely, as though she was reading his mind.

"Arthur, if someone knows...if they've betrayed you...this would be the end. Knowingly impersonating a candidate would be a considered an act of rebellion. You know what they do to rebels." Claire's voice was shaking. Arthur reached for her hand.

"Cain wouldn't let that happen."

But even as he said it, Arthur knew. Secretary Cain wouldn't take the fall. If something went wrong, he would be on his own.

Claire knew it too. She pulled her hand away.

"This is not a joke! I'm so scared. I...I can't lose you. Please, Arthur. I need to know. Are you in danger? Does someone know who you really are?"

Arthur's thoughts flashed back to Martin—the night at the pool, their conversation in the forest. He had given his word that he wouldn't tell anyone that Martin knew his secret. But even as he thought it, he wondered if Martin had meant Claire too. She wasn't just anyone, was she?

"Who is it, Arthur?" Claire had guessed. "Is it one of the other candidates?"

All he had to do was give her the name, and all her fears would go away. If she knew it was Martin, she wouldn't worry anymore. She had known Martin for a long time and would trust him to keep Arthur's secret safe.

But no matter how much he wanted to tell her, to reassure her, he couldn't. He had given Martin his word, and a promise was a promise.

"Claire, please. You're just going to have to trust me. I am safe. They're just rumors."

Gently, he reached across and pulled her close to him, partly so she would stop looking at his guilty expression. It killed him that he

143

couldn't tell her more—that he couldn't take away all her worries and fears.

There was a long pause before Claire spoke again.

"Thank you, Arthur. I do trust you. If you say that there's nothing to worry about, then that's good enough for me."

She spoke quietly, dropping her head against his shoulder. More than anything, Arthur wanted to stop talking about this. If this was their last evening together, the minutes were precious, and he just wanted to enjoy being with her.

As if hearing his thoughts, Claire jumped lightly to her feet.

"Now, I promise to stop spoiling this beautiful night we have together." As she spoke, she reached up coyly behind her and carefully pulled the zipper down the back of her pale-blue shift. The dress fell to the ground, and she wiggled out of it. Then she stood on the very edge of the dock, her toes curling over the wooden trim.

"Shall we?" she said, enticingly, pausing for just a second before diving into the black shimmering water.

"Wait, I can't swim," Arthur protested, but she was already under the surface, ripples dancing across the lake from where she had dived.

In a record time Arthur undressed and gingerly climbed down the dock's old metal ladder. It wasn't exactly glamorous—hanging on for dear life, but there was no way he was missing out on this.

He gasped as he dipped himself into the chilly water, almost turning back. Something creepy tickled his feet under the dark water, and he nearly screamed, as Claire surfaced next to him, laughing. She reached her hand up and pulled him down toward her, kissing him passionately on the lips. He looped his arm over a rung so he wouldn't fall into the water and pulled her up in his arms until they were wrapped close together. If this was going to be his last night as a free man, Arthur thought happily, he was OK with that.

144

Chapter 11

The next day, Arthur stood next to a potted plant in the lobby of Laurel Lodge and waited. People were milling around him in a state of excitement, but he kept his head down and stared intently at the plant, only occasionally looking around, avoiding eye contact. The third and final primary, the test of courage, should have started by now, and a sense of nervous anticipation was growing by the minute.

Harry was standing off to Arthur's right. As always, she seemed calm and composed, taking it all in stride. She had nodded toward Arthur when she arrived, but since then she hadn't so much as glanced in his direction. Kennedy was near the door, pacing like a caged tiger. Now and then, he would stop and shake out an arm or a leg like an elite athlete before a race. Unlike Harry, he seemed bothered by Arthur and gave him a death stare every time he changed direction. At least Arthur had a word for that look now, jealousy. Martin hadn't arrived yet, and Arthur wondered if that was what was causing the delay.

Evan stood shoulder to shoulder with him. Other than a few dirty jokes in the unit, the Scot had been unusually subdued all morning. Arthur appreciated his lurking presence and quiet solidarity. He didn't feel able to have a conversation or make small talk. Especially when he knew that in a few hours, if he lost, he might never see his friend again. He had to focus hard not to let fear about the future creep into his thoughts and overwhelm him.

There was a disturbance by the front door as some Secret Service men walked in, whispering to each other. One of the men stepped into the center of the foyer. Arthur told himself to breathe, his heart was starting to pound. He reached out to stroke a leaf on the potted plant next to him, trying to calm his nerves. Hard plastic. The plant was a good-looking fake. Like him.

"Lady and gentlemen," the agent said loudly, looking toward the candidates. "The primary is commencing. Please follow me."

Arthur instinctively snatched off a small leaf and put it in his pocket with the car emblem and cylinder. He had slipped them in this morning. He knew it wasn't logical, but somehow he felt that they might bring him luck.

Evan patted his back.

"It's gonna be OK, lad," he said kindly.

"Yeah," Arthur muttered. He couldn't speak in case he said something stupid, like what he was really feeling. That wouldn't help anybody.

"Candidates, if you please." The agent indicated the elevator doors. Arthur's heart leaped. He was finally going to see what was under the lodge.

One last pat on the back from Evan, and Arthur walked forward to the elevator doors, taking his place next to Harry and Kennedy.

The doors opened, revealing a disappointingly ordinary

elevator, with patterned, orange wallpaper and wood paneling that looked like it was from the 1970s. The three candidates stepped inside, the doors closing behind them as the elevator started going down, cheesy elevator music playing quietly in the background.

"Where's Martin?" Kennedy asked the second they were alone.

"Gone. He dropped out," Harry said matter-of-factly.

"What?" Both Arthur and Kennedy turned to her, astonished.

"No way. Nobody drops out. No one volunteers to be Retired!" Kennedy was almost shouting. He sounded affronted at the thought that anyone would consider such a thing. Arthur thought of Ben for a moment. But he knew it was different for Martin; it didn't make any sense. Martin had a good chance of winning, and he had Harry. He wouldn't have walked away this late in the game.

"Well, all I know is he's gone. Quit. He'll be sipping martinis on a beach in Martha's Vineyard by now." Harry threw her head back, glaring defiantly at the elevator doors as though she had moved on already, but Arthur could tell she was upset.

Kennedy looked devastated, though Arthur suspected it was because he wouldn't feel his victory was complete, rather than out of concern for Martin.

"I'm sorry, Harry," Arthur said quietly, knowing it was probably the wrong thing to say, and she would probably give him a hard time for it. But surprisingly, she didn't; instead, she just nodded and for just a second looked like she might cry.

Arthur felt a cold sensation. Had Martin gotten into some kind of trouble? Had Cain found out about the "good people," Martin was friends with? A dozen questions popped into his mind, but he forced himself to brush them away. He was being paranoid. Martin was secretive, and there was no way to second-guess why he had dropped out. Right now Arthur knew he had to focus on the primary.

When the elevator finally stopped, he realized that they must be deep underground beneath Laurel Lodge. The old-fashioned doors slid open to reveal a series of polished concrete corridors lined with high-tech access doors. There were people in military uniforms and others in medical scrubs bustling around, many pausing to glance at the candidates as they stepped out of the elevator. A small entourage of Secret Service agents was waiting to escort them along the corridor.

The bunker complex was massive. They followed corridor after identical corridor before turning into a massive hall, several stories high with windows lining the walls and narrow steel bridges crisscrossing above them.

On one side of the hall, a security checkpoint cordoned off a pair of high-tech doors marked ominously with biohazard signs. The only people coming in and out of the doors were medical personnel in lab coats. On the opposite side of the hall, Arthur saw a crowd of people lined up to catch what looked like high-speed metal armchairs. The speed chairs had steering wheels and black visors and were hovering just inches above the ground. As soon as someone got in, the chairs would race off, heading into an enormous circular tunnel at an alarmingly high speed.

Arthur could have stayed and watched all day. He was dying to ride one of the speed chairs. But his chaperones kept hurrying them along, out of the hall.

Everywhere they went, people stopped to stare at them and whispered among themselves. A few even clapped and cheered, pulling out their CDs to capture digital memory snaps of their celebrity heroes. Harry and Kennedy acknowledged the attention graciously, without missing a step. But Arthur felt hugely self-conscious and gave awkward little waves and half-hearted smiles, pausing several times as people called out to him. The Secret Service detail kept nudging him along, obviously in a hurry to get the primary started.

Eventually they got to an ominous-looking medical suite. Four exam tables were set up, evenly spaced across the room, with a cart full of dangerously sharp implements and medical goodies hooked up behind them. They were each instructed to lie down on one of the tables, and several medical devices were attached to them.

Arthur glanced over at Harry and Kennedy. They both seemed calm and businesslike. Kennedy was nodding his head from time to time, muttering, as though he was doing some mental warm-up exercises. Harry noticed Arthur looking over and gave him a tight smile.

Before long, they were plugged in to a handful of devices, and smooth, egg-shaped helmets were put over their heads. Arthur stared into the black inside of the helmet, trying to direct his thoughts away from the feeling of panic that was rising within him.

They won't try to kill me, he kept repeating over and over in his mind. But his thoughts kept drifting to George. Accidents happen.

Through the helmet, a familiar voice was talking.

HOPE: *Ladies and Gentlemen. Take your seats. It's finally here. The moment you have all been waiting for.*

THE VOICE: *Twenty, nineteen, eighteen…*

HOPE: *The third and final primary—the test of courage.*

THE VOICE: *Fourteen, thirteen…*

HOPE: *The most dangerous and daring test these young candidates have ever faced.*

THE VOICE: *Nine, eight, seven…*

HOPE: *Candidates. May you have strength and honor. Good luck.*

THE VOICE: *Three, two, one…*

Instantly Arthur's mind started to drift, taken over by some kind of drug. For a moment, his thoughts seemed to turn in on themselves, and he experienced a wild sense of disorientation, like spinning upside down on a roller coaster in the dark. Then, with a surreal whoosh, everything righted itself, and Arthur found himself standing on the top a towering pillar of red rock in a desert, blinking against the harsh light.

The disoriented feeling had been replaced with vertigo, and Arthur almost dropped to his knees. He craned his neck out, not daring to move his feet yet, and peered down over the edge. A hot wind swept up from the canyon, carrying up the piercing sound of vultures crying out as they circled far below. The drop was easily two hundred feet to the canyon floor.

"Oh, this will be fun." Harry's voice made him turn around. Harry and Kennedy were standing, facing each other on the narrow rock surface. Arthur grinned. This would be a lot easier with these two for company. They were probably the two most capable people he knew. It didn't occur to him that they were competing.

"So, let's see. No way to climb down. No way up. What are we supposed to do? Wrestle each other off the top? Last one standing wins?" Harry spoke jokingly, but Arthur noticed that their stances had become almost imperceptibly stronger, as though readying themselves in case of an attack. Kennedy and Harry were focused intently on each other; no one seemed worried about Arthur. He realized he might as well throw himself off the top, for all the chance he had of defeating either of these two in battle.

"Doesn't seem very brave to me. Isn't this meant to be a test of courage?" Arthur said, trying to diffuse the threat, or at least delay the inevitable. His words had a small effect, and the tension lifted slightly.

"All right Washington. So what is your plan, then?" Kennedy said to him dismissively.

Arthur looked around, completely flummoxed. The only way off this rock was down, and he didn't like the look of that.

"If we die in a simulation…?" he asked tentatively.

"There's a strong chance of dying of a heart attack in the real world." Harry completed his sentence. "They give us drugs to counter our bodies' chemical and physical responses to the virtual death, but sometimes it's not enough." She looked down for a moment, embarrassed, probably remembering George.

Suddenly there was a loud crack. The pillar started shaking hard, knocking Arthur to his knees. The edges of rock were crumbling, great pieces splitting off and falling hundreds of feet to the desert floor. Arthur scrambled away from the edge, just as the ground he had been kneeling on fell away.

Just as soon as the earthquake had started, it was over. Arthur sat stock still, his heart pounding, wondering if he might have a heart attack here and in the real world. Eventually the panic subsided, and he started looking around. The pillar was much smaller now. Harry and Kennedy were both on their feet, facing the center of the rock where two dark bundles had appeared. As he scrambled to his feet, Arthur looked more closely at the bundles. One looked like some kind of backpack and the other an enormous coil of rope. Before he had time to think about it, Kennedy and Harry leaped forward, grabbing for the backpack. Kennedy's extra few inches gave him the advantage, and he snatched it away seconds before Harry could grasp it. He backed off toward the edge of the pillar, his fingers quickly exploring the straps, his eyes fixed on Harry.

"Seriously? Base jumping?" Harry said dryly, standing protectively over the rope.

Kennedy held the parachute tightly. He had his ride, and he wasn't letting go.

"What about this?" he said, indicating the rope at Harry's feet. "See anything to tether it to? There must be something." Kennedy talked fast, redirecting the conversation away from the fact that there was only one parachute, and he had it.

"Look for cracks. With all these tremors something might have opened up," said Harry, moving easily away from the rope and studying the rocky edges. She obviously wasn't too worried that Arthur would try to steal it. He started looking around too, but couldn't see anything that could be used to tie the rope to. Another tremor knocked them all to their feet. The rocky platform was shrinking alarmingly.

"Maybe tie it around the whole pillar?" Kennedy threw out.

"Seriously? You'd trust your weight to that with the whole thing crumbling away under us?" Harry flared up at Kennedy, annoyed that he'd even suggest such a lame idea. For a long moment they looked around, stumped.

Well, if these two perfect humans can't figure it out, I might as well give up now, Arthur thought as he looked across at the two of them, equally beautiful, equally brilliant, unequally sized. Suddenly an idea hit him, and he blurted it out before he could second-guess himself.

"Counterweights! That's how we do it. One of us on one end of the rope, one on the other. Opposite sides of the rock."

Harry actually looked impressed, but Kennedy just shrugged, possibly a little miffed that he hadn't had the idea first.

"Nice, George. And I thought you were just a pretty face." Harry smiled up at him, making him blush. "Slight problem. We would need to balance the weight. Make it as even as possible. I'm all of five feet nothing tall. But you strapping young lads…" As she said it, Harry sidled up next to Kennedy until she was right in front of him, making the size difference even more obvious. Kennedy unsubtly moved the parachute behind him, out of her reach.

"Seriously?" Kennedy did not like the way this conversation was going.

"Do the math," said Harry, enjoying herself.

"No. Find another way. The parachute is mine." Kennedy turned as if examining the rock edges once more. For a few minutes the two of them wandered futilely around the pillar, arguing nonstop the whole time. Arthur, staying out of it, almost considered jumping just so he wouldn't have to listen to the bickering. Eventually he'd had enough.

"Look, just stop. I don't get it. What's the goal here? To survive at all costs or to show that we have what it takes to be president?" He looked pointedly at Kennedy, who seemed subdued by this. "Aren't we supposed to work together, find a way for us all to survive, be a team? Wouldn't that be the presidential thing to do?"

"Damn you, Washington. And you Tubman," Kennedy said grumpily, reluctantly throwing the parachute to Harry, who grinned and winked at Arthur. Kennedy picked up one end of the rope and started wrapping it in a complex harness around himself.

"What are you waiting for, Washington? An invitation?" He threw the other end of the rope to Arthur, who gingerly tied it around his waist, pulling doubly hard on the knots.

Soon they were standing, facing off on opposite sides of the pillar. Harry was organizing the rope so they could lower themselves simultaneously. Arthur didn't look down, but imagined he could feel the wind blowing up at him from the vast void below. He couldn't imagine how he was going to do this. He just knew he had to.

"On three?" said Kennedy. Harry pulled the parachute on her shoulders and clipped on the straps. All three stood for a moment on the edges of the great drop, looking at each other.

"One…two…" Kennedy looked directly at them as he said it. "Three."

Simultaneously they all stepped back into the void. The rope around Arthur's waist snapped him up instantly. He felt like it was cutting him in half and thought enviously of Kennedy's fancy harness. He was dangling just below the rim. He couldn't see Kennedy, but he could feel his movements on the far side of the rock. He knew that this could only work if they kept evenly balanced, and he forced himself to start moving, jerkily feeding the rope through his hands as he started to rappel, his feet struggling to find the rock wall. It was working. He allowed himself a relieved smile and started dropping faster.

Then everything changed. Suddenly the desert, the rope, everything flickered out of sight, replaced by a dark, gray room with the shrieking sound of an alarm. Then, almost instantly, he was back in the desert.

Disoriented, Arthur's grip came lose, and he momentarily lost hold of the rope, which instantly whipped upward out of his fingers. He flailed, desperately trying to catch it, but it was too late. He was falling, gathering speed, crashing once hard against the pillar, and spinning to face the ground as he hurtled toward it. He cried out in fear, but the wind caught his voice.

There was nothing he could do to save himself, as he braced for impact.

Chapter 12

Arthur gasped as he sat bolt upright. His chest felt tight as adrenaline coursed through him. His hands gripped onto the edges of the exam table as he struggled to overcome his terror. *I'm still here, it didn't happen, it wasn't real*, he told himself over and over. He tried to look around, but all he saw was pitch-blackness. A heavy weight pushing down on his head reminded him that he was still wearing a helmet, and he desperately ripped it off, flinging it across the floor, looking around, trying to ground himself.

He was back where he started. Back in the bunker, only it looked different now. The lights were off and there was just an ominous red glow from the emergency lighting. An alarm was shrieking intermittently. The room was empty. All the medical personnel and Secret Service agents had gone, and the exam tables where Harry and Kennedy had been were now empty. The door was wide open and faint, foreboding bangs that sounded like gunfire came from the corridor outside. Arthur sat completely still for a moment, listening intently. Was this still the primary? Was it another virtual test? If so, it was a clever trick bringing him back here to the bunker. He had known the desert wasn't real, but this felt different, confusing.

A loud explosion rocked the room, snapping him out of his thoughts. Real or not, he needed to get out of here. Arthur slipped his legs off the edge of the table, but as he stood up, a jolt of pain in his arm pulled him back down. He still had a bunch of needles and tubes connected to him, and he gingerly started pulling them out, wincing a little each time one came lose. The pain wasn't bad, but Arthur really hated needles.

Soon he was out the door and running down the smoke-filled corridor. He was heading for the elevator, the only exit he knew for sure would get him out of this miserable bunker. He raced along corridor after corridor, easily following the route he had taken when he arrived that morning. Arthur never got lost. It was like he carried around a map in his head.

Rounding a corner by the great hall, he slammed on the brakes, sliding to an abrupt stop. The whole space was filled with smoke and an acrid burning smell. He saw dark figures moving around near the doors to the biohazard area, stepping over shadowy outlines on the floor that looked ominously like bodies. At first he thought they were Secret Service, but as the smoke cleared briefly, he saw that their uniforms were a ragtag mix of government-issue clothes, bits of old-style firefighter equipment, and various bike and motorcycle helmets. They had revolutionary red bandannas tied over their noses and mouths, hiding their faces. They were Red Rebels from the Outside.

Arthur's jaw dropped with surprise. He had never seen a real Red Rebel before. They held an almost mythical status in the Outside, inspiring both fear and hope in equal measure. They had generally left the Outsiders alone, as their enemies were the state and all the rich Zoners, but Arthur realized with a start that he was now considered an enemy. George Washington, a presidential candidate, would be a symbol of everything they despised, and he didn't fancy his odds in a fight.

He shrank back into the corridor and was about to head back the way he had come when he heard footsteps behind him and soft muted voices. Quickly he looked for a place to hide, running to the only door in the corridor and trying the handle. He was in luck. The door opened, and he stepped into a small dark closet filled with cleaning equipment. The door didn't quite shut all the way, and Arthur peered out through the narrow slit.

Two rebels passed him, heading for the hall. Both were equal in height, not tall, but one was well built and muscular, while the other was skinny and moved gracefully. As they reached the end of the corridor, the skinny one paused, grabbing the other one's arm. She spoke to him, small fragments of the conversation loud enough for Arthur to hear.

"I have to try one more time." It was a woman's voice, whispering urgently.

"We are here to get the evidence. Not get distracted." Something about the man's voice was familiar to Arthur. He carefully shifted forward, straining to overhear more. The man was talking again.

"He can take care of himself. He's not the priority." Where had he heard that low, distinctive voice before? Arthur struggled to place it.

"Arthur is my concern," the woman said clearly. Arthur froze. Had she just said his name? He knew it was unlikely that there were two Arthurs in the bunker, as old-fashioned and unpopular as his name was. Why was she concerned about him? He moved even farther forward, struggling to get a better look at the two of them.

The man seemed to be deliberating, turning slowly to face the woman.

"All right. But hurry. Your dad is going to kill me if anything happens to you." He laughed.

The woman quickly turned to go, giving Arthur an unobstructed view of the man's face. Even with the bandanna on, the dark, handsome eyes were unmistakable. It was Martin.

Arthur moved back in surprise, knocking into a broom, which fell, cracking hard against the door and swinging it open. In literally seconds, Martin had Arthur by the neck, pinned down on the floor with a laser pointed at his head.

"Martin, it's me," Arthur said, gasping, his neck squeezed tight by Martin's strong arms.

Martin looked at him in surprise for a moment and then started laughing his deep, warm laugh. He released his grip on Arthur, sat back, and pulled his bandanna down, his face filled with a big grin.

"You are just full of surprises, George."

"You mean Arthur," said the woman's voice. She moved into Arthur's line of sight. Dark frizzy curls had come untucked from under her makeshift helmet. She pushed one back and looked at Arthur with unmistakable blue-green eyes.

"Bay!" Arthur almost shouted, sitting bolt upright.

"Hi," she said, grinning, pulling down her bandanna. Arthur had never been happier to see anyone than he was right now. His eyes drank in her smiling, intelligent face, like he couldn't get enough. God, he had missed her.

"Wha...how? Are you real?" He knew inside that this couldn't be happening. Bay was from a different life. Somehow Cain must have found a way to use his own thoughts against him. This was just another sick twist in the primary. But even knowing this, his stomach turned in knots of happiness, just seeing her again.

"I am real, Arthur. But I know you can't trust that right now.

Anything I do to prove it to you could just be part of the game." She sounded so like Bay. If this was all in his head, he knew her well.

"Either way, it's good to see you, dork." She smiled her brilliant, cheeky smile, and Arthur couldn't hold back. He reached up for her, and they hugged, clinging tightly to each other. She felt real; her awkward, lanky arms wrapped around him. For a moment he sunk his face into her curls, breathing in her familiar, fresh smell. For all the world, it felt like coming home.

All too soon the moment was broken by the shudder of an explosion, followed by gunfire.

"Sorry, to interrupt. But sounds like the security police are on their way. We have got to get out of here." Martin offered Arthur a hand, pulling him to his feet. As he stood up, the car emblem fell out of Arthur's pocket and clattered onto the floor. He quickly scooped it up, pushing it back in his pocket. He didn't want to lose his good luck charm.

"Come on. We can catch up later," Bay said, pulling Arthur toward the large hall. When they stepped inside, they could see that most of the rebels had already left or were leaving, heading down the round tunnel, cramming onto the speed chairs in groups of three or four. A small band of rebels stayed back, guarding the exit to the large corridor that led to the elevator, the sounds of gunfire echoing off its walls. The doors to the biohazard area were blown wide-open, bodies littering the floor around them.

One of the passing rebels sprinted over. He had several dark bands on his left sleeve and spoke to Bay with authority.

"There you are, Commander. We couldn't get the evidence. The lab was empty. Secretary Cain must have suspected we were coming and cleared out."

"Darn it!" Bay slammed the wall in frustration. She paused, shaking off her frustration. "All right, Captain. Give the order to abort. Blow the exit to give us enough time to get out. Asset One is secured. I'll get Asset Two out now." She grabbed Arthur's arm. The man nodded and ran off, talking fast into a head comm.

"I'm going to help them rig the exit," Martin shouted over the noise. He pulled out a handful of what looked like small metal jacks, tossing one playfully into the air and catching it.

"Jesus, Martin," Bay snapped. "You're going to blow yourself up!"

Martin just laughed, giving Arthur a familiar parting whump on the shoulder.

"Good to have you on board, George. Cain must be having a cow right now. Losing his golden boy to the rebels." Quickly, he turned and sprinted off to the exit corridor.

Bay pushed Arthur toward the tunnel. The remaining rebels parted to let them through when they saw who they were, many turning to stare at the famous Mr. Washington.

Several of them touched their right hands to their left shoulders in some sort of salute, bowing their heads toward Bay. She obviously commanded a lot of respect among the rebels, Arthur noted with surprise. Bay moved forward, oblivious to the attention they were receiving. She grabbed a speed chair, reaching in to flick a few switches and activate it. The chair started hovering inches above the tunnel floor.

"Want to drive?" Bay asked. "Stick shift, just like those old beaters we used to jack up in the Outside."

The memory of those hot, desperate days flashed through Arthur's head, and he almost jumped into the humming speed chair. But something wasn't right. Being reminded of Bay in the Outside with him, a world away, made him stop in his tracks. How could Bay be here? If this were part of the primary, riding off with her to join the rebels, betraying Cain and the government, would be the most epic fail imaginable. He would be Retired immediately. He doubted Cain would even bother having a public vote about it.

Bay must have sensed his doubt and moved closer to him.

"Arthur," she said, reaching for his hand. "I can't prove it, but it is me. I am really here. This isn't one of Cain's games. I need you to trust your instincts. To trust me."

Arthur looked into her eyes. He wanted to trust her more than anything, more than anyone. She was probably the one person in the world whom he actually did trust. She had been his best, his only friend at a time when he was a nobody with no future or hope. She knew everything about the pathetic loser Arthur Ryan and had still stuck by him.

Which is why Cain would choose her to test him. Pulling her out of his head, manipulating his purest memories for his own stupid amusement.

"Arthur, please. Look at me." Bay's voice had a new urgency. She seemed to sense that she was losing him.

"Why are you here?" Arthur said, doubt creeping into his tone. He wasn't sure if he was annoyed with her or with himself for getting into this situation in the first place.

"I'm with the rebels. I came for you." Bay spoke directly, looking him in the face.

"No! It doesn't make sense. You're just a kid. A poor, hungry seventeen-year-old schoolgirl from the Outside. Not some rebel fighter. You can't expect me to believe you found a way to leave and secretly join the rebels. Then you made your way across the country to rescue me, all by yourself. It's not possible. It's not real. You're not real." Arthur was convincing himself as he spoke. Of course she wasn't real. What was he thinking?

Bay let go of the speed chair and moved closer to him, but he backed away a step.

"Arthur, you're right. Of course it wouldn't make any sense for the girl you knew to be here now." Bay paused, looking at him intensely, as though trying to read his thoughts. She seemed to be struggling to decide what to say next. Arthur noticed her eyes were burning green. Finally she spoke, quietly but with determination.

"You deserve to know the truth, Arthur. I was never just a poor schoolgirl from the Outside."

For a moment Arthur looked at her, baffled.

"The truth is…I have been a Red Rebel all my life. A year ago, Abel finally managed to track you down, the back-up George Washington. They needed someone to get to know you and earn your trust, without alerting suspicion. I was the obvious choice. I moved to Westgate for you, Arthur. I rode that bus every day so I could befriend you." She looked at him, her eyes reading his expression, seeing his doubt. "That was me in the press section after the primary. I left you a message on the wall? Didn't you see it?"

"Just stop! Please."

Arthur didn't want to hear it. Real or not, her words felt like they were ripping him apart.

His friendship with Bay had been the one true thing he had. Knowing that someone had accepted him for who he was had been his lifeline through all the bad times. Hearing her say that it was all an act felt like the cruelest betrayal of his life. He didn't care right now if she was real or not. He didn't care about the primary or the rebellion. He just wanted her to stop.

"Arthur, please!" Bay sounded desperate. She must have seen the look of hurt in his eyes. "There's so much at stake. Please. I know it's a lot to take on. I know you're confused right now and hurting. But we can figure this out. We can talk about this. Just please come with me now. For our friendship…"

"I don't have friends," Arthur shouted. Surprising himself.

Without thinking, he jumped onto the speed chair and smacked it into gear, swinging it hard around to face the empty tunnel away from the rebel exodus. For a second he paused, the speed chair pulsing with power beneath him. He took one last look at Bay, instinctively reaching his hand into his pocket and pulling out the car emblem, her emblem. He tossed it dismissively on to the tunnel floor at her feet.

Bay slowly bent down and picked it up. Her fingers stroked the edges, and Arthur thought he saw tears of recognition in her eyes. Then she stepped back, her expression sad but determined.

"I'll keep this for you," she said, looking away. "I'm really sorry, Arthur, but right now, you are your own worst enemy. Take him." She called out to two of the rebels behind her.

Instantly, they both turned toward Arthur, grabbing for speed chairs. Arthur kicked the accelerator and his chair leaped forward with alarming speed. He was done with thinking. He put Bay and Martin far behind him as he raced off down the circular tunnel, the speed chair swinging up the curved walls as he cornered. The speed was exhilarating.

The controls were laid out just like an old-style car, so Arthur had no trouble figuring out how to maneuver. However, the rebels were obviously more experienced drivers, and before long they were pulling alongside him. Arthur swung from side to side to force them back and then gunned the accelerator to the maximum as the force threw him back against the seat.

Again the rebels pulled up alongside him. Arthur was easily outclassed by these two, and he realized, with a sinking feeling, that he wouldn't be able to outrun them. One of them had reached for a laser and was pointing it at the back of Arthur's chair. As he fired, Arthur braked hard, almost falling headfirst over the controls, swinging to a complete stop.

He flinched as the shot ricocheted around the walls over his head, spiraling off down the tunnel behind him, the brilliant light momentarily blinding him.

As his eyes adjusted back to the darkness in the tunnel, he realized he had made a big tactical mistake. The two rebels had stopped about a hundred feet ahead and turned to face him, their speed chairs revving menacingly, blocking his escape. Over his shoulder, Arthur saw several more headlights approaching from behind, fast.

He was trapped.

He was breathing hard, and he listened to his breath for a few seconds as he tried to calm himself down and think. He was caught, he knew it, but he was not ready to quit. He quickly assessed his situation. His best chances were to go forward, away from the bunker, he decided, focusing on the two speed chairs ahead of him. They could easily have shot him by now, so he had to assume they wanted to capture him, Asset Three, alive. That gave him a big advantage. But how could he get past them? They were completely blocking the tunnel. Running into them headfirst would be suicide. As he looked along the smooth, curved tunnel walls, he started to get an idea. It was risky, but it just might work.

The headlights had stopped behind him. One of the rebels called out.

"Please, sir. Come with us. Don't do anything stupid."

But it was too little, too late. Arthur was focused on his idea, his eyes calculating the odds. He knew it was dangerous, but he wasn't afraid. He knew what he needed to do. He allowed himself a little smile, slipped the speed chair into gear, and started accelerating toward the two rebels.

As he picked up speed, he started swinging the speed chair up the walls, back and forth, low at first, then higher and higher. He had to time it just right. As he neared the two rebels, his chair was swinging so high it would momentarily be suspended in midair at the top of each swing. Arthur mentally counted down to the final moment. On the last upswing, seconds before he was about to crash, he threw his full weight onto the accelerator, propelling the chair up the curved wall and over the heads of the waiting rebels. For a brief, exhilarating moment, the speed chair raced upside down across the tunnel ceiling, its momentum carrying it forward.

But it wasn't quite fast enough. Midway across the roof, the chair started to drop, free-falling upside down. For a few terrifying seconds, Arthur thought he was going to be dashed headfirst onto the ground. But then the bottom edge of the chair clipped the wall of the tunnel and righted itself, bouncing violently as it hit the floor. Arthur was thrown backward and forward like a rag doll. His head smacked hard into the control panel, and everything became a scary blur of sharp light and shooting pain.

When Arthur could finally focus again, the speed chair was still spinning uncontrollably along the tunnel floor, one side dragging along the ground in a cloud of sparks. He had made it past the rebels and briefly allowed himself a self-congratulatory smile. But as he reached toward the controls, he found that his hands weren't doing what we he wanted. His vision kept swimming in and out of focus, and he could feel something warm and sticky running down his face. He tried reach up and push it out of his eyes, but his arms fell weakly to his sides. The driverless speed chair crashed and bumped along, but Arthur could do nothing to help himself. He slumped sideways, dangerously close to the edge of the chair, unable to grab on to something. A wave of nausea and dizziness overwhelmed him as he felt the sensation of falling, darkness slowly closing in until there was nothing left.

Birdsong. That was the first thing Arthur noticed. A warm feeling flooded him as he remembered the last time he had heard the beautiful sound. Slowly he struggled to open his eyes, but his eyelids felt too heavy. He lay still for another moment, collecting his strength. The familiar smell of fresh cut grass and a ripple of fresh air blew across his face. He smiled, sure of his surroundings even before he opened his eyes just enough to let in the warm, golden light of his bedroom. He was home in Mount Vernon.

It was a few more minutes before he felt strong enough to move, tentatively lifting his aching head off the pillow, propping himself up on his elbows. He looked around the room, realizing he was not alone. Claire was sitting by the open window, the white net curtain wistfully blowing beside her. She hadn't noticed that he was awake, and he took a moment studying her profile.

The soft light fell gently across her pale skin, giving her the timeless appearance of an exquisite, marble statue. But there was something else too—an air of sadness, as she sat silently staring across the fields. As he watched, she absently reached a hand up to her face, her fingertips softly pushing a strand of white-blond hair away from her cheek. The small gesture made him ache inside.

"Claire?" Arthur's voice sounded croaky, like it hadn't been used in a long time.

She started slightly, turning to look at him, her expression still distant. Slowly she seemed to collect herself and smiled.

"Mr. Washington," a man's voice said, making Arthur jump this time. He turned quickly in the direction of the voice, his vision taking a few seconds to catch up. To Arthur's surprise, Secretary Cain was standing in the doorway, his familiar, easy smile on his face.

Cain walked into the room, perching himself comfortably on the end of Arthur's bed. Arthur pushed himself up to sitting, feeling horribly underdressed in his pajamas. He glanced over nervously at

Claire, but she had turned back to face the window, her cool distant expression restored.

"The hero of the hour. How is your head?" Cain asked in a tone that implied he couldn't have cared less about the answer. He was looking at Arthur appraisingly, as if inspecting a piece of machinery that was broken.

"Fine...sir," Arthur croaked, immediately regretting the sir. It was an old nervous habit and not something presidential.

He swallowed as a pulse of pain throbbed through his head. He reached his hand up tentatively to feel a bandage taped across his forehead. Cain watched him silently. Arthur could feel himself blushing, but was too nervous to speak first. He swallowed loudly and looked down at the bedsheets, trying to avoid eye contact. He wasn't sure why, but in spite of Cain's outward friendly manner, he always made Arthur feel desperately uncomfortable.

"You've come a long way since we first met, Arthur. Further than I would have anticipated." Cain paused and seemed to be considering something for a long moment. "The way you handled yourself in the final primary was courageous...heroic, even presidential, one could say." Cain smiled at him thinly.

Arthur's thoughts flashed back to the bunker. To the rebels, Martin and Bay. Maybe this was his chance to find out what was really going on and clear up some of the confusion in his head.

"Sir," Arthur mentally kicked himself. "I mean, Secretary Cain, sir. The primary...the bunker...none of it was real?"

"Of course, Arthur." Cain stood up and started pacing the floor. He had an athleticism about his movements that was at odds with his slightly overweight physique.

"The whole primary was an illusion. But a beautiful one. You see our technologies have improved to allow us near seamless integration of the subject's own thoughts and ideas into preset scenarios. It is, if I do say so myself, flawless."

Cain's obvious enthusiasm made him more animated than usual. He talked fast, waving his hands to illustrate his points.

"Arthur, you are confused. I can see it in your expression. Let me put it simply. During the primary you encountered people, things that only you know about. No doubt you started to wonder if you were still inside the primary simulation, or if somehow you had broken through into real life. Our rebel bunker attack plot line was designed to reinforce this doubt. Only this way could we really test your loyalty, your strength of character, and your commitment to your country."

Arthur saw Bay in his mind, the way she looked at him when he threw the car emblem on the floor before her. The flash of green in her intelligent eyes as she had looked at it sadly. Her dark, wild curls of hair falling forward as she bent to pick it up. Her voice when she told him that she would keep it for him.

Was that really all an illusion?

As if reading his mind, Cain spoke again.

"The simulations integrate your own psyche. There were things in there that you put there. Things you needed to face, or process." Cain looked hard at him. "People you needed to say goodbye to. It's rather beautiful. Playing out your own personal, little neuroses on a very public stage. Welcome to our brave new world." Cain sat back down on the bed, smiling a little smugly as he considered his proud creation.

Of course Cain had to be right.

Bay wasn't a secret rebel sent to watch over him. How dumb was that idea? She was like him, just a poor Outsider. Someone unimportant to anyone but him. It wasn't as much of a stretch to imagine Martin as a cool, rebel leader. But as Arthur thought of the two of them together, Bay and Martin, fighting the good fight against the government, dressed in motorcycle helmets with red bandannas, he blushed at how ludicrous his fantasy had become.

Even more mortifying was the realization that people all across the UZA had probably watched his imaginary adventures play out. Bay might have watched it from her one bedroom apartment in the Outside.

Cain stood up.

"Needless to say, your valiant escape from the rebel hordes was highly entertaining. You won an easy victory; by popular demand, you are one of the final two nominees for president." Arthur felt a pang of relief. He had almost completely forgotten what the primary was for. He had actually won!

"How did Harry, I mean Tubman, do?" Arthur asked quickly.

"Not so well. She found the rebel cause a little too compelling. You will be running against John F. Kennedy." Arthur could imagine Harry facing Martin in her version of the primary. It would have been an irresistible choice to make, given her feelings for him.

Cain seemed to be getting impatient, walking briskly to the door.

"Well, I have enjoyed our little chat, as always. But now, business attends. Claire, a pleasure as always." He nodded in the direction of her chair. Arthur turned to see her response, but as he moved his head a flash of burning pain in his temple made him stop. He lowered his head into his hands for just a moment, waiting for the pain to subside. He had forgotten about his injury.

"Wait!" he cried out suddenly. Cain froze in the doorway, his back turned to Arthur.

"My head. How did I get injured if it was all a virtual game?" Cain paused for a long moment. Too long. He finally turned, a stiffness in his manner.

"While you were in the primary, you broke free of your

physical restraints. One of the nurses had not adequately secured you, and you fell from the examination table, hitting your forehead on the floor. Your subconscious cleverly fit the injury into your primary narrative. A speed chair accident, I believe. Regrettable, but as the saying goes, no harm no foul."

Arthur starred at Cain. All of Cain's easiness had gone. His expression was calm, but there was something forced about his voice. Arthur could have sworn he was lying.

There was an awkward silence as Arthur and Cain stared at each other. Cain's eyes had narrowed, and there was something dark and dangerous in his expression. Unusually, this time Arthur met his gaze, not intimidated. He needed to know if his instincts were right. If Cain was lying about the head injury, was he lying about the primary too? Was it possible that it had actually happened? Doubts started closing in on Arthur as he held the older man's stare, his own expression hardening.

Surprisingly, Cain was the one to break first, giving a small playful bow.

"Well, Mr. Washington. It really has been a pleasure. But time is ticking, and I have a nation to oversee. So glad we had this chance to get to know each other a little better." As he said this, he smiled, his composure back in full force.

"You really should rest. Tomorrow you start the campaign trail. It is time you returned to your true home, don't you think? It's time you go to Washington."

With that, Secretary Cain turned and was gone.

Part 3

The Election

Chapter 13

George for Washington.

Arthur almost choked on his coffee when he saw the slogan splashed in enormous red, white, and blue letters across the campaign bus, stars and 3-D flags rippling across the surface. For the next few weeks, he had to ride in this thing across the entire UZA on his campaign tour to Washington. They would hardly be missed, he thought, imagining Outsiders on their farms stopping work to have a laugh at them as they flamboyantly wafted by. Mortified, he wondered if he could perhaps ask to ride with Evan in his unmarked black unit instead.

The bus doors silently slid open, and Ty bustled out, surrounded by a cloud of clipboards and personal drones. His goatee seemed to have morphed into a new, angular shape that looked like it was about to crawl up his face and escape. As soon as he noticed Arthur, he hurried over.

"George! I knew you could do it. Didn't doubt you for a second. Let's have a look at you. Phew. No scars. Still pretty. Makes my job, so much easier."

Ty was ecstatic. His own candidate had made it to the final round. This was the big league.

"Well, jump on board, settle in. We leave in five. O M fricking G. So much to do." He rushed off, swatting at the personal drones, barking orders at anyone who came within his sphere of self-importance.

There was an excited bustle as everyone prepared for the month long road trip. Secret Service agents were all over the place, loading Arthur's expensive leather suitcases, moving units into place on either side of the bus. A security detail of police units flanked the convoy, their officers standing around, shooting the breeze in full body armor, armed to the teeth with lasers and other unidentifiable weapons. Arthur spotted an unwelcome figure among them. Uncle would be joining them on the ride. He should have guessed. Cain would want his attack dog back now that they were heading into uncharted territory.

A prickle of anxiety pulled at Arthur, and he swallowed nervously.

"And so, it begins," the professor said, pulling her wheelchair up next to Arthur. It was the first time he had seen her since the primary, and he would have hugged her if there hadn't been so many people around. He grinned, relieved to see his friend.

"Are you coming?" he asked hopefully.

"No. No. Wheelchairs don't do well on long bus journeys." She smiled back. "Besides, you don't need me anymore. You are doing very well on your own now."

Arthur didn't feel like he was doing well alone. He thought of his conversation with her brother and what had happened in the primary, and he desperately wished they could have just five minutes alone to talk privately. He had so many questions. But any minute now, the bus would be pulling out, and Arthur had no idea when, or if, he'd be back to Mount Vernon. Quickly, Arthur turned to the professor.

"Professor. Your brother…" As if reading his mind, the she reached forward, pulling on his sleeve so he bent down.

"My brother is not to be trusted, Arthur," she whispered. "Whatever doubts you're having. Follow them to their natural conclusion."

"It's just—I don't know what to believe anymore."

The professor smiled at him affectionately. "Your instincts are good, Arthur. Always. What you lack is the confidence to trust in them. You are and will always be your own worst enemy."

Arthur looked at her for a long moment. She had changed since the day they met. He hadn't seen her take a drink in weeks, and her bitterness seemed to have been replaced with a subdued melancholy. He knew enough of her past to understand where the sadness was coming from. What he didn't know was how to help her.

"Same could be said for you," he said with a resigned smile.

The professor laughed.

"Yes, indeed. We are quite a pair of losers, aren't we?" She grinned.

Arthur jumped at the sound of a loud voice announcing that it was time to board the convoy. Instantly all the black-suited figures started disappearing into the different vehicles, ready to hit the road.

Arthur turned to the professor. He would miss her. Quickly he wrapped his arms around her and gave her a big hug. At first she went rigid, surprised by the show of affection. Then slowly, she relaxed, her hands came up, and she tentatively hugged him back.

"My turn?" Evan's voice cut in. Arthur stood up. The shorter man was carrying his duffel bag, dressed in his military-style uniform for the road. He nodded to the professor. She smiled back, a warm smile. Arthur felt a tug of affection for them both. The three of them made a dysfunctional group. They had absolutely nothing in common with one another beyond the walls of Mount Vernon. But somehow they had wound up here together, and they felt like family in an odd sort of way. He swallowed down a wave of emotion and was almost glad when another announcement ordered everyone onto the bus. Time to go.

Reluctantly the two men turned and started walking toward the convoy. Arthur couldn't help noticing that Evan kept looking back over his shoulder at the professor. He was about to ask him what was the matter, but then he saw the expression on his friend's face. For a moment he was speechless.

Evan liked the professor? Not just liked. *Liked*. Arthur was momentarily grossed out, but rallied quickly, telling himself that old people could have crushes too.

"Wha'?" Evan asked him, noticing his funny expression.

"It's just…you like her? Don't you?" He gestured toward the professor who had almost arrived back at the house.

"Och, Arthur. She's a beau'iful woman, wi' a fine mind." Evan turned back to look at the professor, longingly. "A'course she'd no chose to be wi' an oaf like me."

Arthur stopped in his tracks. He reached up and put his hand on Evan's shoulder, turning to face him.

"You're a good man, Evan. The best man I know."

For the briefest moment, Arthur thought that Evan was going to cry. But instead, the military man sniffed loudly and pulled himself up to his full height. He nodded to Arthur, silently thanking him. Then with a last look at the professor, he headed to one of the black units, hefting his duffel on his back.

From the door of the bus, Arthur turned back one last time. The rising sun was just clipping the top of Mount Vernon, giving the house a pale yellow glow. Its peaceful, simple facade with its ordered symmetry gave Arthur the same feeling of calm he'd had the first time he had laid eyes on it.

Silently, Arthur made a wish, that one day, no matter what happened next, he would be back. He would come home again.

The bus doors slid shut, and the bus pulled away.

The front of the bus had the look of a slick, corporate office. One side had rows of comfortable seats made out of buttery soft white leather. The other side had a miniature meeting area complete with several VT screens, a large map and a coffee maker, all the essentials. Ty and Van had already taken over the office and were busy bossing around a group of overdressed, overcaffeinated aides.

Arthur quietly tiptoed past them and headed to the back of the bus, to an area where cabin-like bunks lined the walls. Each bunk had a sliding screen door that rippled with bland, but beautiful nature imagery. As Arthur walked past each one, the occupant's name floated across the screen.

Jackson and Washington were together, Claire and George. Of course they wouldn't separate the sweethearts.

Arthur climbed up a small ladder to the bunk with his name. A blue light scanned him and the lush rainforest on the screen door slid silently open, monkeys and birds running to the side to avoid being sucked into the wall. His cabin was not much bigger than a bed, wrapped around by shiny-white walls that concealed myriad shelving and discreet cup holders. One entire wall was a window with a view across the dawn-touched fields.

Somehow, despite its size, the cabin didn't feel claustrophobic; it felt safe and peaceful. Gratefully, Arthur fell back on the soft silky sheets, turning on his side to watch, as in the far distance, the rooftops of Mount Vernon finally disappeared from view, swallowed up into the landscape. The last thing he could see, his cupola, caught one last shard of dawn sun, giving him a final, affectionate wink. Arthur winked back, as he turned to face the road ahead.

The long days and nights on the campaign trail, soon settled into a kind of routine. Arthur spent the time alternating between listening in to drama-filled strategy sessions, rehearsing prescripted speeches for upcoming rallies, and staring out the window. Something about being on the road, constantly moving, felt good. Even though they were cooped up inside a giant, metal can, there was a kind of freedom to it. It was so different from anything in Arthur's restricted childhood, that he relished the feeling and spent countless hours watching the world flickering past behind the window.

They were in the Outside, safely traveling on the endless miles of elevated highways that crisscrossed the giant dust bowl, like lifelines feeding the hungry Metrozones. For a lot of the time, all they could see was the inside of stark, high-security walls. But now and then, there would there would be a break in the wall, and a stretch of barbed wire where Arthur could look beyond, across the familiar red landscape.

The Outside was mostly empty and desolate, but whenever they approached a Metrozone, dusty little towns and farms would start to appear. The people looked rough and hardened as though the sun had baked them inside and out. There was an air of resigned desperation about them as they peered out of widows, or stood in silent lines outside food drops, their matching government-issue clothes giving them a bland uniformity. Somehow they didn't seem like living people, their humanity buried deep beneath the surface. If he hadn't been one of them, Arthur could see how he might have been afraid of them.

Occasionally he would look across at Claire, wondering if she was thinking the same thing. But she was always sitting impassively, eyes turned down to look at her book, an old-fashioned paper copy of *A Tale of Two Cities*. Arthur wanted to talk to her, but something about her manner made her seem closed off, distant. As though she wanted space, even from him.

Before long, he started to worry that he had done something to upset her, racking his brain to replay their last meetings. Had she watched the final primary? Had she seen Bay? Was she disappointed in him, or maybe…jealous?

Whatever she was feeling, he missed her terribly. The long hours cooped up were tedious, and Arthur longed to be able to talk, really talk, to someone.

By the third night, things changed.

Claire started coming to him in the small hours of the morning. She would knock softly on his cabin screen, then slip in and curl up beside him. They never spoke. Instead they held each other, their bodies folded together, their arms wrapped around, holding them close. Wordlessly, they would lie there, together in the dark, silently watching as the Outside raced by.

Every few nights they arrived at a new Metrozone, shuffled in through wall security in the early hours of the morning, when they would attract the least attention.

It was always the same—tree-lined city streets, posh old hotels, overly obsequious hotel managers, bowing and scraping to impress their celebrity guests. A Secret Service detail would accompany them everywhere. Often, Uncle would head up the detail, a lurking shadow, like a snake waiting for its moment to strike. Arthur tried to ignore him, but his constant presence always put him on edge.

The hotel suites seemed like museums to Arthur. Everything was old and precious, designed to make the guest feel like royalty.

They would all shower and dress in some obscenely expensive eveningwear, then head out for the night to a series of society events with the upper echelons of Metrozone life. Arthur and Claire attended a whirlwind of operas, art galleries, and parties held in their honor. The parties were always filled with flamboyant food and drinks, music and lights, and posh people crammed into immaculate outfits in brilliant, joyful colors.

These hot Metrozone nights were the worst part for Arthur. He was George Washington, the nominee, and everyone wanted a piece of him. All eyes followed him from the moment he entered some glittering event or other—a constant succession of shiny, bling-covered people throwing themselves at him, fawning all over him. Arthur was caught like a deer in headlights.

He would have been lost if it hadn't been for Claire.

Everyone adored her. She was perfect, gracious, and beautiful, with a knack for making everyone feel as though, for one brief moment in their lives, they had touched the stars. Night after night, she redeemed Arthur, brushing his awkwardness away with her glorious presence. Night after painful night, he watched as people fell under her spell, wondering if he was no different from the rest.

Arthur could never sleep after one of these Metrozone nights. He would lie awake in his crisp, cool sheets and think about the Outside. He would see faces of people he remembered, people he had seen from the bus—haunted, dirty faces. Hungry, desperate, hopeless. He would imagine that their eyes were watching him, dressed up in his fancy clothes, eating from the buffets piled high with the freshest fruits and delectable treats. As he closed his eyes and tried to sleep, he thought he could hear their voices—*You know us. You're one of us. Have you forgotten us?*

The faces often stayed with him into the next day, when he would have to give some pre-scripted rally speech in some dark lecture hall. Each time he bumbled and stuttered his way through, half-heartedly, his face flushed. The speeches always sounded flat, the words jumbling meaninglessly together as he read off the prompter. However, the crowd had obviously been primed to cheer and fake enthusiasm. Between some favorable editing on *The Democracy Games* and Claire's unstoppable popularity, George Washington somehow seemed to be scraping by in the polls. By the time they were nearing Washington, DC, Arthur was only narrowly trailing behind Kennedy.

Just days away from their final destination, as Arthur was staring out of the window, there was a loud bang. Two of the front units swerved off the side of the road next to the bus, crashing into the wire fence. Suddenly another explosion made the bus swing violently sideways, cups and books flying as everyone grabbed for something to hold on to. For a few brief moments, the bus was sliding sideways along the highway, slowing to a stop.

The doors flew open, and Uncle jumped on board.

"Stay calm. Our tires have been taken out," said Uncle. He walked over to Ty and Van, holding up a small metal device that looked just like a jack. Arthur recognized it as the same thing Martin had been playing with in the primary. How could he have imagined that?

"Darn rebels. They throw these on the highways from time to time. They usually get picked up by highway security in the mornings, but looks like they weren't doing their job today." He looked angry that anyone would dare inconvenience him.

Evan came aboard, his hands covered in oil.

"All gone. We've no got enough spares for this. It's goin' a take an unscheduled wee stop." Evan spoke calmly, but his words had an instant impact on the people on the bus. They were going to have to pull off the highway into the Outside. Ty had a look of horror on his face, as though all his worst nightmares had piled on top of him. Van stood tall, trying to pull off a show of strength, but Arthur noticed his hands were shaking wildly. He looked at Claire. For once she had looked away from her book and was watching with a look of mild interest. Arthur tried to catch her eye and exchange some kind of meaningful look, Outsider to Outsider, but she resolutely kept her eyes off him.

It was decided. They would head to the nearest town, 1134, less than a mile away. The convoy would limp in slowly, trying not to do any further damage. There was bound to be a place where they could get replacement tires or patches. Uncle would oversee security, while Evan would get the parts needed. The people on the bus were instructed to stay on the bus and keep their heads down.

The convoy pulled slowly off the protected highway and crawled into a disused gas station. Small scrappy houses lined the run-down streets of Town 1134, abandoned cars dotted around, Outsiders stopping to look at the unusual sight. The tension on the bus rose palpably. Arthur realized that for most of them, this was the first time they had ever been in the Outside.

As they pulled to a stop, the black Secret Service units surrounded the bus. Several agents got out, all heavily armed. Uncle and two other men headed over to the bus, opening the doors and standing just inside the entrance. Arthur saw Evan and a handful of other men heading toward the gas station convenience store, people dashing to get out of their way. A couple of girls, who were walking out of the store, were pushed and shoved roughly out of the way by the agents. Arthur couldn't hear what they were saying, but he saw one of the girls break into hysterical tears as the other pulled her away.

Slowly a crowd was gathering down the street. More and more Outsiders, finding strength in numbers started appearing. They were curious. Many of them had probably never seen a sight like this. Arthur knew that he would have joined them in the old days. He would have wanted to see, to understand what was happening. A change was an unusual event. Even if it brought something bad, like the paravirus or some new police action, people wanted to know what was going on.

Evan and his men were still inside the store. Uncle was getting nervous. The Secret Service men were all turned to face the gathering crowd. The two girls had run over to join them and were surrounded by people asking them questions, pointing at the bus and the store. They had the familiar look of Outsiders, sunburned and underfed, wearing a ragtag collection of olive-and-beige government-issue clothes, tinted by a sheen of red dust and sweat. All of them looked hungry.

The store door finally opened, and Evan and his security detail came out. They had a bag with the supplies they needed and headed straight to the back of the bus. Slowly, almost imperceptibly, the crowd was starting to shuffle closer. At first they moved slowly, but as more and more people joined them, the sheer weight of numbers pushed them forward. The Secret Service agents had moved to form a defensive wall. Noises came from the back of the bus as Evan and the drivers tried to do a hurried fix.

Arthur could hear something else now. Something different. The crowd was chanting, their voices building. He couldn't make out their words, but he could see them raise their arms and pump their hands in the air to the beat of the chant. They seemed energized, their previous fear melting away as they stood as one. They were less than a block from the first unit. The Secret Service men, although heavily armed, were starting to look desperately outnumbered.

Uncle leaped out of the bus and sprinted a few feet toward the approaching crowd. He was talking fast into his head microphone.

"STOP WHERE YOU ARE. DO NOT APPROACH THE BUS. ANYONE WITHIN FIFTY FEET WILL BE IN VIOLATION OF THE LAW, AND WE WILL TAKE ACTION AGAINST YOU." Uncle's voice boomed across the streets.

The crowd slowed, and the chanting weakened as people looked at each other in confusion.

"Oh my god, oh my god, oh my god…" Ty had curled up under a table in a small ball.

An ashen-faced Van was standing stock-still.

Finally a young man in a red hat, not much older than Arthur, stepped forward and turned to face the crowd. He seemed to be shouting to them. The crowd responded to him, cheering and laughing. The chanting started again, louder this time. They shouted excitedly, still moving slowly toward the bus. Frustrated that he couldn't hear what they were shouting, Arthur moved toward the open bus doors, stepping out into the stifling heat. At last he could make out what they were chanting.

"Wash-ing-ton! Wash-ing-ton!"

They had seen the name on the bus. They weren't rioting. They were excited because George Washington was here, their celebrity favorite from *The Democracy Games*. They were cheering for him.

The security police didn't see it that way. They saw a dirty wild crowd gathering momentum, cheering and chanting and egging one another on. They saw danger, a threat. They had snapped into a military formation as soon as the chanting had picked up again. Uncle was outside the bus, feeding them orders over his head microphone.

"When they pass the corner, Unit A, take out the ringleader. Units B and C, restraining fire on the front row. On my count." Uncle spoke fast. "Three…"

"No, wait. Stop!" Arthur shouted. He ran to Uncle. "Stop!

They're not dangerous. They just want to see what's going on. You don't need to do this. Don't do this!"

"Get him inside now," Uncle ordered. The closest Secret Service agents grabbed Arthur.

"Two…"

"No! Don't hurt them. No…" Arthur was wrestled back toward the bus, struggling violently, kicking and punching at the agents. He was roughly dragged through the bus doors and held, pinned hard against the wall. The crowd was roaring now, the excitement outside the bus inciting them.

"One." Ordered Uncle. "Fire."

The chants turned to screams.

Through the window of the bus, the scene turned to carnage. Clouds of red dust were kicked up from the road as people scattered in fear. They ran desperately, pulling one another into doorways or behind old cars, looking for cover. Sharp blue lasers silently cut through everything and everyone in their path; indiscriminately people fell to the ground.

It must have only lasted a few seconds, but everyone on the bus, everyone on that street, would remember what they saw that day. No matter how hard they would try to forget.

Arthur watched helplessly, tears filling his eyes.

The lasers stopped almost as soon as they had started. For one long, awful moment the scene looked still and unreal, like a painting. The red dust was settling over the street, shapes slowly appearing out of the clouds. Several shadowy outlines were strewn across the ground where the crowd had been standing. As the dust cleared, Arthur made out the young man with the red hat, unmoving in the dirt. Arthur saw the girls from the store—one holding the other's limp body, swaying back and forth. A man and a woman wrapped in each other's arms lay still, lost in time.

Arthur's legs gave in, and he slumped to his knees, the arms that had been pinning him down, finally releasing. Everyone was silent.

What happened next was a blur. Somehow everyone stumbled back onto the bus and into their units. Somehow the bus started, and the units pulled into line. Somehow the convoy got out of Town 1134 and back onto the highway, back behind the walls and ribbons of barbed wire and fences.

Arthur hadn't moved from the floor. No one said a word. The bus just drove on, heading away, people turning their backs to Town 1134, as if it had never happened.

For the next few days, Arthur stayed inside his cabin. He had no desire to talk to anyone and nothing to say. His final speeches had been cancelled, because of a "head cold."

He spent hours fuming over the VT news. There was not a single mention of what had happened at Town 1134. It was as if it had never happened. The massacre didn't rate a mention, but hours were spent discussing Claire's last dress, its empire line creating a wave of speculation about whether she might be pregnant. Cynically, Arthur wondered if Cain had picked that dress for her deliberately.

At night, Arthur's thoughts were consumed with guilt and horror. He could barely close his eyes without images of the townspeople popping into his head, the chants ringing round his ears. Wash-ing-ton. Wash-ing-ton.

Wash-ing-ton, the coward who had watched them die. Wash-ing-ton, the fake, the phony leader. They had been calling for him, excited for him. Maybe they thought he would be their hero, someone who would change things, help the Outsiders. Maybe they were just excited that someone like him had bothered to stop in their town. Maybe they thought he cared about them.

184

Well, they paid the price for believing in false gods. For believing in him. He had failed them and in the long dark nights, he didn't know how he could live with that.

For the first few nights after the town, Claire had come to him, softly knocking at his bunk door, interrupting Arthur from his anguished thoughts. But he didn't open the screen. Instead, he lay silently listening, just feet from her. After the third night, Claire stopped coming.

Arthur's shock was giving way to a deep, powerful anger, an emotion that was unusual for him and scared him. He was angry with himself and the world, but also at Claire, Ty, and the rest. They had stood by and watched as the SS agents had held him down, without even trying to help, or stop Uncle.

He tried to rationalize it, asking himself what Claire or Ty or any of them could have done. But the answer always came out the same. Probably nothing, but they didn't even try. He had never felt more distant from them than on that day, and it wasn't a feeling you could shake easily.

Sometimes he wondered what Bay would have done if she had been on the bus with him, instead of Claire. Would she have stood by and let it happen? He saw an image of her in his mind, wearing her rebel uniform, her wild curls escaping from her ponytail, her blue-green eyes smiling at him over her red bandana.

Then he pictured the girl on the school bus, sitting next to him, sucking on a pencil while she thought of what she wanted to draw for him in their scrappy notebook. He didn't know who she really was—how much was real, how much was in his head. But he did know she was strong, and in his mind he wanted to believe that she would have been different, that she would have done something.

The only one Arthur wasn't mad at was Evan. He had been under the bus, fixing the wheel when things had gone down. When he saw what had happened, he went ballistic, demanding accountability. When Arthur had finally come out of his cabin after his self-imposed exile, both Uncle and Evan were sporting some nasty bruises. Arthur never asked about them, but he could guess what had happened.

On the final night, before they were due to arrive in the Washington Metrozone, Arthur finally ran into Evan on one of his trips to the bathroom. He had the feeling that the older man had been waiting for him.

Evan looked as rough as Arthur felt. His face still had the bruises from his run-in with Uncle, and he looked like he hadn't shaved or slept in a while.

"Were you waiting for me?" Arthur asked, already knowing the answer.

"Thought we should have a wee chat afore we arrive an' all."

"Were you sent to talk to me?" Arthur would have trusted Evan with his life, but he still had to know for sure. These days he felt like everyone was on Cain's side.

"Ha, no. They would'n a sent me, kiddo. Secretary Cain does'n like me very much these days. I was worried abou' you."

Arthur was touched, swallowing down his feelings. He felt like he was keeping a huge well of emotion just beneath the surface and knew that anything could set him off.

Evan also looked like he was having difficulty finding the words he wanted.

"When I was a bairn, no much older than you, I was called up to fight in t' Pan Global Conflicts." Arthur looked at Evan in surprise. He knew he had been in the army, but Evan had never mentioned that he had fought in that terrible war.

"Och, war is a messy business, Arthur. It changes a man, changes how they see t' world. You do thin's...see thin's, what

186

people are capable of…Take away t' rules, add a wee bi' o' fear, and we are all animals. Monsters, just below t' surface."

Evan's expression was distant, as though he was seeing something from a long time ago.

"You once tol' me I were a good man, Arthur. But I'm no." He held up his hands, looking at his rough fingers with contempt, his eyes flooded with memories. "But when 'tis all said and done, when you come home an' have t' find a way t' live agin…knowing what y' know abou' people, abou' yerself…well, tha's when your real fight begins. Many a good soldier, didn'a make it. Survived t' war only to fall, here, surrounded by people they loved." Evan looked at Arthur, his face tortured.

Arthur hadn't realized it, but his cheeks were wet with tears.

"Y' make a choice, Arthur. Each an' every day. To gi' in to the demons, or t' fight 'em. It nair goes away. T' darkness is somat all soldiers carry wi' us, in our souls. It's t' choices we make tha' define us."

The two of them stood silently together, swaying slightly from the motion of the bus. Lights flashed past. Outsider checkpoints, tunnels, nameless towns. Arthur knew why Evan had chosen to tell him this now. He knew what the older man wanted him to do. He just didn't know if he had the strength to do it. To put his feelings of guilt and anger behind him and to choose to fight the darkness that had threatened to envelop him since that day at Town 1134.

"How?" he whispered.

"Y' jus' do, son." Evan put his hand on Arthur's shoulder and then turned and walked away, leaving Arthur alone.

Arthur looked out the window at the lights flashing by. His reflection stared back at him. For the first time, he didn't see his own face; he saw George Washington. He reached up, touching the cool glass that came between him and the man he was supposed to be. A soldier, a leader, and a hero. A man who had fought the darkness a thousand times over and had won. For the first time, Arthur felt a connection to the man he saw before him.

At long last he understood the man he was supposed to be.

Chapter 14

Washington Metrozone seemed different from the others, though Arthur wasn't sure if that was just because he was biased. After all, it was his city.

The convoy pulled up by the old, venerable Jefferson Hotel, and everyone decamped from the bus, standing silently, watching as it pulled away for the last time. Forever, in Arthur's memories, that bus would be associated what had happened at Town 1134. He closed his eyes as images from that day resurfaced, threatening to overwhelm him. But as quickly as they came, he pushed them down, somewhere deep inside.

The Presidential Suite was refined and peaceful, a series of expansive rooms that was larger than most of the houses Arthur had grown up in. Soft-yellow paneled walls gently radiated warmth over the rooms filled with antiques and old paintings.

Best of all were the balconies, with expansive views across the sleeping city. Arthur could see the Washington Monument, lit up like a beacon in the dark. His skin tingled when he saw it, and he held his breath, wondering if it had the same effect on everyone, or if in some weird way, he was connected to the slumbering monolith.

As he looked around, another landmark glowed brightly among the city streets. For a moment he didn't recognize it, finally realizing that he was looking at the most famous building in the UZA. The White House. This time he shivered slightly, for the first time feeling the chill in the night air.

Over the next few days, the main topic of conversation was the upcoming presidential debate, the final event before the election. At last, in front of millions of viewers, Washington and Kennedy would go head-to-head. The days were spent on lockdown, the entire team, hunkering down in the suite's fancy living room, drilling Arthur over and over on what to say, how to say it, how to stand, how to move. The latest polls showed the damage that Arthur's lackluster speeches had done. The two nominees were neck and neck, but Kennedy had momentum in his favor, and everyone knew that Arthur would have to pull out a winning performance to have a chance at the presidency.

But as the big day drew close, tensions rose. Arthur's heart was not in it, and no amount of hard work could fix that.

When he got to bed on the last night before the debate, Arthur was so mentally exhausted that he fell asleep fully clothed. But as usual, the nightmares came calling. By midnight he had climbed out of bed, looking for a distraction so he wouldn't have to lie there listening to his own thoughts. Evan was on duty, outside the suite door, and he was more than happy to accompany Arthur downstairs to the hotel lobby for a change of scene.

Everything was quiet downstairs. The only place open was Quills, the hotel bar. While Evan stood watch by the bar door, Arthur went in alone.

It was mercifully dark and peaceful inside. The gentle glow of light from the bar gave the place a safe feeling, like being inside a sanctuary. Obviously that was why people came here. He wasn't the only straggler. A handful of lonely-looking people sat in corners alone, nursing drinks to keep their own personal demons at bay.

One of the loners was seated in a wheelchair at a small table near the open fire, her hand holding tight to a small whiskey glass. Arthur knew her instantly, his heart jumping for joy. He ran over and hugged her. The professor was both happy to see her favorite prodigy and a little drunk. She ordered him a root beer and herself another round; once they were settled, they started talking.

"I adore this place, Arthur." She waved her hand to indicate her surroundings. For a moment, Arthur thought she meant the bar.

That was no surprise. But then she continued.

"Washington, District of Columbia. Our nation's capital. Named in honor of my little friend here." She bowed her head toward him, making him blush. He was glad it was dark.

"So much history. So much hope and glory, poured into the very stones. Right here, Arthur. You can feel it. Hope for a new nation, one that will do better, that won't repeat the mistakes of the past. Hope, ah, it's intoxicating, isn't it?"

"Yes," Arthur said with a laugh.

Something was intoxicating her, for sure. He didn't have the heart to tell her that he hadn't seen any hopeful stones yet. That he'd spent his entire time in Washington sitting in one hotel room.

She continued, waxing lyrical about the glories of the Capitol, and Arthur happily sat back and listened. The sound of her voice took him back to Mount Vernon and their long mornings in her study. He would have gladly listened to her all day. Her passion for the past was infectious.

But as she talked about the great and the good, Arthur felt a darkness stealing into his heart. Was she really naive enough to believe all that grand philosophy? Had she ever been to the Outside?

Did she even understand how cruel the real world could be? Once again he heard his name, quietly in the back of his mind. Wash-ing-ton, Wash-ing-ton.

The professor had stopped talking and was looking at him.

Arthur wanted to tell her what was upsetting him, but it felt as though the words were stuck in his throat, behind a protective wall that concealed his worst feelings. But he didn't need to say anything; she already knew.

"Evan told me what happened. I'm so sorry, Arthur." The professor put her whiskey down and sat back in her chair, rubbing her eyes. The fire crackled, as the two of them sat silently in the warm glow. When the professor finally spoke, her voice was quiet.

"There was a time when our leaders were also our heroes, and people knew right from wrong. When the future lay before us, ours for the taking. Now it's just the dust beneath our feet, and the worst part is we did this to ourselves."

"So what do we do about it?" Arthur asked. "Do we just accept it? We blew it, so quit complaining?" His voice was uncharacteristically bitter.

"No, Arthur. We fight." It was an easy, trite answer, and Arthur had expected better from the professor.

The now familiar anger swelled inside him.

"Right. We fight. We choose. What does any of that really mean? I stood by and watched Outsiders massacred like cattle, and I could do nothing, *nothing*, to stop it. You think I can fight this? I am nobody. Cain's pathetic pet, his puppet. I wasn't born. I was made. Made for one purpose alone. And if I fail, Cain will destroy me. How can I fight this?" Arthur felt tears rising to his eyes. The guilt he felt cut him so deeply, he could barely control his words. He closed his eyes and breathed in, his breath ragged and shaky as he willed himself to calm down.

192

When he finally opened his eyes, the professor was watching him.

Self-consciously, he wiped the back of his hand across his eyes and turned away to face the fire.

"Don't be afraid of my brother, Arthur. You have more in common than you know." Her voice was soft, thoughtful. "There's something I should have told you long ago." Arthur turned to look at her face. She seemed to be conflicted, as if deciding how to continue.

"I had another brother. Many years ago. He was eight years old when he died."

Arthur started to mumble how sorry he was, but she waved her hand at him dismissively.

"Oh, I barely knew him. I was just an infant. His name was Paul." She paused. Arthur blinked, momentarily confused. Why would both her brothers be called Paul? It didn't make sense.

"My mother, the brilliant Dr. Jane Cain, never got over Paul's death. She was consumed by grief and made a terrible choice. It was within her technical ability to play god, and she decided to bring her lost son back."

Arthur looked up at her quickly, shocked. Was she really saying what he thought she was? Cain was a clone, like him? The resurrections were said to have started when the walls were raised. This must have been twenty years earlier. How was this even possible?

"She made a deal with the government. In exchange for the funding she needed, she agreed to clone a second child too, a government experiment. They were the first of your kind, Arthur. The two boys were raised together, constantly studied and examined, like lab rats. They even brought in a third child, an abandoned baby boy to act as a constant—a human baseline. I grew up hanging around the lab, with these three boys. A strange childhood, not altogether unpleasant. They were almost like...brothers to me." A fleeting look of nostalgia crossed her face, quickly replaced by sadness.

"But there are many reasons why mere mortals should not play god. The least of which is that we don't have the mental capacity to cope with the consequences of our actions. My mother had her beloved son back, but he wasn't my brother. His life, his memories were different. He grew into his own person, but still looked and sounded like the boy she had lost. By trying to bring him back, all she had succeeded in doing was perpetuating her own grief with a living, walking reminder of everything she had lost. She grew to loathe Cain with a hatred most reserve for only themselves. He was her terrible mistake, and she never forgave him for that."

For the first time in his life, Arthur actually felt sorry for Cain. Through no fault of his own, he had never stood a chance. He grew up hated, unwanted by his own mother. An ill-thought-out idea turned to flesh and blood. No wonder he had turned out the way he had. Driven, ambitious, and ruthless.

The professor turned to Arthur.

"Arthur, I told you this, because you need to know that my brother is not someone to be feared. My mother's avarice changed him, shaped him into the man he is. He is powerful and dangerous; that is indisputable. But he is no god. He has weaknesses and vulnerabilities, just like the rest of us. You of all people can understand that. You of all people can stand up to him."

"Why me?" Arthur wasn't sure what she was getting at.

"Because you are George Washington! You are born of one of the greatest rebel leaders in history." She leaned forward and took his hand. "You don't have to accept anything. You do what Washington did. You get up, even when you don't feel strong enough. You hope, even when your cause is lost. You lead, even when you have no idea where you must go. Where you see injustice, you fight back, Arthur…you rebel."

She pulled her hand back, leaving something hard and sharp in Arthur's closed fingers. He looked at the object. At first it made no sense. He just stared at it, wordlessly. Then slowly a smile crept across his face. Of course. He should have known.

His fingers slowly rubbed the metal oval, brushing over the three stars. It was a car emblem, similar to the one he had last seen on the floor of the bunker, at Bay's feet, where he had thrown it. So the professor was a rebel supporter. Secretary Cain's own sister was secretly trying to bring him down. The professor, Bay, and Martin. They were all making a stand, fighting for what was right. He wasn't alone.

He looked up, grinning, but the professor had already turned away and was heading for the door. He watched her as she wheeled up to Evan, reaching out to take his hand, the two of them talking quietly, affectionately together.

Arthur didn't follow. He wasn't tired and stayed a little longer by the fire, finishing off the professor's whiskey, thinking.

Twelve hours later, Arthur found himself standing face-to-face with Kennedy in a dark, empty lecture hall. They had been primed and primped, a cloud of people dressing them and touching up their hair and makeup. Biometric scanners had been taped to every inch of them under their suits. Arthur kept scratching at them uncomfortably, the tape pulling on dozens of different hairs every time he moved.

Each nominee was standing on a raised, circular platform, another heavy, round disc suspended ominously in the air above them. Arthur briefly wondered if they were planning to cut the top circle loose and squash the debate loser. He wouldn't put it past Cain.

It would make great VT.

Claire had come to wish him luck. For a moment they stood together, spotlighted, just looking at each other, her white-gold hair glowing radiantly under the lights like some kind of halo. Arthur couldn't help wondering which of the two Claires he had come to know was standing in front of him now. The cool, fake girlfriend or the sweet, vulnerable Outsider he had come to love. She seemed able to switch between roles at will, so he never knew where he stood.

As everyone filtered out of the hall, Claire stayed, still looking at him. It felt as though she was trying to communicate something to him with her eyes. As usual, he had no idea what she was trying to tell him. Finally, she stepped forward, close to him, still not touching him. He could smell her—her sweet breath and her soft perfume mingling with the warmth of her skin. She was intoxicating. She turned her face up to him, a small smile playing across her lips as she softly whispered just one word, so only he could hear it.

"Win."

She stepped back, her eyes on him for one last lingering moment, then turned and walked out of the hall.

And then it was just the two of them, Washington and Kennedy, standing alone in the dark, glaring at each other. Arthur scratched nervously at an awkwardly placed biometric monitor, wondering if he sweated too much he might get electrocuted.

Eve's standard issue voice announced that the debate would begin in two minutes. Kennedy began his usual, shaking-out warm-up moves.

"You have to be the lousiest public speaker on the planet, Washington," Kennedy growled, probably hoping to psych out the competition.

"Yeah. Probably true." Arthur half laughed. He'd even managed to put his own campaign manager to sleep at one of his speeches. He wondered if he should limber up too but didn't want to make the monitors pluck any more hair out than was absolutely necessary.

"You have no right to be here. You've done nothing. You just show up when you're told and say what you're told. You're not a real leader. King, Tubman, even fat Ben had more right to be standing there than you."

Once again, Arthur didn't disagree.

"If you're trying to put me off my game, try telling me something I don't know." Arthur was ready for the debate to begin for real.

"Something you don't know? OK." Kennedy stopped moving and faced him, a blindingly perfect white smile on his handsome, boyish face. "Your girlfriend works for Secretary Cain. She's your handler." Finally Kennedy had hit the mark.

Loud debate music suddenly swirled around them; thousands of virtual faces appeared in the air. Hope's voice announced the commencement of the presidential debate.

Arthur felt a wave of nausea in his stomach. It was as though Kennedy had voiced his deepest suspicions. But was he lying? Maybe he was just jealous. Desperately Arthur tried to put Claire out of his mind; he had a job to do.

The excitement was rising. Hope's dramatic introduction was wrapping up.

"Gentlemen, you know the debate rules. Please…meet the people."

As suddenly as it had started, the swirling stopped. Arthur could hear voices now. "I want to know what you're going to do about school closures." "We are not represented by our own government." "We need more…" "We need less…" The voices crashed over him like a wave, some people appearing on the stage next to him, others floating in the air around him, all talking, asking their questions.

Tentatively Arthur reached his hand out toward a random person. Instantly he was standing, next to Kennedy, in a school gymnasium, surrounded by crowds of kids on bleachers, cheering ecstatically to be on VT. The woman he had tagged was standing in front of him, one hand on her round pregnant belly, the other holding a microphone. Her name, Lois, Baton Rouge Metrozone, floated over her head.

Arthur swallowed nervously. This was going to be a lot harder than he thought. He waved shyly at the kids and then nodded nervously toward Lois. Kennedy smoothly stepped forward.

"Hello, Lois, and hello, Baton Rouge Metrozone!" The cheering went through the roof.

"Oh my goodness! I can't believe you're really here." Lois struggled to pull herself together. "Hi, Mr. Washington, Mr. Kennedy. I am the mother of three, well almost four children." The crowd laughed. Encouraged, Lois continued. "My children attend the Lower Ward District Schools. In the last month, these schools have been locked down fifteen times, all because of the dangerous and reckless behavior of Outsider students. Now, I feel for these kids as much as the next person, and I agree they have a right to be educated. But putting them in schools with our kids. Well, it hurts everyone. They're different. Their needs are different. Frankly, sir, they are bringing us all down."

A few shouts of support filled the air. Lois looked around, excited by being the focus of attention.

"My question to you both is this. If you are elected president, are you going to segregate the school system, once and for all?"

Someone shouted, "Get them Outsiders out," followed by laughter and heckling.

"Thank you, Lois. That is an excellent question…" Kennedy had easily swooped in and was talking smoothly, convincingly to the enraptured crowd.

Arthur quickly turned around. He knew exactly what he was looking for and finally found it—the Outsider section, at the back and in the corner farthest from the stage. He looked over at the straggly bunch of kids, all sitting silently, their heads bowed in fear and shame. His heart was there with them, always.

Kennedy was talking animatedly, his words rousing and engaging the audience. Arthur had no idea what he was saying. It didn't matter now. He knew what he had to do.

"Unless my fellow candidate disagrees?" Kennedy had finished. All eyes turned to Arthur. He took a deep breath, willing himself to have the courage to do what he knew he had to do.

Slowly, he raised his hands, instantly silencing the crowd. All his self-consciousness had gone. Last night in the bar, after the professor had left, he had made a promise to himself. Now it was time to carry through, no matter the consequences.

Turning to face the Outsiders, he spoke from his heart.

"The truth is I don't know anyone who isn't afraid right now. Our land is ruined, our nation ripped apart by crime, our future uncertain. We are all scared. But what happens if we give in to that fear? If instead of facing the world we have created, we hide from it?" He looked around, at the sea of youthful faces watching him. The plump, pale Zoners looked clean with their hair brushed and shiny, and the Outsiders' lean, tan faces peered at him from under a curtain of dust.

"We built walls to protect ourselves. And as our fears grew, our walls became bigger and stronger. Then one day, we woke up, and we couldn't see the sky anymore. We didn't keep danger out. We built ourselves a prison. Look at us, trapped inside like rats in a fancy cage, while our own brothers and sisters are out there, living on their knees."

There were a few cheers from the crowd. Arthur could feel their anticipation. They were listening, really hearing him. The Outsiders weren't hiding their faces anymore. They were watching Arthur closely, warily, as though trying to figure out if he meant what he was saying.

"The dangers facing us are real. Starvation, disease, and crime...they are real. But we are not." He pointed to himself, then slowly raised his arm to point at Kennedy.

The crowd was silent, confusion and expectation in equal measures on their faces. Kennedy had turned to face him square on, a dark look on his face.

Arthur turned around to take in everyone.

"But we...the candidates...are not real. We are not who you think we are."

The silence was deafening. Crushing. A sea of faces, uncomprehending faces, watching him, confused. Arthur knew he had to carry on, before Cain figured out what he was up to and pulled him out.

"My name is not George Washington. It is Arthur Ryan, and I am an Outsider. George Washington, the man you think I am, died in a terror attack on the first primary. I was a spare, drafted in by Secretary Cain to replace him, to trick you into thinking I was him. I am a fake—all of us are, really. We are not the great leaders you want us to be. We are just kids, copies of great people sent to entertain you and distract you from what's really going on..."

The cheers faded as the auditorium around him flickered and disappeared. He was being pulled out. Arthur shook his head, trying to snap himself out of the moment. He was back on the podium in the dark, thousands of faces floating around him.

Kennedy was standing, unmoving on the podium next to him. He was staring at the ground, his fists clenched tightly, the muscles in his jaw working. Slowly he looked up at Arthur, his eyes burning with anger.

"Is it true?" His voice was dangerously quiet and controlled.

Arthur nodded.

"So there are spares of us? They can just throw us out and replace us with another…clone?"

Kennedy's expression had shifted from disbelief to anger.

"I'm sorry, John. Cain's been playing us. All of us. None of this has even been about us."

Kennedy turned away, his body slumped slightly. Arthur looked at his back and for the first time felt pity.

All Kennedy wanted, more than anything in the world, was to live up to expectations. He was born, "made," to be a king, a leader, a hero, like his clone father. His entire life was devoted to that one purpose. And yet, unbeknownst to him, that position was already filled. Kennedy was a puppet in someone else's grand game. He could never be his clone father, no more than Arthur could. He was a good man at heart, potentially a great one. But he had never really stood a chance. He deserved better.

Arthur reached around tiredly for the microphones stuck to his chest. He wouldn't be needing these anymore. He was sure Cain would be coming for him any second now; he just had to hope that he had done enough. That he had been heard.

But before his fingers could pull the tape off, a disorienting rush made him drop to his knees.

Carefully steadying himself with his hand, he looked around.

The podiums had disappeared and been replaced by a makeshift concrete room, piles of rubble pushed into the shape of crude furniture, lights flickering in his eyes. A feeling of familiarity turned to surprise as he turned to face the source of the light. Broken glass hanging where the wall should have been, framing the view across a ruined city, the colors of late afternoon touching the sky. He was in the castle.

Slowly, Arthur looked around, breathing it all in, a smile crossing his face. He had no idea how or why this had happened, but it was like standing in one of his dreams. He wanted to walk over to his favorite concrete couch, but knew he couldn't step off the podium or this world would be lost to him.

"This is mad," he half whispered to himself.

"I know. Crazy times, huh?" It was Bay's voice—her quick intelligent voice was unmistakable. It always sounded to Arthur as though her words couldn't keep up with her brain. She had appeared in front of the missing wall, the sunlight catching her from behind, lighting up her frizzy dark hair and giving her a halo of gold. Her sea-blue eyes sparkled warmly at him, and she grinned a cheeky, teasing grin. Arthur felt a warmth stealing over him. Seeing her always felt like coming home.

She walked over toward him, coming close. Slowly she reached her hand up. Without hesitating, he put his hand up too, holding it in the air next to hers. For a moment they stood still, the world forgotten, imagining they could actually touch each other. Both of them smiled.

From this close, he could see the lines of exhaustion that crossed her face, the bruises and smears of dirt on her hands and neck. For the first time, he noticed her uniform, the rebel red bandanna, his car emblem clipped to her dirty jacket with safety pins.

So it was real. The primary had happened. He dropped his hand.

It was not like he hadn't guessed. In his heart he hadn't trusted

Cain's version of events. But there had always been the possibility that it was just another part of this crazy game he was playing. That Bay had still just been the schoolgirl he had known. His best friend. Not someone sent to recruit him to the rebel cause. He looked down, shaking his head to clear it, trying desperately to process his thoughts.

"So…it was real? The tunnel? You being one of them…a rebel?" Arthur stumbled over the words. Bay nodded, but didn't answer, maybe afraid to provoke a response. He had made it quite clear the last time that he felt betrayed by her.

Arthur dropped his eyes. He couldn't risk looking at her. Everything about her felt right and good; he couldn't help but trust her when he looked at her. So he kept his eyes down. He had so many questions, but he knew that time was short. If she had found a way to hack into the debate, it wouldn't be long before they would get shut down.

Quickly he asked the question that had been weighing on him since the primary.

"Remember that day on the school bus, the day they came for me?" The memory of the day this all started, still burned in Arthur's mind. He could feel the fear and shock as if it was yesterday. "If you knew who I was all along, why did you let them take me? Why didn't you warn me? I thought we were friends." It was easy keeping his eyes down. He didn't want her to see his look of hurt.

Bay looked taken aback. For a moment she seemed to be struggling to find the right words.

"I'm so sorry, Arthur. I wanted to warn you, to pull you off the bus and get you out of there." She paused. A look of sadness crossed her face like a shadow. "But, I was ordered to keep you in play."

"Keep me in play? Ordered? By who? Who gives you the orders?" He looked up at her face, searchingly.

"Abel." For the first time, Bay looked nervous, unsure of

herself.

Arthur was taken aback. Bay was getting orders directly from the rebel leader himself. He was surprised that Bay and he warranted the attention of the mysterious Abel.

"But how did you get orders? We were on the bus…it happened so fast."

"Digital communications are monitored, so we often have to go old school." Bay waved her hand around her, and Arthur actually noticed the colorful graffiti for the first time. It was always there, in the background, all over the Outside. No one paid any attention. With a flash, Arthur remembered the tunnel through the West Gate, how Bay would study the freshly graffitied walls each morning. She was picking up her orders.

Suddenly a small fat duck flashed in the corner of the room, quacking loudly. Surprised, Arthur recognized Mr. Sandwich. He must have been the one to hack the rebels into the debate.

"That's our warning alarm. Time's almost up. They'll kick me out of the loop soon. When they find out Mr. Sandwich got us in, Cain's going to be pissed."

"Mr. Sandwich works for the rebels?" Arthur couldn't help asking.

"Mr. Sandwich works for no one." Bay grinned, her eyes flashing warm green as she looked at him. Her expression darkened.

"Arthur, I came to give you a message. You're in danger. Cain's needed you up till now. He's needed you to be his champion, his George Washington. But he won't let you risk destroying everything he's worked for. He doesn't trust you; he knows you are a wild card, and he's taking steps to…control you, to reign you in. As soon as the election's over, he's going to make his move. We can't protect you from the Outside. You're in too deep. You have to get yourself out."

Arthur actually laughed.

"I think it's a little late for that."

Bay looked at him, confused.

"What do you mean? What's happened?"

"You'll see when you watch the debate."

"Arthur, what did you do?" Bay looked worried, a furrow creasing between her eyes.

"I did what I had to do, Bay. I told the nation who I really am. Who Cain really is. That we are all frauds—that this is all a lie."

Bay was staring at him, her eyes focused intently on his, but he could tell her mind was elsewhere, racing ahead, calculating the repercussions of what he had just told her.

Arthur shuffled uncomfortably from one foot to another.

"Look, I'm sorry. I had to do something…"

"I know. I know you, Arthur." She smiled, a shadow of sadness crossing her face.

Slowly, she reached her hand up to his face, her virtual fingers moving across his cheek; unfeeling, untouching. Arthur closed his eyes and willed himself to feel her—just this one time.

When she spoke, her voice was low and urgent.

"Arthur, you need to run. You need to get to the Outside."

As he opened his eyes, he saw that she was fading, black lines streaking across her as the castle flickered in and out of view. He nodded, instinctively reaching for her, his arms coming up empty.

She was fading now, blackness swallowing her as the debate hall flickered briefly into view around him.

"Get to the Outside. I will find you."

Everything swirled around Arthur in one last disorientating loop, falling slowly into place. He dropped to his knees, his hands pushing into the shiny metal floor of the podium as he steadied himself. Bay was gone. He was back, and he was in big trouble.

Under the harsh stage lights in the dark hall, the shadowy

outlines of several Secret Service men were appearing, moving quickly toward him. He quickly looked around. Kennedy was gone, all the exits were guarded. There was nowhere to run.

"Sir, step down. You're coming with us."

He raised his hands in the air and stepped forward, Bay's parting words ringing in his head.

"Get to the Outside. I will find you…I promise, I will find you."

Chapter 15

Arthur couldn't understand it.

All hell should have broken loose by now.

But he was far from dead or locked up in some godforsaken dungeon. He didn't even seem to be in trouble. In fact, the Secret Service had very politely escorted him back to his hotel suite, even stopping to offer him a nice cup of coffee and a pastry on the way.

It was as though the debate had never happened.

By the time they reached the hotel suite, his team was already there. Claire, Ty, Van, even Uncle and Evan, were all lounging around watching postdebate analysis on *The Democracy Games*.

Claire looked up when Arthur entered.

"Hey there." She turned back to watch the VT.

Arthur stood stock-still. It wasn't the reaction he was expecting. He quickly looked around at the others. Van was at the side table pouring tea. Ty was picking his nails, lounging comfortably across half the sofa. Uncle just looked bored. Evan smiled at Arthur and stood up to offer him his armchair.

They looked relaxed and happy, as though nothing had changed.

"So, how did I do?" Arthur asked, trying to provoke some kind of a reaction.

"Great. Come listen. They'll be getting the first polls in soon." Ty didn't even look up. "Ooh, I can't wait. It's so exciting. I reckon you won this one from that nasty Kennedy boy."

"You better believe it!" Van hustled over, spilling tea everywhere. Every inch of his enormous frame was awkward and uncoordinated. Claire yelped as he almost landed in her lap.

An excerpt from the debate was playing. Arthur saw himself standing, handsome and professional, in a school hall, pregnant Lois in front of him. For all the world, it looked as though he was really there.

"My question to you, Mr. Washington, is this. If you are elected president, are you going to segregate the school system, once and for all?"

Arthur remembered everything vividly.

He remembered how Lois had kept turning nervously to the crowd, how the Outsiders had sat silently in the back of the crowd, and how hard his heart had been beating as he had steeled himself to say what he was about to say.

He watched Kennedy eloquently field Lois's question.

He held his breath in anticipation of what was going to happen next. Handsome George nodded sympathetically and then spoke.

"Lois. I feel for you. Our great nation is at war with itself. Good citizens like you have been tyrannized too long by the weak and greedy who want what you have but lack the guts to work for it. Let's face the truth; our great nation is being dragged down by a few bad apples."

It wasn't him. He had never said those words. But there he

was—same tie, same suit, same immaculate hair, and same voice.

"Well, when I'm president…that ends. No one gets a free ride. The Outsiders don't have an inalienable right to share our resources—our schools, health care, and food. They have to earn that right."

Arthur felt sick to his stomach. He jumped to his feet, recoiling from the VT. A feeling of loathing for himself, for the man standing before him, flooded through him.

"Sometimes, doing the right thing means making tough choices. And I'm not afraid to do that. When Outsiders come into our own schools and break our own rules, they lose the right to be there. When I am president, I will end this. For the future of your children, of our great nation…I promise you, I will close the gates to troublemakers and send them to their own schools. I will make the UZA great again."

The audience was cheering wildly. It looked like the speech was a great success. The news cut back to the commentators, but Arthur couldn't bring himself to listen.

He felt angry. Powerless and angry.

"That wasn't me." He spoke in a low, almost menacing growl. His hands were shaking as he squeezed them into fists, trying to control his emotions.

"Always your own worst critic. George, enjoy this moment. You worked hard for this. Those people are cheering for you." Ty seemed delighted with the outcome.

"That wasn't me. Those…aren't my words." Arthur looked around furiously.

Ty kept waffling on about how it was good he had kept to the script, but Arthur didn't listen. He had noticed Claire. She was looking at him, her expression impassive but hard.

She knew. She knew it wasn't him. He didn't know how, but

she knew.

"What the hell is going on? How could you do this?" Arthur spoke directly to her. The iciness in his voice stopped Ty in his tracks, everyone turned to look at Arthur.

Claire stood up and walked calmly toward his bedroom. She obviously wanted to keep the conversation private. Infuriated, Arthur followed her, slamming his door shut behind them. For a long time, neither one said anything, both standing tensely facing away from each other. Finally Arthur calmed down enough to speak.

"I didn't say any of those things. That wasn't me. But you already know that, don't you?" he said accusingly. He remembered Kennedy's parting words to him—She works for Cain.

"Arthur, you just went off script a bit. You're not at your best when you improvise." Claire's tone was placating. She was handling him.

"Off script! I didn't say that. I don't believe any of that. Those people aren't voting for the real me, they're voting for a fraud."

The instant he said it, Claire turned to face him. She looked almost as angry as he was.

"Grow up, Arthur. They were never voting for you. They were voting for a myth, a legend…never you." Her tone was harsh and critical. Arthur was shocked. He hadn't expected her to say that. He thought she would try to talk him down, convince him to bide his time. Tell him that everything was going to be OK.

Claire walked up to him until her golden head was inches below his. He breathed in her irresistible smell. He was pointedly aware that she was doing this on purpose, pulling him into her net. She looked up at him, sweetness in her eyes, erasing the sharpness of her last comment.

"Arthur, you have to play the long game here. If you want to make a difference, alienating Secretary Cain is the worst thing you can do. You have real power…"

"Are you working for Cain? All this…you and me? Is this just…your job?" Arthur was terrified to hear her answer, but the time had come. He had to know for sure, one way or the other.

Claire stepped back, shocked. But she didn't answer.

Arthur began to feel a dark fear inside him. Had she been sent to watch him? All those nights, had they been an act? Images of the touches, the kisses, the soft words whispered between them, flashed through his mind. It couldn't all be an act, could it? He wasn't sure if he could bear it. If he could bear to lose her. They stared at each other, the air between them icy. Finally Claire spoke, her voice barely above a whisper.

"How could you even think that?"

Her voice was tinged with disappointment, her eyes clouded with tears. She turned her back on him and walked over to the french doors to the balcony. Arthur watched her back, her slender frame, the delicate way her dress hung over her shoulders, her hips. She looked vulnerable as she stood facing the city, her arms folded protectively around herself.

Arthur felt deeply ashamed for hurting her and mentally kicked himself for asking. He should have kept his suspicions to himself, shouldn't have let Kennedy get into his head like that. What kind of friend was he if he chose not to trust her?

"I'm sorry, Claire. I just…" He tailed off, unsure what to say.

She turned, still not looking at him, and walked to the door, but as she opened it, she paused. The VT was still playing in the living room. George Washington was standing in front of them both, larger than life.

"For the record, that is the 'real' you. It was recorded before the accident." She looked at the handsome, smiling, waving young man, a shadow of grief crossing her perfect features. Then without a backward glance, she left.

Arthur sank down onto the bed. Out of their whole conversation, the thing that Arthur couldn't let go of had nothing to do with Cain or who she might or might not be working for. It was the way she had looked at George's hologram.

She loved George, still. That much was obvious. Arthur had wanted to believe that she had feelings for him. But he was a shadow of his predecessor. A messed-up, damaged shadow. A reminder of the man she had loved. Just like Cain was a poor copy of his dead brother. How could he have let himself think that a girl like her could fall for an idiot like him? He felt sick to his stomach.

Arthur walked over to the french doors and stepped onto the balcony. He needed air. As he stood looking over the professor's beloved city, he breathed in deeply, the coolness of the stone balustrade sinking into his hands, calming him as he struggled to make sense of his emotions.

The only thing that felt right at that moment in time—the only person he wanted to talk to—was Bay. He needed to get away from Claire and Secretary Cain and all the fancy hotels and smart suits and find her. Even though she had lied about who she really was, she was one of the few people who knew him, the real him. She understood. He needed to get to the Outside somehow. She would find him, as she had promised.

It was evening by the time everyone finally left the suite. Arthur breathed a sigh of relief. He had spent the entire day plotting his escape, impatient for the moment when he could put his plan into action. Amicably he had pretended that he was going to shower and dress for dinner, even going so far as to ask for advice on which tie to wear, hoping to allay suspicions.

Minutes after the door closed on Ty and Van, he had changed

into a plain dark hoodie and pants and was listening at the door. There would be two security police officers outside, but at this time, it wouldn't be Uncle or Evan. He didn't want to run with Uncle hunting him down, and the last thing he wanted to do was get Evan into trouble. They would be starting their shifts in twenty minutes, so Arthur knew this was his moment.

As he left the suite, he nodded to the two guards, mumbling something about needing a bit of fresh air. Instantly both men started talking into head comms, walking briskly after him. It was time for Arthur to put his plan into action.

He paused at the elevator. As it dinged and started opening, he darted to the stair exit at the side, slipped quickly behind the door, pulled his shoe off, and counted. It took just three seconds for the guards to push the door open. Quickly Arthur tossed his shoe into the stairwell. It clattered down noisily, just as the guards stepped in, running down the stairs in the direction of the noise.

So far so good. Arthur silently caught the door and slipped back into the corridor, sprinting to the stairwell at the other end. Just in the nick of time he crashed through the exit doors as he heard voices in the corridor behind him. He peeked through the tempered glass lite and saw several people running out of Claire's suite, heading away from him. Van came out last. His low, loud voice was audible through the door.

"Totally wigged out when he saw the broadcast. Started ranting about how it wasn't him. I'm not surprised…"

Arthur kicked himself into action, sprinting down several flights of stairs until he heard the sound of an exit door opening far below him. Voices carried up the long stairwell. Secret Service. Pulling his hood up, he slipped through the nearest doors, aware of the security camera drones floating in the corridor corners. Walking briskly, but calmly, he pretended to stroll along the corridor, until he heard a door open. Quickly Arthur turned and pretended to be unlocking a door. A middle-aged couple stepped into the corridor and started walking toward him in the direction of the elevator. As they passed, Arthur turned to walk close behind them.

The couple seemed a little unnerved by his presence. When they stopped by the elevator doors, they turned to look at him challengingly.

"Have you seen a dog? Small, kinda puggish, brown?" Arthur smiled winsomely. "He ran out of my door, and I can't find him anywhere."

The couple relaxed, relief crossing their faces.

"No. I'm sorry," the woman said sympathetically, looking at the handsome young man. She frowned, studying his familiar features. The older man pushed his Redskins cap back on his head to get a clearer look at Arthur. The elevator doors opened and the three of them got in, talking about the missing pug.

As soon as the doors closed on the elevator, the woman finally put the pieces together.

"Wait a minute. You're George Washington! Oh my goodness. I'm in an elevator with George Washington!" She reached into her bag for her comp disc, flipping the disc into the air and telling Eve to take a photo. Arthur obliged, posing smilingly next to them, and then turned. Exercising a charm he hadn't known he had, he explained his predicament to the excited couple. By the time the elevator reached the ground floor, he had posed for dozens more photos, swapped jackets with the man, and was wearing the Redskins baseball cap, pulled low over his features.

As the doors opened, the three of them stepped out into a chaotic lobby filled with hotel guests and Secret Service agents racing around, trying to locate the missing nominee. They walked forward, huddled closely together, heading toward the front doors, the woman with her arm in Arthur's. To an outside observer, they looked like a couple and their teenage son.

As they approached the main entry, Arthur saw security stopping and searching guests as they left. His tenuous cover wouldn't hold up to that kind of scrutiny, so as they passed the entrance to the bar, he quietly thanked his new friends, promising to return the hat and jacket, and slipped through the door to the bar.

Quills was almost empty. Arthur had noted the layout on his last visit and walked directly past the counter, slipping through the staff door, flashing a friendly smile at the surprised barman. Once inside, he sprinted past a few uniformed employees in a break room and hurried down the service corridor until finally, he saw what he was looking for—an exit door.

Arthur crashed through the door and into the cool night air, pausing to catch his breath. He was standing in an alley filled with Dumpsters; the sounds of city streets echoed down the narrow walls. Car headlights flashed past the end of the alley, silhouetting city folk as they passed by, heading home for the day. He had made it out of the hotel. Now it was just a simple matter of walking to the corner and disappearing among the passersby.

For a moment, Arthur felt a buzz of elation. He knew that this was just the first step, that getting through the Metrozone wall would be nearly impossible, but he told himself he was going to make it. He had made it this far. It was just a matter of time before he got to the Outside. It struck him as amusing that he was trying desperately to get outside the wall, after a lifetime trying to get in. Arthur half smiled, pulling up the zipper on his jacket as he turned toward the street and freedom.

But his happiness was short-lived. He had barely taken a few steps when he felt a sharp sting on the back of his neck. He swatted at it, his hand smacking a small black object, knocking it hard into the alley wall. A drone. Arthur knew instantly he was in trouble.

He tried to hurry toward the street, but his feet seemed to be failing him. He stumbled, crashing hard onto his knees. He tried desperately to push himself back up, but it was useless. His vision was starting to fog, the car headlights blurring into a mess of bright colors. Still he struggled to fight it, trying to drag himself forward.

"Stupid, stupid, stupid." The voice sent a chill down Arthur's spine. Uncle.

A dark shadow filled his view, blocking all the light. Despair filled Arthur's mind. He was caught; there was no way out now. Moving instinctively, he tried to stand one last time, but the effort was too much. He fell forward onto the ground, his head smacking hard into the ground. For a long moment, he stared at the sideways street, watching uncomprehendingly as Uncle's shiny black shoes with the red stripe filled his vision. Then slowly, as one shoe moved forward to prod him, rolling him onto his back, blackness took over everything.

Red.

At first Arthur thought he had made it to the Outside. His eyes slowly opened, his mind struggling to make sense of his surroundings. The red was wrong. It was bright, unnatural, not the rust color of the Outside. His hand reached up to touch it, brushing against the red, exploring the soft, textured fabric.

By the time Arthur figured out he was on a sofa, he was already sitting up, fighting the heaviness behind his eyes. The room was brilliant white, sunlight cascading through immense floor-to-ceiling glass walls. The furniture was minimal, in vibrant hues, each piece standing alone like a work of art. In the center of it all was a man, dressed in white, his back turned to Arthur as he hunched over a desk. Several floating screens surrounded him, as he reached up casually, efficiently flicking through them at high speed.

"Hello again, Arthur." The man spoke without even turning around. Arthur wondered how he knew he was awake. "You're looking well. Zoner life suits you." Did he have eyes in the back of his head?

"Secretary Cain," Arthur said matter-of-factly. He looked around, taking in the state of the art surroundings. He guessed he was in the secretary's office. Every time he had seen Cain, he had been surrounded by old, venerable historical things. It was oddly fitting that his private world was the opposite, a bastion of technology and cutting-edge design. It suited the two sides of his duplicitous nature—a public and a private face.

Cain swung around in his seat, flashing Arthur one of his friendly, easygoing smiles. It was incongruous with the man he knew, the power-hungry mastermind pulling the strings behind the government. When Arthur had first met him, he had been drawn in by the charming act. But now, he just found Cain's manner disturbing.

"Where are we?" Arthur asked coldly.

Cain seemed to notice the tone, instantly dropping the smile. His face hardened.

"The CDC. The Centers for Disease Control. We are in the RIP wing."

"RIP?" Arthur remembered talking about it on *Air Force One*.

"The Resurrection Innovation Program." Cain paused and looked at Arthur appraisingly. "This is where you were made, Arthur. Where you first came into this world. Welcome home, son!" He laughed, pleased with himself. "This is the very desk I sat at when I generated your DNA. That's the screen I used to scribble my notes upon, calculating what I needed to make you exactly what you are. And that's the same view I stared at when I got bored with working on you." Pointedly Cain stood up and walked over to the wall of glass, looking out across the wide expanse of Washington Metrozone. He pulled an apologetic face. "What can I say? You weren't my first."

Playing games. It was always games with Cain. He seemed to relish manipulating other people's lives, with no care for their feelings or suffering.

"That said, you were a bit of a favorite." Cain was smiling again. "Well, both of you. You and George. Now that was fun. Two identical clones for the price of one. Never been done before. I kept you together at first. Here. You used to play in the laboratory next door. George in blue, you in green, so we could tell you apart. Fascinating. Not identical twins, but the same exact person, playing with themselves.

Cain walked briskly over to the desk, swiping at the CD screen.

"Eve, show Arthur some home movies. Show him 'Data Log 17—Hopeful Monsters.'"

Instantly two identical plump babies were floating in the air, surrounded by technicians in lab coats. Digital stats and data kept popping up over their heads. A much younger Secretary Cain appeared holding a rattle. He put it equidistant to both babies and stepped back. Arthur was transfixed. He kept looking at the baby in green, himself apparently, though there was no way to tell.

"This is a personal favorite. You have to imagine this. Both those babies are the same person. The exact same person. So what happens when confronted with the same situation? What should they do? The exact same thing, right? But, watch."

Both babies turned toward the rattle, both paused. Then at almost the same time, both put out their chubby right hands, reaching for the rattle. Realizing it was too far, both babies pushed themselves forward, scooting toward the rattle. It was unnerving, the babies were responding to everything identically, as though they were watching a mirror image. Both babies reached for the rattle, both grabbed one end and pulled.

"Here, Arthur. Here watch this. Watch what happens next." Cain almost shouted, he was so excited.

Both babies pulled on the rattle then looked at their challenger, noticing the competition. For a few more moments they kept pulling, both babies getting frustrated and starting to make little crying noises. Then it happened. The baby in green let go. Delighted, the baby in blue, started gurgling happily and shaking the rattle up and down. The baby in green sat still and watched.

"Amazing! Did you see that? You developed different traits. One of you, George obviously, took on the more dominant role, despite being exact equals. He consistently led, and you consistently followed. Nurture beat nature." Cain was delighted, rubbing his hands together gleefully. "Obviously when the time came to pick one of you to be our hero, we kept George. He had displayed far superior leadership instincts. You became the spare and were dispatched to the Outside."

That was it. That was Arthur's life. Slow on the uptake as a baby and summarily dispatched to his life of foster homes and lessons from Uncle. What would have happened if he hadn't let go of that rattle? He could have lived as a Zoner, well fed, nurtured, and secure. He had failed even then, even though he was made perfectly. Something inside him was broken, different.

"But, I think I might have made an error in judgment, and it has taken until now for me to realize it." Cain was watching him closely, with the same expression of scientific interest his younger self had in the home movie. "I underestimated you." He turned back to the babies.

The baby in blue had lost interest in the rattle and had thrown it down on the ground. The baby in green sat still watching. Then, instead of reaching for the rattle and taking his turn, the baby turned and looked at young Cain. Cain reached forward and shook the rattle, trying to catch the green baby's interest. But the baby seemed more interested in Cain than the rattle. Even when the rattle was put in his hand, the baby just opened his fist and let the treasured rattle drop to the floor, turning back to watch Cain.

"What I took for innate passivity, a weakness, was actually something far more dangerous. Coming second to George, coming second in everything in your life, it gave you something else. It gave you the instinct to rebel." Cain's expression had hardened.

Arthur realized with a jolt that he was doing the same thing as the baby in green. He was sitting quietly, watching Cain closely with a guarded expression. If someone had put a rattle in his hand right now, he would probably have dropped it too. He guessed he hadn't changed that much after all.

Cain ordered Eve to close down the CD screen and then walked over to the desk, standing for a moment, pushing his knuckles into the desktop, apparently lost in thought. When he finally spoke, his voice sounded oddly bitter.

"We have more in common than you think, Arthur. I know a little about coming in second." Cain's face had darkened, something dangerous lurking behind his eyes. He walked up to Arthur. "Imagine making a human being, flesh and blood. Choosing every cell in their body, crafting them, shaping them into your vision. Then standing before the person you built, and all you see are the flaws in your work. Pity you can't just throw away a person like a piece of paper with a bad idea written on it."

Bitterness laced through Cain's words as he stood inches from Arthur. For a moment the two of them stared at each other, eye to eye, but not as equals. As a parent might stand before a troublesome child. But oddly, Arthur was not intimidated. He understood the meaning behind Cain's words.

"You're not talking about me, are you? You're talking about yourself and your mother." Arthur's words hung in the air between them. Cain's mouth dropped open in surprise. He rolled back a few steps. It was the first time Arthur had seen him at a loss.

"Well, I see you have been talking to my sister. Exactly how much did my darling, loyal sister decide to tell you, hmm?"

Arthur felt the hairs rise on the back of his neck. Cain was making him nervous. He had never seen him like this. There was something menacing about him, all of his customary friendliness had gone. It felt like Arthur was seeing the man behind the mask for the first time, and it was disturbing.

"Wait, let me guess. She told you that I am a clone, like you. The reincarnation of a much-loved dead boy. You know that my own mother, my creator, couldn't stand to look at me." Cain moved forward, threateningly, his face red with anger. "But did she tell you that I grew up in a laboratory, like a lab rat, in the shadow of one of you. The first resurrection. A king among men. Adored and worshipped by everyone around him, including my mother." Cain was practically ranting. Arthur subtly moved back. "An Abel to my Cain."

Arthur felt as though somehow he had always known. Cain and Abel. Two "brothers" whose jealousy had set them on a destructive path that was now threatening the entire country.

"Well, where is the golden boy now? Where is the great hero? I'll tell you where. Out there, in the dust, pretending to lead a pathetic bunch of rebel nobodys. And look at me. I own this country. I made you, I control you, and I toss you away when I'm done. Who's the king now?" Cain was almost nose to nose with Arthur.

Arthur wasn't sure what made him do it, but he instinctively reached into his pocket, pulling out the car emblem that the professor had given him. He tossed it lightly into the air in front of Cain's face, catching it with one hand. Without a word, he raised his chin and stared back defiantly at the older man.

Lightning fast, Cain hit him in the face, hard. Arthur fell to the floor instantly, pain and surprise blinding him momentarily. Arthur reached up to his cheek, feeling a tender lump already swelling up. He could taste blood in his mouth.

Cain stepped back, looking shocked by his own actions. Losing control was obviously not something he was comfortable with. He turned away to face the expansive view, opening and closing his fists as if desperately trying to control his rage.

Arthur pushed himself to sitting, slowly, keeping his face down, avoiding eye contact. He knew how to take a beating. He stared at a spot on the floor, thinking about everything Cain had said and the things he hadn't.

There was a long wait until Cain had pulled himself together enough to talk. His voice was so low and quiet that Arthur had to struggle to hear him.

"I resurrect one of history's greatest rebels; I really shouldn't be surprised when you rebel. I underestimated you, Arthur. I won't make that mistake twice. So now we will play this a little differently." He walked over to the door.

"No more rewards for good behavior, Arthur. Now you will do exactly as instructed, or I will crush you and everyone you care about. If you doubt my word, here's a little demonstration." Cain put his hand on a panel by the door, and instantly one entire wall became transparent. The room behind looked clinical and sterile, like some kind of medical laboratory. In the center of the room was a single, unoccupied chair.

"Just remember, you work for me, Mr. President." Cain smiled, his shallow charm creeping back. Then, touching the panel again, he walked out. Arthur stood up slowly and walked toward the glass wall, a feeling of dread in his stomach. What had Cain meant? What was he going to do?

A door inside the laboratory opened, and two familiar figures walked in. Uncle was half dragging Claire, pulling her toward the chair. She seemed to be trying to resist him, talking to him, begging, her words lost through the glass wall. Her eyes looked around wildly, briefly finding Arthur through the glass. Her hair and clothes were disheveled. Her hands were shaking with fear. Arthur had never seen her like that before. Desperately he shouted her name, banging hard on the glass wall, but she didn't seem to be able to hear him.

Uncle forced her into the chair, clipping restraints over her tiny wrists and ankles. Then he turned to face the wall where Arthur was standing, bowing low, a cruel, familiar smile on his puffy face. He knew Arthur was watching.

Arthur ran to the door, desperately trying the panel, but it wouldn't open for him. He called Eve, but there was no response. He beat hard on the door, but he already knew there would be no way out. No way to get to Claire.

Uncle was walking around Claire, whispering menacingly in her ear, reaching out to touch her hair, her shoulder, softly. Claire was crying. Her eyes were fixed on Arthur, imploring him to do something.

Whip-fast, Uncle hit her hard in the stomach. She doubled over in shock.

"No!" Arthur screamed. He grabbed one of Cain's designer chairs, flinging it hard against the wall. It bounced off uselessly, not even making a scratch.

Uncle had a sadistic smile on his face. He laughed at Arthur's desperate efforts to stop him, mockingly putting his hand to his cheeks, feigning surprise.

Grabbing everything he could get his hands on, Arthur smashed at the wall, over and over, futilely. But there was nothing he could do.

Finally he stopped, pushing his hands uselessly against the glass. Claire looked up, her tear-streaked pale face turned to him, her enormous eyes, ringed by black streaks of makeup, finding him. He dropped to his knees. He would have given anything at all, anything in the whole world to swap places with her. But he couldn't.

Uncle turned back to her, slowly balling his fists, coiled like a snake ready to strike, savoring their fear in the moment before he unleashed his power.

And then he began.

"I'm sorry. I'm so sorry. Oh god, I'm so sorry," Arthur whispered. But Claire couldn't hear him.

Chapter 16

The shower was so hot it almost felt like it was burning his skin. Clouds of stifling steam wafted around, clouding the bathroom, obscuring the walls and mirrors. Arthur liked it that way. He liked standing in the streams of water until it hurt, testing himself to see how long he could bear it.

It was Election Day.

Dark thoughts and unanswerable questions raced through Arthur's mind. Each followed by another, then another. No resolution. Just more questions, piling up, one on top of the next.

In just a few short hours, Arthur, Kennedy, and President Lincoln would stand shoulder to shoulder on a giant stage in front of the Lincoln Memorial, to hear the election results. Arthur wondered if close-up he would be able to tell how Cain had made Lincoln his puppet president. Had he been "fixed," his brain rewired to obey his master? Would his eyes have a vacant expression, like someone whose free will had been surgically removed? Would his hands have a giveaway tremor, his eyes a glimmer of fear as he cowered under

Cain's threats to destroy those he loved? Arthur wanted to know. He wanted a clue as to what Cain was planning to do to him if he won.

It was an odd sensation. While he stood in the shower, trying to forget what day it was, all across the UZA people were voting, scanning their retinas in the privacy of their own homes and offices, registering their selected nominee. Some would be voting for him, some for Kennedy. Many would care passionately, putting up signs, or wearing T-shirts with slogans. There would be breakout parties as the excitement built. Even in the Outside, where most people didn't bother to vote, people would know it was Election Day.

In a few hours, the nation would gather around VTs to watch as the nominees rode old-school motorcades through tens of thousands of fans, thronging across the National Mall, Kennedy on one side, Washington on the other. They would gossip over Claire's outfit, comparing her to past first ladies, to Lucella. Everyone out in full force to unknowingly celebrate the death of their democracy. The election of another fraud to the White House. A handsome hero with a great name. Washington or Kennedy. It didn't matter which. They were interchangeable.

The familiar feeling of being trapped rose up inside Arthur, claustrophobic panic threatening to overwhelm him. He forced himself to focus on the burning heat in his shoulders as the scalding water poured over his red skin. This time it took several minutes for the panic to subside.

Arthur stepped out, wrapping a towel around his waist. As he walked into his bedroom, the sound of an excited crowd filtered through the open french doors. He stepped out onto the balcony, the icy wind biting his hot skin.

Peering over the stone edge, he saw a surreal sight. The streets below were pulsing with red, white, and blue masses. Throngs of people, looking like a living sea, flooded the city streets, chanting

"Wash-ing-ton!," "Ken-ne-dy!" Over and over, as though they were heading to the Super Bowl to watch their favorite team. They were euphoric, exhilarated. All the years spent watching the clones grow, maturing into these young heroes, had led to this day. It was pure, unadulterated, first-rate entertainment.

And Arthur had a starring role.

He turned back and started dressing in the beautiful wool suit and coat that was set out for him. No point in thinking. He was Secretary Cain's next puppet, and there was nothing he could do about it.

Breakfast was almost silent. The usual grand fare of delicate pastries, omelets, exotic fruits, and coffee went barely touched. Arthur had no appetite, and his mood seemed to affect those around him. For a week now, since the terrible day at the CDC, he had barely been able to bring himself to talk or smile. He did what was asked of him, but no more. His heart wasn't in it, but he didn't dare risk angering Cain again.

Claire had returned to the Jefferson Hotel a few days earlier, but he hadn't been able to talk to her alone. Two new Secret Service agents had been assigned to her. Everywhere she went, they lurked just behind her, their enormous frames twice her size, looking like they could snap her in half. It filled Arthur with terror to see them, knowing that they were there because of him. A warning. One step out of line, and we will crush her.

As the team ate silently, Hope Juvenal appeared on the VT, reporting "live" from the National Mall. A giant tent media city had sprung up around the Washington monument. Fancy multistory tents dotted the grass filled with news reporters and swarms of drones. Hope was high up in one of the CBN election hub tents, a sweeping view behind her across the mall, swarms of people covering every inch of ground.

"Washington is still leading in the polls, but it's too early to call. It's just two hours before the results are in, and our new president is announced. Park services estimate the crowd to be hundreds of thousands of people, the largest at any election results rally, ever. It is just amazing to see such an outpouring of enthusiasm over these two outstanding young candidates. Very exciting. Very exciting indeed."

Arthur glared at her over the top of his coffee cup, wondering how an operating system could know what excitement felt like. Normally Ty and Van would have been delighted to be watching and analyzing the news. But today, they were subdued, glancing nervously at Arthur from time to time. Everyone knew that something had changed for him and Claire, but no one dared ask him what. Instead, they all watched Hope in silence.

"Soon now, the motorcades will be leaving the hotels. I know I'm not the only one who can't wait to see what our future first ladies will be wearing. Let's talk to our next guest, Vogue *editor..."*

Something was odd about Hope's face. As she prattled on about the big day, her nose was stretching longer and longer. At first Arthur thought it was his imagination, but by the time it was a few inches long, he started smiling for the first time in a week. It didn't stop there. Hope obviously wasn't aware, even when there was a good twelve inches of it. Soon everyone was laughing, even Claire, especially when Hope swung around to interview the fashion editor and her virtual nose poked him in the eye. A small fat duck waddled onto the corner of the screen, quacking loudly. Mr. Sandwich must have hacked CBN.

The mood in the suite had changed, thanks to the rogue hacker. As always, there was a flurry of panic, as all devices were powered down. Arthur was escorted to his room, to wait out the incursion.

Arthur flung himself onto his bed, glad for the excuse to be alone. Rolling onto his back he watched the sunlight reflect off the glass doors on to the white ceiling. As he lay there, he imagined the shadows and patterns of light moving, dancing around, forming pictures and words. BEN PRESENT. Arthur sat up quickly. There was no way that that was in his imagination. He looked around. A small drone painted rebel red was hovering next to the bed, projecting the message faintly onto the ceiling. Ben present?

Suddenly Arthur understood. He leaped off the bed, reaching deep inside his pillowcase, his unsophisticated hiding place, to pull out the small silver cylinder. He twisted it the way Martin had shown him, and instantly a series of small crashes gave away the location of several hidden security drones as they switched off and dropped to the ground. The only drone still flying was the red one.

Arthur looked around expectantly, waiting to see who was trying to reach him, jumping when he noticed a fat, yellow duck floating inches above the bedsheets between his feet.

"Mr. Sandwich?" As he spoke, the letters "shhhhh" appeared above the duck. Arthur nodded, although he had no idea if the duck could see him.

"TODAY—PARADE—REBEL   ATTACK—STOP   THE CAR @ 12TH—"

The words appeared in a stream like news headlines. The rebels were coming for him. Arthur felt the first glimmer of hope in a week, his feelings of helplessness momentarily fading. But then he remembered Claire.

"I can't. I'm sorry." He whispered, feeling crushed.

"?" appeared above the fluffy yellow head.

"I can't help you. I'm sorry. You'd better get out of here before someone sees you." Arthur felt deeply ashamed of himself. The rebels were fighting a war here, and he was letting them down because of his feelings for one person. He realized how selfish he was being, but he couldn't help it. He couldn't risk Cain hurting Claire again.

The duck froze. There was a long pause, as if the Mr. Sandwich was consulting someone. Finally the words "BRING CLAIRE" appeared.

The words floated in the air like a beacon of light. The rebels must have guessed what was holding him back. He could rescue Claire. They could leave together. This was happening. This was actually happening. He felt a buzz of hope for the first time in weeks. He nodded happily.

"STOP @ 12TH—SIT PARKSIDE—DO NOT FORGET 2! DUCK!"

Arthur felt his heart beating, excitedly. The rebels were coming. Everything was going to be all right. The avatar actually looked pleased with itself. It did a little victory dance that looked oddly familiar. Very familiar. Everything about the duck reminded him of something...someone.

At long last, Arthur finally started to connect the dots.

He looked down at the powerful little cylinder in his hands, in surprise. Ben's IMP. Quickly he turned it over in his fingers, looking for the letters SW. He flipped the cylinder upside down and read the letters again. MS. Mr. Sandwich. How could he have missed it?

"Ben?"

The duck came close to him, quacking happily.

"RICHARD SANDERS, AT YOUR SERVICE"

Arthur laughed out loud, quickly coughing to cover the sound. Richard Sanders had been Benjamin Franklin's favorite pseudonym. Hence Mr. Sand-wich.

If he could have, Arthur would have hugged the little yellow avatar. Of course Ben hadn't minded being Retired. It didn't matter where he was. He had the whole world at his feet, as Mr. Sandwich— the legendary hacker. There was no prison on earth that could hold him.

The faint humming of waking drones warned them that time was up.

Instantly the duck disappeared, and the red drone looped wildly around the room before shooting out of the french doors.

Quickly Arthur put his face in his hands, trying to hide his goofy grin. Ben was OK, better than OK. And in a few hours, if all went well, Arthur would be free. He felt a lightness that he hadn't felt in days. Everything was going to be all right.

He slipped the cylinder in his pocket and walked to the bathroom to splash water on his face, studying himself to see if he looked suitably depressed and hopeless. He didn't want to attract any attention.

By the time Arthur was allowed back into the living room, he looked convincingly sullen; the only giveaway that something had changed was a small tremor in his hands, which he kept firmly tucked in his pockets. He willingly went along with preparations for the parade, counting down the minutes and seconds until he would be able to escape.

Two hours later everyone had made their way to the underground staging area for the parade. The vintage open-top cars were parked, engines idling, surrounded front and back by black units. Kennedy must have been allocated the red car, as his girlfriend Lucella was already in the back seat, her red jacket coordinating perfectly with the car.

Kennedy was standing next to the car, glaring at his handheld CD, probably watching the latest exit polls. Their entourage bustled ferociously around them, touching up hair and makeup, rearranging stray items of clothing.

Arthur walked toward the other car. Predictably baby blue with cream trim, a surefire hit with whatever Claire would be wearing. Van helped him into his smart gray wool coat and light-blue scarf. Now he would match the car too, he thought grumpily, scratching uncomfortably at the neck. He hated wool.

Ty had shown him the parade route, back in the suite, pleasantly surprised that Arthur was actually taking an interest. Washington had been allocated the north side of the National Mall, Kennedy the south. So Arthur and Claire would need to be seated behind the driver to be parkside. The Twelfth Avenue intersection was about a third of the way along the mall. As Arthur stood by the car, mentally preparing himself for the great escape, he noticed that Kennedy was striding purposefully toward him.

"Washington." Kennedy nodded. "Or maybe I should call you Arthur Ryan?"

Arthur glanced around quickly, looking to see if anyone had overheard, but they were alone. Both their teams had fallen back, giving the important men their chance to speak in private.

"I would usually come out with some rubbish like, 'may the best man win.' But you and I both know this whole thing's rigged." Kennedy's voice was odd, bitter.

Arthur nodded. There was nothing to say. He was glad Kennedy knew the truth. He deserved that much.

"And I think we both know who it is rigged for." Kennedy's eyes flashed impressively.

"Yeah, maybe." Arthur sighed, resignation in his voice.

No matter what happened, when he tried to escape, he would be handing the presidency of the entire UZA over to Kennedy by default. The election wouldn't matter if one of the nominees had run away to fight with the rebels. Maybe in just a few short hours,

Kennedy would be thanking him.

"You don't even care about this election, do you?" Kennedy was studying Arthur's face, confused. "I don't understand you."

"Look. John, if you win, if you become president, can you do one thing for me?" Arthur's tone was serious, but placating.

Kennedy laughed, confused, wondering if he was being mocked in some way he didn't understand. But when Arthur didn't respond, still looking at him with the same intense expression, Kennedy stopped.

"All right. Fine. I have no idea what your little game is, but I'll go along with it for now. What do you want me to do if I'm president?" Kennedy folded his arms across his chest defensively.

"Just, please…be the president for all your people." Arthur looked him in the eyes.

It was pointless. Kennedy would be forced to do Cain's bidding, no matter what. But somehow Arthur felt he had to try.

Kennedy looked at him for a long time. It felt as though he was trying to figure him out, to see what made him tick. Then slowly, he raised his hand and offered it to Arthur. Arthur took it, and they shook hands. A solid bonding handshake.

"Wouldn't have it any other way," Kennedy said, his voice straight speaking. He nodded and walked away to his waiting red car.

Arthur watched his back. Kennedy was a good man. He knew it. A strong leader who would try to do right by his country, given the chance. In a different time and place, maybe they could have been friends.

"Arthur?" Claire was standing behind him, waiting patiently.

He turned to her, his heart skipping a beat. She had never looked more beautiful. The chill morning air had brushed her cheeks with a soft touch of rose. Her eyes seemed almost luminous, taking in the chaos around them. As he had predicted, her soft blue coat matched the car perfectly, but somehow, everything around her looked shabby by comparison.

He felt an irresistible urge to tell her that soon everything would be better, would be OK. That he was going to get her out of here, out of Cain's reach. She would be free, once and for all. But he bit back the words, knowing that he couldn't take that risk. Instead, he reached out his hand, his fingertips brushing hers.

"Shall we go?"

The motorcade pulled out of the staging area and into the Metrozone streets, the bright vintage cars standing out distinctly among the surrounding black units. Shouts and cheers erupted from the rows of people already lining the streets. Arthur waved as they moved forward, slowly but steadily, heading for the National Mall.

Arthur had given the seat on the driver's side to Claire, so she would be parkside. He had shuffled as close to her as he could without alerting suspicion. He wasn't sure what the rebels were planning to do, but he imagined those small, but powerful explosive jacks might be involved. Uncle was in the front, next to the driver, looking dangerous in his dress uniform, dark glasses, reflected in the rearview mirror. Evan was walking with a handful of Secret Service agents alongside the car, moving discreetly around the car, checking and reviewing security.

As the motorcade turned into the National Mall, the crowd erupted. Tens of thousands of people thronged across the mall, a sea of red, white, and blue, covering every inch of the green grass. Their voices raised in a roar of cheering and chanting. It was intoxicating and terrifying at the same time. As though, together, the people formed one vast and powerful creature, changeable and unpredictable. If anyone had ever doubted the power of the masses, seeing this would change his or her mind.

Claire's hand slipped into his. Her fingers clutching his tightly, holding on for support. She must have been feeling as overwhelmed as he, but like a good first lady, she just kept smiling and waving. Two Outsiders, two frauds, paraded like royalty through the city. Arthur forced himself to focus on faces, individuals, picking out people to wave to. It made it easier, less daunting somehow. An old man with a cane, a group of kids with holo flags and signs floating over their heads, a group of servicemen and women in uniform, saluting as they passed. Virtual Arthurs hovered in the air, dotted across the crowd, also smiling and waving as the words "VOTE WASHINGTON" appeared and disappeared. Above everything, the Washington Monument soared peacefully, the stone obelisk standing tall against the crisp blue sky.

They inched past the National Archives building. They were getting close now. Arthur squeezed Claire's hand hard. She looked at him, confused.

"What is it?"

"Just excited, I guess," Arthur said, trying to laugh casually, but sounding strange even to himself. Claire studied him a moment longer, then turned back to the crowd, all smiles. Arthur tried to calm himself down by waving, but he felt queasy. Twelfth Avenue was coming up.

Just then, he noticed Evan, walking far off to the right, checking the barrier. Mr. Sandwich, Ben, had been explicit. Arthur needed to be on the park side of the car. But Evan was as far away from the park as it was possible to be. Dozens of scenarios raced through Arthur's mind. Were the rebels going to blow something up? Would they sweep in, guns blazing on the street side? He had no idea what they were planning, or even what they were capable of. He only knew that they wanted him as far away from Evan as it was possible to get.

A wave of pure panic hit Arthur. He could see the junction approaching. If the rebels were going to attack, they would see Evan as Secret Service, the enemy. They wouldn't hesitate to take him out. He would be front and center in the line of fire. He couldn't risk that.

"Stop! Stop the car." He stood up, shouting loudly.

The car jerked to a halt, abruptly.

"Sit down!" Uncle hissed at him, careful not to let the crowd overhear him ordering around their hero. Evan had stopped inspecting the barriers and stood watching him. They were a stone's throw away from Twelfth Avenue.

"I, er…want to walk. Among the people," Arthur shouted as loudly as he could. The crowd went wild, chants of "Wash-ing-ton!" ripped through the air. Claire looked at him in shock.

"Keep driving," Uncle ordered the driver, who sat momentarily confused as to the chain of command. Arthur quickly seized the opportunity, grabbing Claire's hand and pulling her ungracefully over the side of the car.

"Evan, walk with us," he shouted. Evan looked up, nodded and started walking toward him.

"Damn it!" Uncle shouted. He leaped out of his seat and started clambering over the back of the car, scrambling to get to the wayward nominee.

Arthur pulled Claire over to the park barrier. Hands reached across, desperately grabbing for them, people calling out for them. Everyone wanting a piece of their heroes.

"Arthur!" Claire called out in alarm. "Arthur, wha…" But she never finished the sentence.

It felt as though it happened in slow motion. First a massive explosion, followed by a powerful wall of burning hot air that leveled everything in its path. The baby-blue car flew several feet straight up into the air, hovering surreally for a second, before smashing to the ground, instantly bursting into flames. Then the worst part came, a horrifying, shocked silence that hung in the air as though time had stopped, as slowly, the panic and fear set in.

The Red Rebels had arrived in Washington.

Chapter 17

Arthur slowly sat up, his ears ringing. He looked around him in shock. Several people lay unmoving on the ground. The barriers had been blown away, ripped clothes and shredded posters littered the ground where he had been standing just moments before. Lasers cut through the air, the sound of gunfire hammering all around. Claire was next to him, pulling herself to her feet, blood on her hands and knees where she had fallen hard.

"Are you OK?" Arthur grabbed her arm. She nodded, her face ashen.

Uncle was lying face down just feet in front of him. He wasn't moving, and his arm looked wrong, like it had been bent the wrong way. His clothes were burned and ripped. He must have been blown off the car when it exploded. Suddenly Arthur had a terrifying thought. Evan had been behind the car, walking toward him. He must have been right where the explosion had happened.

"Evan…no."

Arthur was on his feet instantly. He had to find Evan. He had to help him. But as he started toward the burning car, the security police appeared in front of him, running forward, securing the area. They seemed to be panicking, firing indiscriminately into the crowd, at anyone wearing red. It was all Arthur and Claire could do to scramble out of their path and duck behind a bench. There was no way Arthur could get to Evan without either getting shot or taken into custody. He peered through the bench slats, hoping to at least see his friend and find out if he was all right, but the smoke and flames blocked his view.

"He's here," a voice said.

Arthur looked up to see a short woman, dressed like everyone else in the crowd in a bland gray coat; a red, white, and blue scarf bundled around her face; and a hat low on her head. Oddly, she was holding a large laser rifle. "Secured Washington and his plus one." She spoke into an ear microphone, squatting down calmly next to them, pulling down her headscarf. It was Harry.

"Harry!" Arthur exclaimed, delighted to see her. She was the last person he was expecting to see here.

"I guess I should call you Arthur now, right?" She grinned broadly. "I knew there was something weird about you." She looked happy and far too relaxed, considering their current situation. Several explosions farther along the road propelled them into action.

"Come on, both of you. We have got to get you somewhere safe. This place will be swarming with SS soon." She stood up, pulling Claire to her feet. But Arthur didn't follow.

"I can't, Evan is back there. He might be hurt…"

"Evan?" Harry looked confused.

"His Secret Service bodyguard. They're close," Claire said quickly, by way of an explanation. A look of comprehension crossed Harry's face.

"Oh yeah. Redheaded guy. Look, they take care of their own,

Arthur. If he's hurt, he will get the best medical care there is. There's nothing you can do to help him now."

Arthur knew she was right. His presence would only add a distraction and delay medical help from getting to Evan. But it still felt wrong to leave his friend behind, without even knowing if he was OK. He took one last desperate look through the bars on the bench, then reluctantly stood up and followed Harry and Claire into the chaos.

The massive virtual screens that were spaced out across the National Mall were showing a very different picture from before. A breaking news alert kept flashing across the bottom of images of chaos, warning that there was a terrorist attack on the Election Day motorcade. As the three of them ran into the scattering crowd, Harry picked up various items of clothing left behind in the chaos, throwing them to Arthur and Claire.

"Cover up. You're too recognizable," she ordered.

Soon Arthur's fancy wool coat had been replaced with a dark hoodie jacket and sunglasses, the hood pulled low over his face. Claire was looking faintly ridiculous in a knitted hat with kitty ears, glasses, and an enormous blue poncho with white stars. Arthur wondered if Harry was deliberately picking embarrassing clothes for her. There was no love lost between those two.

They hadn't gone far before they had to stop. Perimeters had sprung up everywhere, thousands of security drones floating in lines crisscrossing the National Mall. Each drone projected a continuous vertical wall of blue light. As panicked people darted forward, the light scanned them, instantly assessing their security threat. If they were unidentified, or considered dangerous, lasers fired from the drones, stunning them. Unconscious people were strewn across the meridian, piled up in some places, awaiting collection from the security services.

"Darn!" Harry groaned. "We are going to hit all the buttons if we try to cross that."

"Wait!" Arthur reached into his pocket, pulling out the IMP. "We can use this."

"Benjamin's finest." Harry smiled. "But we can't use it here. They'll be looking for disruptions in the perimeter field. If we shut down this section of drones, it'll draw them right to us."

Bursts of laser fire and screams rang out all around them. Security police seemed to be appearing from everywhere. It was chaos.

"What now?" Claire asked, her voice sounding more impatient than scared.

"You got a suggestion? Or you just waiting to be rescued?" Harry glared at her. She was not into girly girls, and delicate little Claire with her *save me* eyes was nothing short of an insult to women, as far as she was concerned.

Claire returned her hard stare, but remained quiet. Combat strategy was out of her comfort zone.

"All right then," Harry continued. "We get into the cover of those buildings. The rebels have a safe room in the basement by the north corner." Harry pointed out a large venerable-looking building in front of them. Some sort of government department with official-looking flags and signs decorating every available surface. "We just need to distract these monkeys long enough to get you there."

"Oh, I think I can help with that." Arthur's heart leaped at the sound of the voice. He looked up to see a young woman, dressed in slacks and white trainers, wearing an oversized baseball jacket and a visor with 'I heart JFK' printed loudly across the front. He would have thought she was some crazed Kennedy fan from some Midwestern Metrozone, if the voice hadn't given her away.

"Bay!" He leaped to his feet and hugged her. He couldn't believe he was actually touching her, for real this time. He breathed in her smell, wrapping his arms around her lanky shoulders. She felt so unbelievably good. He could have stayed like that forever, forgetting the world around them, but Harry's voice cut in.

"Seriously not the time for a love-in, guys. Come on, give me a break." Harry's tone was firm, but when Arthur looked at her, she was smiling.

Claire, however, was not. She was studying Bay with an odd expression. Arthur wondered briefly if she might be jealous, but then wrote the idea off as wishful thinking. She was probably just trying to figure out who this new person was and if she could be trusted. He turned to her.

"Claire, this is an old friend of mine from the Outside. This is Bay."

"That's Commander Bay to you," Harry added, laughing. Arthur looked surprised. It still sounded strange to hear his old friend deferred to in that way. She would always just be Bay to him.

Bay was already talking into a head comm wrapped neatly around her visor. She was giving orders to some unseen rebels.

After a few moments she turned to them, outlining the plan to get them to the safe room. Bay was going to head off and start a large distraction, enough to give Harry time to get Arthur and Claire to safety.

As they stood up ready to go, Arthur caught Bay's hand briefly.

"Wait. Don't go. Or at least, let me come with you." Bay smiled at him, her eyes crinkled warmly.

"No offense, but you'd be a liability out there. Go with Harry. I'll be right behind you."

"That a promise?" Arthur hated how he sounded, but he didn't want to let her out of his sight, now that they had finally found each other.

"Yeah, sure." She squeezed his hand softly. Then as quickly as she had arrived, she disappeared back into the chaos.

They didn't have to wait long. About five separate explosions rang out simultaneously around them. As predicted, the SS instantly headed out to secure the area, leaving a clear path for them, across the Mall.

They half walked, half ran, making it quickly across the road and down to the basement entrance. The door was already open, so they quickly made their way along a gloomy corridor to what looked like a disused office. As soon as they were inside, a figure stepped forward, out of the shadows, pushed back his hood, grabbed Harry, and kissed her passionately on the lips.

Arthur stood frozen in surprise, unsure if he should tackle the man to the ground or cheer him on, until he heard Harry giggle.

"Get your paws offa me, MK." She pushed the man away, and Arthur saw his face clearly for the first time.

"Martin!" He almost shouted, he was so delighted to see him. "What are you doing here? It is so good to see you!" He hugged Martin, only realizing as he pulled back that their relationship wasn't quite at the hugging stage yet. Martin shuffled from one foot to the other, embarrassed.

"Should I be jealous? Something you boys ain't telling me?" Harry was highly amused.

"Shut it, Minty," Martin growled in his low voice, only making Harry laugh harder.

For the first time, Martin seemed to notice Claire, standing in the shadows quietly behind Arthur.

"Claire." Martin nodded. "Nice outfit." Claire glanced down at her poncho as if seeing it for the first time and blushed.

244

"Picked it out myself," Harry said, still in high spirits. "It is so darn good to see you." Harry reached up and kissed him hard on the lips.

Embarrassed, Arthur turned away, glancing around the room. It had the look of an old basement office. Boxes of dusty files were stacked along one wall, and old discarded chairs and tables were scattered around the edges of the space. A door with a restroom sign led off in one corner. A small row of windows had been taped over with thick cardboard, and one corner had been stocked with food and sleeping backs. Martin walked over to the supply pile and pulled out a couple of candles, lighting them and propping them in the center of the floor.

"Welcome home. The janitor's a rebel sympathizer. The Reds have been using this place for years. There are enough supplies to last a few days if needed. We are going to have to wait until dark before we make a move, so might as well make ourselves comfortable."

Arthur gladly sat down. Now that the excitement was wearing off, he felt exhausted. They had made it this far! They had escaped and were with the rebels. He knew their situation was far from secure, being stranded underneath a government building in a Metrozone. But he was so happy to have gotten to this point that he decided not to worry about what would happen that night. Washington, King, and Tubman. Together again. That would be a tough act to beat.

Harry and Martin were chatting, catching up on rebel gossip. Arthur tried to listen in, but understood only half of what they were saying. He let his mind wander, small sharp points of fear starting to cut into his thoughts, now that the elation was wearing off. Was Evan OK? Why was Bay taking so long? He glanced around to look at Claire. She was sitting, pale faced, propped up against a large pile of boxes in the corner, as far back from the lantern light as she could be.

"Are you OK? You didn't get hurt, did you?" Arthur shuffled over to her slightly.

Claire shook her head but didn't answer him.

Arthur looked at her, concerned. For the first time, he realized that she was probably in shock. He had known about the escape, planned for it as much as he could. But she had had no idea that any of this was coming. Suddenly Arthur felt guilty for not finding a way to forewarn her. It might have been easier now.

"Claire, we escaped. We did it. Cain can't hurt you anymore now." He smiled encouragingly, hoping to get a reaction out of her. But she just stared at the floor.

She had probably never been in such a scary situation before, Arthur told himself. It was pretty brutal out there. And he was used to it after the primaries and everything. He reached out to hold her hand, half expecting her to pull away. But she let him hold it. That was something at least, he told himself.

Martin had dropped a comp disc in the corner of the room, and the news was replaying quietly. This time, there was no denying that the incident was rebel related. There had been too many witnesses with personal recording devices for anyone to claim it was another random accident. Statements were issued and "confirmed" regarding the events that had taken place, and it was repeated over and over that the nominees were safe and in secure locations. Arthur laughed to himself when he heard that. In a way it was true, for now.

A noise in the corridor set them all on edge. Instantly Harry and Martin were on their feet, backs to the wall behind the door, lasers ready. Arthur and Claire ducked behind a table. There was another noise. Someone was definitely outside. Slowly the door handle turned, and the door creaked open. A dark figure slipped into the room, and instantly Harry was upon the figure, tackling him or her to the floor roughly.

"Wait. It's me," the dark shape said. Arthur recognized the voice with relief. Harry pulled back off Bay, laughing.

"What took you so long, Commander?"

Bay took off her "I heart JFK" visor, tossing it to one side and moved forward into the candlelight. Her face was flushed, blood crusted down her cheek, her hair wild. She looked around, finding Arthur. Her eyes were a steady green, calm and collected, but intense.

"Hey," she said softly.

That was all it took. Arthur stepped out from behind the table and hugged her, his cheek pressed to hers. His eyes closed, and for a long moment he felt some of her calm rub off on him. She made him feel like he was home. Not the Outside, but somewhere safe and familiar. Maybe the castle.

Bay's breathing was abnormally fast, and as Arthur let go, she gasped almost imperceptibly. For the first time, he noticed blood on her jacket. A burned slash was cut through the shoulder.

"You're hurt!"

"It's fine," she said, but her voice was laced with pain.

She sunk to the floor, and Arthur helped her struggle out of the heavy jacket. There was a deep gash on her arm just below the shoulder, laser from the look of it. The security police lasers could cut through anything like butter, but the only good thing was that they seemed to cauterize and sterilize the wounds they inflicted. There wasn't much they needed to do other than bind the area. Bay shrugged off any attention, slipping a small tin with tablets out of her pocket. She popped one under her tongue and then lay back against an upturned chair, closing her eyes. Arthur watched her, concerned.

"Way I see it, we got one shot at getting out of here with these two." Martin was back to business, nodding toward Arthur and Claire. "Anyone in touch with HQ? Bay, does your comm still work?"

Bay shook her head.

"Secretary Cain's got lockdown on all comms. We are on our own. We should stick to the plan. Wait till dark, then head out to an extraction point." She reached forward, wincing in pain, flipping the comp disc into the air between them. A three-dimensional map of the area popped up, rotating slowly. "The extractions are here and here." She was pointing toward two locations on the south and east end of the National Mall, both on water. The rebels must have access to boats.

"We should split into two groups. We will attract less attention and increase the odds of at least some of us getting out alive," Harry suggested.

Everyone nodded in agreement. After quite some discussion, it was decided that Arthur would go with Martin and Bay. Claire would go with Harry. Neither of them looked thrilled at this arrangement, but it was agreed that their odds of escaping would be vastly improved as two women traveling alone. No one said it, but it was commonly understood that the government would be looking for Arthur. George Washington was the prize.

Once all was said and done, they settled in to wait out the hours until nightfall. Martin borrowed Arthur's hoodie, pulled it low over his face, and headed out into the streets to look for a change of clothes they could use to disguise themselves. After all, four out of the five of them were among the most famous living celebrities in the UZA. Sneaking out would be tricky, even under the cover of darkness.

The rest of them opened cans of food and made seats out of old crates and upturned chairs, snuggling in a circle around the candles. Harry even found some cans of beer in the supply stash and passed them around. The warm flickering light gave the gathering a cozy feel, as though they were just a regular group of friends, hanging out. It was surreal; yet for the time they had, it felt good.

Arthur was sitting between Bay and Claire, which he found a little awkward. Neither was particularly chatty and whenever he spoke to one of them, he had to turn his back on the other. He knew it was silly, but he thought he could sense friction between them. Women never took to Claire. She seemed to rub them the wrong way before she even opened her mouth. But Bay had always had a natural warmth and grace about her that drew people close. It was one of the things he had found so amazing about her in the Outside. How someone like her had become friends with a dork like him. Of course, now he knew why.

It was Harry who jokingly suggested a round of truth or dare. After all, as she put it, chances were at least some of them would be taking their secrets to the grave with them in a few hours. They took turns to spin an empty can, asking the person on the open end a question. At first the questions were joking and light, a little flirtatious, like a regular group of teenagers trying to kill some time.

But as the time to leave was coming closer, tensions rose, and the questions became more challenging. The light from behind the cardboard blind was fading, and they all knew time was running out.

Claire spun the bottle, and it landed on Arthur. She looked down for a long time, as if deciding what to say. Then finally, she met his eyes; her expression was sad.

"It's OK." Arthur reached his hand out to her, his natural instinct to protect her and make her feel better. "What is it?" For a brief moment his imagination ran away with him. Maybe she was going to thank him for rescuing her, or declare that she had always secretly loved him.

"You really want this?" Claire's voice was trembling, but there was a core of anger in her tone. "To go back...there? My God, Arthur! Think of what we are giving up. How can you want to go back to that place? To the...Outside?"

Arthur was shocked. The room was silent; even Harry didn't joke.

"Claire..." Arthur started, but couldn't finish. He was trying to understand what she had just said, but it just didn't make any sense to him. Was she trying to tell him that she wanted to stay, with Cain watching over her, living like a prisoner?

"How can you forget what it was like? The fear and hunger, the diseases and suffering. So much suffering. Living every miserable, waking moment trying to stay alive, for what? Just think about what we are giving up. Think about Mount Vernon. Your home. Your friends. Security. The chance to live a good life, to have a future. Why are you making me do this?"

Arthur heard her, and he understood.

For him, there was no choice. He couldn't stay and pretend everything was all right, sitting at his fancy table in Mount Vernon, stuffing his face, while knowing that there were people in the Outside who hadn't eaten in days.

But it was different for Claire. She was a survivor, forged in hellish circumstances. He wasn't angry or disappointed in her. This wasn't a fight she had chosen. In her eyes, she had suffered enough, paid the price, and all she asked was for the rest of her life to be decent. Arthur felt sick that he had brought her here, forced her to do this. He had never even asked. It had just made sense to him. He had thought that she would feel the same.

"Leave her here." Harry's voice was filled with contempt. "If that's what she wants. When they find her, she can bat her baby-blue eyes and say we forced her to come with us. The rebels don't need someone like her anyway."

Claire didn't react to Harry. It was as if she didn't exist. Her eyes, her attention were focused on Arthur alone.

"Arthur? Please."

"I'm so sorry." His voice was barely above a whisper. "I'm really sorry for doing this to you. But we don't have a choice now. You can't go back." He took Claire's tiny hands in his. He felt terrible that he had put her in this position. "If I go without you, Cain will destroy you to punish me. You aren't safe here anymore. I'm so sorry, Claire. I promise I will do what I can to make things better for you out there. I will keep you safe. I promise."

Claire pulled her hand from his and looked him intently in the eyes.

"Stay! If I'm not safe here without you, then stay here with me. If you care about me at all, you will stay with me. Arthur...I'm begging you."

Arthur sat back. Was she serious? She wanted him to pretend none of this had happened, to volunteer to be Cain's next puppet. To live a lie?

"I...I can't, Claire."

Claire's eyes instantly looked darker than he had ever seen them before. The softness had disappeared. She looked like a survivor—strong, determined, and angry.

"George would have. He knew what was at stake here. He would never have gotten himself into this mess. Everything started going wrong when I met you, Arthur Ryan. Everyone you touch gets pulled into your world and winds up hurt or dead. You don't deserve to share his name, his face. I hope you're proud of yourself." She turned away from him, from the group. Her hands hid her face.

Arthur stared at her, a deep sensation of guilt rising up inside him. He remembered the people at Town 1134. How they had come to the bus because of him. He remembered what had happened to them. Was Claire right? Did he hurt people?

Self-doubt crept into his mind. He could still fix this. He could take Claire's hand, and they could walk out the door together. Turn themselves in to a patrol. It might take some convincing to get Cain on his side. He'd be risking a straight-up lobotomy. But that was no greater risk than what they were about to do.

His thoughts were broken by a clattering noise. Bay had kicked the can and as its spinning slowed, she nudged it with her toe so the open end faced Claire.

"My question," she muttered quietly, sitting back, holding her injured arm carefully. "Claire, why don't you tell us where you go when you are not staying at Mount Vernon?"

Claire looked flustered by the unexpected question. But she quickly rallied.

"Georgetown University. Here in Washington, DC. I'm studying law."

"Yes. But tell us where you stay all of those long weeks, when you're in town?" Bay's expression was unreadable, but Claire looked deeply uncomfortable. She shifted around on her makeshift chair.

"You want me to tell him?" Bay asked, nodding in Arthur's direction.

"Arthur, it's not what you think. Please don't jump to conclusions." Claire glared at Bay as she spoke. She reached for Arthur's hand, but he moved it slightly away. He knew he was about to hear something he didn't want to.

"Arthur. I stay at one of Secretary Cain's houses. It's the house I grew up in." Arthur didn't listen to the rest. He felt like a wall of hot anger had hit him. All those days and nights, he had waited for her at Mount Vernon, wondering when she'd come home. All those times, she was living with the enemy.

"You live with Cain?" He laughed a nasty, sarcastic laugh.

"Makes sense. You're perfect for each other."

"It's not what you think!" Claire reached for him, talking intently. "How do you think I got out of the Outside? You never asked. Secretary Cain was touring the field hospitals, and he saw me there. I was just a little kid, desperate and alone. He felt sorry for me, and he gave me a second chance, a home and a new life. That's all. I hardly ever saw him growing up. He was like a distant benefactor. But I owe him my life."

"So you pay him back by working for him? You seduce the candidates gullible enough to fall for it? First Kennedy, then George, and me. Is that it? Work Cain's agenda from the inside? You've been manipulating me this whole time. People warned me, but I didn't listen. God, I am so stupid."

"No! Arthur, that's not true. I have never worked for Secretary Cain, and he would never ask it of me. I met Kennedy at the CDC one day, and we liked each other. Until I met George…and you. I never lied to you. Not once. You just never asked."

Suddenly the door crashed open and Martin hurried through, carrying an armful of clothes. He threw them on the floor.

"Have you heard?"

"Heard what exactly?" Harry stood up.

"Oh man, you have got to see this," Martin said. He was grinning widely. The comp disc was lying on the floor by the candles where they had left it after their planning discussion. Martin grabbed it and tossed it front and center. In a flash, Kennedy and Washington flickered into existence, floating inches above the flickering candles. Hope was standing between the two men, talking excitedly.

"An unbelievable day. Despite the chaos and disruption caused by the rebel attacks, our democracy has prevailed once again. For those of you just joining us, an announcement was made within the past hour. The people have spoken, and despite the efforts of a handful of malcontents, your voices have been heard. Ladies and gentlemen, we have a new president-elect. The fifty-seventh president of the United Zones of America...George Washington!"

Everyone was looking at Arthur. He couldn't believe it. Just hearing it made him feel like his world had upended. Quickly, he jumped to his feet and walked over to the window, pretending to inspect the cardboard blind, keeping his back to the others. He didn't want them to see his face. He didn't want them to see that he was smiling.

It was stupid and completely inappropriate, but he felt happy, exhilarated even. Arthur Ryan had never won anything in his life. He was the ultimate loser. If the high school yearbook had a category for most likely to lose, Arthur's picture would appear right there. But he had won this one time. He was smart enough to know that the victory wasn't real; it was a trick manipulated by Cain. But just for now, he felt awesome.

Arthur Ryan, the weedy Outsider kid from the back of the bus, had just been elected president.

Chapter 18

The streets were ominously dark when they finally emerged from the safe house. Debris littered the roads, remnants from the earlier chaos. It was close to midnight, and they had been hiding out for almost twelve hours. Secretary Cain must be seriously worried about his puppet president by now, Arthur thought with no small amount of satisfaction.

Harry and Claire had left ten minutes earlier, heading west. They had synchronized their timing and would be setting off several simultaneous IMP breaches in the perimeter fields in just under five minutes. Then all hell would break loose. Harry and Claire would hightail it to an extraction point behind the Lincoln Memorial. Arthur, Martin, and Bay would head south across the National Mall to the Tidal Basin.

As she was leaving, Claire had come up to Arthur one last time, to say goodbye. He had barely been able to look at her, still struggling to reconcile the fact that she lived with Cain and yet hadn't bothered to mention it to him. He felt like something had broken between them, an unspoken trust they had shared after everything they had been through together.

Claire could obviously sense his animosity, and hadn't pushed it, instead simply asking one thing of him before she left. "Things aren't what they seem. Please don't give up on me." Arthur hadn't answered her.

Her words kept going around Arthur's head as they approached the National Mall. He had realized too late that they might not see each other again. They were heading into a dangerous situation, and there was a fair chance of capture or worse. He didn't want to think about it, about never seeing her again, and he tried to push her from his thoughts.

They walked forward, hidden beneath layers of the clothes Martin had managed to procure. Random groups of people were wandering around in a daze, dragging tattered flags and banners. Squads of security Police patrolled street corners, lasers out, randomly stopping and searching people.

As they squatted behind a tree near the shimmering perimeter field, Bay winced in pain. She had taken another pill before they left, but her face was getting whiter and whiter, and she clearly needed medical attention soon.

"Are you OK?" Arthur asked, concerned.

Bay just nodded and gave him a short half smile.

"You?" She glanced up at him. She looked calm despite the dangers that lay ahead. The only giveaway that she was nervous was the steady green of her eyes.

"Yeah. I'm fine," Arthur lied.

"We've got this." Bay smiled.

"Yeah." He grinned back. They had come a long way since their days hanging out at the castle. There wasn't anyone he trusted more at his side in a situation like this. He believed in her, and after everything, he hoped she felt the same about him too.

"Time's almost up," Martin said, glancing at his CD. "I'd better get into position." He stood up, turning to go.

"Martin, wait…" Arthur wasn't sure what to say, and they just looked at each other, nervously. All hell was about to break loose, and they were going to be right at the center of it.

"Just…be careful, OK?"

Martin nodded, reaching out and putting his hand on Arthur's shoulder.

"You too, Mr. President." For once Martin didn't smile. They both knew how much danger they were in. "Better go. We should be getting the signal any time now." He sprinted off into the darkness without a backward glance.

Arthur closed his eyes for a moment. If anything happened to any of them, to Bay or Claire, Martin or Harry, he knew he would never forgive himself.

"Arthur, look," Bay said sharply. "Harry's signal."

There it was. First a distant flash of white light, high above the buildings, then several sections of the blue perimeter flickered and disappeared. Quickly they both activated their IMPs. More holes appeared in the shimmering blue wall.

Instantly they were both on their feet, heading for the perimeter. They walked fast, heads down, trying not to attract attention. Shouts were breaking out all around as the security police realized something was up. People started panicking and running, afraid another rebel attack might be starting. There wasn't much time.

As soon as they were clear, they slowed to a fast walk, keeping close to passing groups of people to avoid attracting attention. They had made it past the security police patrols, and no one had noticed. Arthur started breathing again, a sense of relief washing over him. He glanced over at Bay and could see she was smiling. They were almost in the clear. The plan had worked.

Far behind them, the blue field flickered back up as the effect of the IMPs wore off. On either side, lasers fired and smoke and panicked shouts filled the air. "They're just warning shots," Arthur told himself. "Martin's fine. We are going to make it. All of us."

Quickly, they headed toward the extraction point. The lights of the deserted media tent city were close, offering cover around the exposed base of the Washington Monument. The elaborate tented structures glowed from the reflected light of immense floating news reports, flashing in the air above them. Arthur saw himself and Kennedy, appearing and disappearing, animated voices and salacious headlines wafting around them eerily.

Towering above them all, the calm, strong stones of the monument soared, like a finger pointing toward heaven. It was surreal, but beautiful, and Arthur found himself stopping, momentarily overwhelmed.

His predecessor had inspired this. He had inspired men to rise from the blood and ashes of war and to raise their faces to the sky. Arthur knew that if Washington had been alive today, he would have fought for his nation again. He would have stood for freedom and equality for all. He would have been a rebel.

As he stared upward, Arthur felt closer to his genetic father than he ever had before, and he briefly wondered if Washington would have been proud of him.

"OMG, it's you! It's really you!" Arthur spun around. A passing group of drunken young adults had staggered to a stop. One of them was staring at him, snapping pictures furiously. Arthur realized with a jolt that his hood must have fallen off while he was looking up. Quickly he pulled it down over his face, but it was too late.

"It's George Washington! He's here!"

Bay grabbed his arm, trying to pull him forward, but the group followed them, pictures snapping, selfies instantly posted, announcing his exact whereabouts.

"No. No. I'm not George Washington. I just look like him. My name's Arthur…" Arthur desperately tried to put them off, but they either didn't hear or didn't care. As far as they were concerned, they were standing on election night, under the Washington Monument with the new president.

Nearby people started drifting over to see what all the fuss was about. Whispers were spreading like wildfire. Before long, Arthur was completely surrounded. Bay reached for him again, but was pushed back, edged out by the excited crowd. security police were turning to look, wondering at the commotion.

"Wash-ing-ton. Wash-ing-ton!" The chant started quietly, but it was picking up fast. Drones started sweeping in, dotting the sky above them. Over their heads, news images started flickering and changing, one by one. Images of the hooded celebrity appeared, close-ups catching his half-hidden face. A security police patrol was heading in their direction. Arthur tried desperately to push through, but the crowd wasn't letting him go anywhere. He knew he was in big trouble.

Suddenly there was a flash and a loud bang off to one side. The crowd fell apart instantly. People started screaming and running away, fearing another rebel attack. Arthur glanced over toward the source of the explosion and saw a familiar figure in the distance, briefly outlined against the flames. Martin. He must have seen the commotion and created the distraction.

Gratefully, Arthur and Bay sprinted toward the Washington Monument, diving gratefully into the cover of the deserted media tents, winding their way quickly through the canvas structures. As they ran, Arthur clicked on the IMP and the drones that were following them dropped to the ground. It gave them a little cover, but not enough. The security patrol had already seen them and was in pursuit. He could hear them, not far behind, stumbling over wires and poles, crashing through canvas, dogs barking. As they stumbled into an opening, they almost ran, smack into a wall. Looking up surprised, Arthur saw that they were at the foot of the monument, outside the entrance to a sleek-looking stone building that wrapped around the base.

Bay had started around the building, and Arthur turned to follow her, when a low growling noise behind made his blood freeze. He slowly turned around.

Two large guard dogs were standing on the edge of the clearing, fur raised, heads low. Their menacing growls warned him not to move. But he had no choice. He backed away slowly at first. Then, after a mental count of three, he turned and sprinted as fast as he could for the cover of the tents.

All the training he had done at Camp David had given him the advantage of speed, but even that was not enough to outrun these brutes. He only made it halfway across the clearing before razor-sharp teeth pierced his left ankle, as one of the guard dogs latched onto him, easily pulling him to the ground. Arthur cried out with pain, desperately struggling with the dog, trying to pull him off. But the dog had locked down.

The second dog stood over him, barking loudly, alerting the security patrol to the location of the fugitives.

Suddenly both dogs yelped. He felt the viselike grip on his ankle release as the dogs, whimpering, backed away, turning and running back in the direction of the approaching patrol.

Bay's hands grabbed Arthur's hoodie, pulling him to his feet. She had her laser in her hand.

As he stood, Arthur put weight on his ankle. The shooting pain almost made him fall to his knees, but he forced himself to stay upright as they half stumbled toward the doors to the monument. Bay pointed the laser at the lock and the doors fell open.

"Arthur, listen to me. You can't outrun them like this." She gestured at his ankle. "I'll lead them away from here. Stay inside. I'll let the rebels know where you are. They'll come for you…"

"There's no way I'm going to hide in there, while you risk your life for me," Arthur protested angrily. How could she even think he would do that? "I'm coming with you, Bay."

Bay turned to him, her eyes serious.

"Arthur, you don't realize how important you are. You are the next president, and in Cain's hands, you are dangerous. All of this, tonight, has been for you. Good people have died to get you out." Arthur saw Evan in his mind's eye, running toward the open-top car just before it exploded. He squeezed his eyes shut, trying to force the image out of his head. He wasn't worth dying for. No one should be risking their lives for him.

The patrol was close by, their shouts getting closer by the second.

"Arthur, go!" Bay pushed him toward the doorway. But Arthur didn't move. He knew what she had said made sense, but he just couldn't do it. Hiding while Bay risked everything for him was wrong.

"Bay, I ca…" Bay kissed him. She grabbed him passionately, her lips finding his, her good arm pulling him hard against her. Arthur could feel her. His hands reached up, stroking her wild curls. It felt as though everything before had led to that one, perfect moment. Bay.

Just as suddenly, Arthur found himself lying facedown on the cold stone floor inside the monument, where Bay had pushed him down. Her hand laser dropped on the ground by his feet, the heavy doors slamming shut behind him.

Too slow, Arthur jumped up, grabbing at the door handles, but a fizzing flash knocked him back. Bay must have fused the doors together with one of the explosive jacks. He was sealed in.

Arthur took a deep breath. Seriously? Had Bay really done that? Had she just kissed him to distract him? He mentally kicked himself. Between Bay and Claire, he fell for it every time. He made a quick promise to himself that if he survived that night, he would never be that gullible again. Nope, he would be a changed man where it came to women. Tough, unassailable, and no more kissing.

For a moment, he leaned his forehead against the cool metal doors. There was nothing for it. He had no choice. Reluctantly picking up Bay's laser, he turned and limped forward into the darkness under the Washington Monument.

As his eyes slowly adjusted to the dim light, he made out an enormous staircase and elevator spiraling up into darkness high above his head. Everything had gone quiet. The giant stone walls shut out all the chaos, leaving him standing alone in the cool, dark silence. It was oddly peaceful, and Arthur paused, closing his eyes for just a second, trying to steady his racing heart.

But, it cost him. When he opened his eyes again, a small black security drone was hovering just inches from his face. The security patrol must have sent drones in to search the place. Arthur activated the IMP, but it was too little, too late.

He heard a loud crash against the door behind him. They had seen him. They were coming for him.

His heart racing, Arthur looked quickly around. There was nowhere to hide and only one way to go. Up.

He hobbled painfully across to the elevator, stumbling twice when his ankle gave out. The car was waiting, faint emergency lights on inside. There was power. He fumbled for the button, bashing it hard, pushing through the doors before they were halfway open. Slamming his back against the wall and pointing Bay's laser at the doors as they slowly started closing.

Too late, he noticed a small silver object on the floor, ten feet from the elevator. The IMP. It must have fallen out of his pocket when he stumbled. He started toward it but stopped himself as the entrance doors crashed open. He was out of time. The black-clad security patrol ran in, fanning out military-style, flashlights cutting through the dark.

"There, in the elevator. Go, go, go."

Arthur slid to the floor, keeping his head low in case they started shooting randomly at the elevator door. He counted slowly in his head, trying to calm himself, his hands shaking as he pointed laser at the doors.

"One one thousand, two one thousand, three…" There were sharp bangs against the doors and the ominous crackle of lasers searing into metal. But the heavy doors were holding up for now.

"Four one thousand, five one thousand." Even in his head, Arthur's voice sounded shaky. At last the elevator started moving up, the muffled sounds of the agents' voices falling away as it rose higher and higher. His leg was burning, and he could feel blood dripping down onto the floor, but he could move it a little, and a little was all he needed.

It can't have taken more than a few minutes, but it felt like a lifetime when he finally stepped out of the elevator onto the observation deck. Quickly he pulled a nearby fire extinguisher off the wall and wedged it in the doors. The elevator beeped angrily at him, opening and closing hard on the extinguisher. There was nothing he could do to block the stairwell. It was little more than a hole in the ground. As he peered into it, a black security drone swooped in through the opening, followed by several more. The first wave was here. Missing the IMP, Arthur backed away into the shadows.

Now what? He was at the top of the Washington Monument, with nowhere else to run. He was trapped.

A horizontal window emitted a faint glow on the wall behind him. Arthur looked out. He was high above the city, the lights fading below a purple sky far below, the golden ring of the Metrozone wall surrounding it. It was magnificent. Washington, DC. His town.

"It is beautiful, isn't it?" Arthur spun around, his heart instantly racing.

Secretary Cain's face was floating in the center of the room. His features were made up of dozens of drones, undulating backward and forward in sync, creating a three-dimensional image. He was smiling at Arthur. "I like to come here alone sometimes at night. Peruse my domain." Cain smiled to himself. "I would join you now, but it's a little hard to appreciate the subtleties, like this." He nodded his head, indicating the drones. More and more drones were sweeping up from the stairwell, the resolution of Cain's face becoming finer as they joined the moving image.

Arthur's senses were heightened. His fingers gripped the handle of Bay's laser. He could hear faint sounds coming from the stairwell. The security patrol was getting closer.

"Eve, order the security forces to stand down. President Washington and I need to have a little chat." Instantly the noises from the stairwell ceased.

"I'll be honest with you, Arthur. Much as I hate to admit it, you have something special, something George didn't have. People connect with you. They see themselves in you. More importantly, they want to follow you."

Arthur was only half listening. His brain whirred as he ran through his options. The security patrol would break through in minutes. As soon as they got to him, it would be game over. He could keep Cain talking. Encourage his megalomaniacal need to brag. But all that would gain him was time, and what was the point? No one was coming.

"Sadly, I must admit that I do not have that quality. Oh, I have a brilliant mind, visionary thinking, et cetera…I just never quite managed to get all those sheep out there to worship me, the way they worship people like you. That's why, I need you, Arthur. More than I care to admit. Together, we would be unstoppable, powerful. We could transform this nation."

"You actually think I would help you? You're sicker than I thought." Arthur laughed shortly. Cain's hubris was breathtaking.

The drones pulled into an affronted expression.

"You think I am the bad guy?"

"Yes!" Arthur thought the answer was obvious. But Cain looked at him challengingly.

"Why?"

"Because you helped raise walls that divide us, that keep half of us starving in the dirt. Because you turned democracy, the one hope we had, into nothing more than a game…"

"Oh, you're right. I'm sorry. *Democracy* is not a game…it's a joke. History's greatest failure—and do you want to know why? Because little people don't see the big picture. They can't think beyond their own petty little needs and desires. Giving them the power, well that's a really bad idea."

"People are good. They care. Given the right information, the right leadership, they will do the right thing…"

"I'm afraid you are wrong, Arthur. History is on my side. Fifty years ago, we had a chance to save our world, to change the future. But 'we the people' chose greed and prejudice. We destroyed our climate. We closed the doors to other countries and allowed gun violence and terrorism to rip the very heart out of our nation. In less than a decade, this country will die by the hand of its own people. The last few resources will be gone, and those of us who don't die from disease and starvation will probably have a violent death. And what brought our great nation to this sticky end? Democracy."

Secretary Cain's chin dropped so fast the drones struggled to keep up, his face momentarily turning into an angry black cloud.

Arthur was speechless, but at the same time he believed Cain's dire prediction. The Outside was getting perceptibly hotter. Supplies seemed to be getting shorter each year. Was a decade really all that they had left?

"Oh don't look so worried. I won't let that happen, Arthur. I am not the bad guy. I'm the only one with the guts to do what needs to be done. The resources must exceed the demand. And if you can't increase the resources, you must reduce the demand. It's painfully simple. All this, the walls, *The Democracy Games*, the paravirus…they're not for my own amusement. They are part of the only possible solution."

"The…paravirus?" Arthur was way behind Cain, his mind slowly piecing together what he had just heard. "You must reduce the demand." He half whispered Cain's words, gasping slightly as he connected the dots. "Oh my God. You created the paravirus. You're going to kill the Outsiders."

"I prefer the term 'cull.' It's tough love, Arthur. To survive, we must pay for our mistakes. The best and strongest are our only hope. They must have all of the resources available if our nation is to survive…"

"You're sick. You're a monster!" Arthur shouted. Memories of the kids who had died, the Outsiders from the bus, flickered through his mind. "Oh my God…all those people. My God."

Arthur felt bile rise in his throat and almost retched. He was shaking from head to toe with anger. This man, this one man, had done this. Destroyed lives, brought about pain and misery on an imaginable scale.

"Grow up, Arthur! People die. I'm no monster. I'm a pragmatist who has the guts to do what no one else can do. I will be hailed as the savior of humankind. I'm offering you a place at my side. A place in history. You could outdo even the real George Washington. You think he didn't make hard decisions, make sacrifices? He did what he needed to get the job done. This is your chance. Are you with me?"

Arthur glared at the drones. His fists were clenched tight. Game over. This was it. He would never help Cain. Cain would mess with his brain, destroy his mind, just like Hamilton, and then he would force the new president to run the country into the ground. He had lost.

"If freedom of speech is taken away, then dumb and silent we may be led like sheep to the slaughter." As Arthur whispered George Washington's words, he understood. He had one choice left. One real choice. He nodded to himself. He could do this.

Cain's look turned cold. He was angry. "You want to play at quotes? Well, try Lincoln—'You cannot escape the responsibility of tomorrow by evading it today.' I'm the hero now, and you can quote me on that! I've wasted enough time on you. Put the gun down and get on your knees. Eve, if you please."

Instantly the security patrol started shouting orders, charging up the stairs.

Time was up.

Before he could change his mind, Arthur turned. Raising the gun, he fired at the small window. The laser cut through the glass like ice, splintering the window into a fragmented pattern. Quickly he hopped over to the glass, his fingers grasping at the frame as he swung himself up, shattering the remaining glass. Using his good leg, he kicked and propelled himself forward, outside onto the top of the stone obelisk.

Behind him Cain was shouting something, but Arthur couldn't make out the words. He had to do this quickly, before he changed his mind. Just a few more seconds, and it would all be over.

He slid several feet down the steeply angled stone, before he managed to slow himself enough to dig his fingertips into a crack between the large stones. His grip was weak, but by pushing the soles of his shoes hard against the rock, it was enough to hold him, for a few final moments. The height was dizzying. A strong, cold wind flapped against him, threatening to send him sliding down into the terrifying drop into nothingness below.

Several feet above him, he heard the sound of the security police storming their way onto the observation deck.

They couldn't reach him here. No one could stop him now. He let the wind carry their voices away, as he held on to the moment for as long as he could. The skyline of the Washington Metrozone, glittered all around him, like a sparkling sea. That's it, he told himself, it's just like diving into the sea.

The smallest movement would do it. So easy now. He just had to lift his fingers and let go. His heart was beating fast and hard. His strong, good heart, wanting to keep pumping, to keep him alive. Every instinct, every fiber of his being told him not to do this. To stay alive. But it was too late.

He didn't want to die. All he had ever really wanted was to live a quiet life, with the people that he loved. That was all. Simple really. But it wasn't his destiny.

Arthur could hear noises from the window above. A wave of panic and nausea rose inside him, almost making him fall. But he steadied himself and clung on, the last few seconds left to him, more precious than any before.

A dark cloud of small spheres was dropping one-by-one from the sky, circling the monument until they found him. Security drones, like a dozen shiny black eyeballs. Here to witness their brand-new president commit suicide live-on-air. Great VT.

The faces of the people he cared about flashed in front of Arthur, taunting him. Evan, the professor, Ben, Martin, Harry...Claire.

He thought of Claire the way she had looked at the lake, her hair wet, smiling and laughing as she teasingly tried to pull him into the cool dark water. Claire, who he would never see again. He remembered bitterly the last time he saw her, how she had begged him not to give up on her.

But he had, hadn't he? That was his last and only chance to set things right. To tell her that whatever she might have done, whoever she was, he didn't care, because he loved her. And now she would never know. The pain cut him like a knife, deep inside. He shook his head hard, trying to let go of her, of the sadness that was consuming him.

But there was one person he couldn't let go of. One person he couldn't push out of his head. In his last frenzied seconds, he saw her. Her dark curls blowing in the wind, her cheeky smile and brilliant eyes. He imagined her before him, watching him, understanding what he had to do.

His best friend. The person who understood him better than anybody.

He knew now, as he faced the end, that he had always loved her. Ever since the first time he had laid eyes on her, clambering onto the school bus, covered in dust and sweat, pushing her frizzy hair out of her eyes. He would never know if she had loved him back, not like that. But as he faced his death, he finally knew his own heart. He loved Bay.

Beams of flashlights cut through the sky. The soldiers were at the window. Time was up.

He was shaking so hard he slipped closer to the edge. One hand lost its grip. One foot kicked out in thin air. For a brief moment he wondered if he had the courage to do this. But then something else took over.

He saw her. Bay. In front of him, her green eyes soft and kind, telling him it was OK. Everything was going to be OK. He could let go now.

He slowly lifted up his free hand, middle-finger raised, and facing the cloud of drones, gave his best screw-you smile for the cameras.

His fingers let go. Softly he lifted the soles of his shoes off the stone beneath him and that easily, he started to slide, slipping silently over the edge and falling into nothingness.

Epilogue

ONE MONTH LATER

The first thing Arthur noticed was low, murmuring voices, whispers almost. He felt a sense of relief not to be alone in the blackness that engulfed him. If he was dead, if this was some kind of afterlife, he was glad he wasn't on his own. The sensations that gnawed at him were strange, distant almost, as if he was imagining them. He tried to move or speak, but it was as though he wasn't connected to his body. Nothing happened. Slowly, peacefully, he sank back into the darkness.

This time the murmurs had colors. Reds, yellows. Warm colors that flickered faintly, dancing slightly as the murmurs grew louder. Forming sounds. Sounds that slowly became words.

"Waking up…Arthur…Arthur."

"Follow my voice…Arthur, follow my voice. Come on, you can do it."

It was an impossibly huge effort, but he managed to move his fingers, just the smallest amount. The voices became clearer, more urgent.

"Come on, Arthur. Please."

He focused his blurry, swirling mind and slowly a crack of brilliant white light appeared.

"He's opening his eyes! He's doing it. Get my dad, quickly please."

The light hurt his eyes, but he held onto it. Anything not to return to the darkness. Slowly dark shadows appeared, moving around him. He tried to reach his hand out but couldn't make his body work. He tried to talk, moving his mouth, his tongue dry, his lips cracked, but no words came out. The effort was too much, and Arthur closed his eyes for a moment. He felt something on his hand, something warm. Someone was holding his hand. Hot tears welled up in his eyes—the feeling was so good.

"It's OK. It's OK. You're safe now. It's over." Bay's voice gently whispered into his ear. He slowly opened his eyes and saw her blue-green eyes close to him, looking intently at him. Lines of worry and exhaustion crossed her face. She looked like she hadn't slept in days. Arthur stared at her, not ready to believe this was real, that this wasn't some cruel dream. That he wasn't still falling, dying.

But she wasn't going anywhere, and soon other people moved into view. He slowly turned his head, fighting back sharp pain as he moved. He was in a sand-colored space, and bright light and heat radiated all around him. It looked almost like a hospital room, with drips and curtains and ominous-looking medical equipment all around. Only as he looked closer, he realized that the sand-colored walls were moving, swaying softly in the hot breeze. He was in a tent.

A figure in a chair behind Bay shuffled closer. It was Martin. The two of them smiled with relief when he looked at them, but their expressions were sad, worried. Something was very, very wrong.

"I...am alive?" It wasn't sophisticated, but he really wanted to hear someone say it.

"Yes. Yes. Amazingly." Bay reached a hand up and gently stroked his forehead, pushing his hair back. It felt so good to be touched, Arthur wanted to close his eyes again but was afraid of returning to the darkness. He looked at her, drinking her in. She had never looked more beautiful to him.

"I fell?" His voice sounded rough and scratchy.

"Yes. You certainly did." Bay paused, glancing over at Martin. He smiled.

"You are one lucky son of a…an ex-president." Martin laughed. "We saw you fall. Talk about going out in style."

"But, how did I survive? That fall…I should be dead."

"You hit CBN's press tent. Crashed through three layers of canvas before you landed. Flattened Hope Juvenal mid-interview." Bay's frown lightened at the memory. "It was kind of awesome. Abel's team managed to scrape you off the ground and get you out of there. Don't move!" Arthur had tried to push himself up but nothing seemed to be working the way it should. He gasped in pain and sank back into the pillow.

"You broke a few things," Bay said by way of explanation.

"Ha, that's an understatement," said Martin. "You looked like a rag doll when we found you—an ugly one."

Arthur tried to suppress a laugh, but still managed to cause a shooting pain through his ribs. Everything hurt, nothing worked, but he felt unbelievably happy. It didn't seem possible that he could have survived, but here he was.

Where was he?

"Is this the Outside?" He had never imagined the day would come when he would actually want to be in the Outside.

Bay nodded. "Welcome home, Arthur Ryan." Her voice was weighed down with sadness.

A cold feeling flooded over Arthur. Something was wrong.

"Where's Harry? Where's Claire? Are they here?" he asked hopefully, already knowing what the answer would be. Martin stood up, knocking his chair back roughly. He was angry.

"They didn't make it to the extraction point. They're still inside," Bay said quietly. Arthur had to swallow back the feeling of helplessness that hit him. He couldn't think about this yet, not now. He was struggling to hold on as it was. He closed his eyes and counted slowly to five.

When he felt strong enough, he opened his eyes. Wincing, he tried to move, flailing a little. He had to get up. Bay and Claire were still inside. He had to go back for them.

"Arthur, don't." Bay gently pushed him down.

"I have to go back. Can't leave them."

"Arthur, you don't understand. Things have changed since we found you."

Arthur looked at her in confusion. "What things? What do you mean? How long have I been out?"

"It's been over a month. You've been in an induced coma for most of it. You were really messed up. It's a miracle you survived. There were times when...when we didn't think you'd make it through the night." Bay spoke fast as if trying not to remember the feelings of those long days.

"A month," Arthur whispered in shock. No wonder he felt so terrible.

"You have a long road ahead of you before you will be going anywhere. Right now, you have to focus on recovering, getting strong. Focus on the fact that you're alive, and that's more than we had thought possible."

Arthur felt sick to his core. He had never felt so helpless before. Tears of pain and frustration welled up in his eyes. He tried to steady himself, to be strong. He didn't want Bay and Martin to see how weak he felt.

"OK, then." He smiled weakly, looking at his friends.

For the first time, he noticed that someone else had entered the tent—a tall man, wearing a long, dusty jacket, with dark shoulder-length hair, laced with gray. He was standing quietly in the corner, watching a VT, his back to Arthur. Bay noticed Arthur looking at the man and stood up.

"I guess it's time I introduced you." She walked over to the man, talking quietly to him. He nodded, turning to face Arthur for the first time.

Arthur looked at the man's lean face, his gaunt high cheekbones, and wide-spaced blue eyes. He had a messy beard streaked with black and gray and impossibly heavy brows. He wasn't a handsome man, by any standard, but somehow, despite his dishevelment, he looked distinguished. Arthur knew for a fact that he'd seen that face before somewhere and stared at him, confused.

Bay moved next to the man, putting her arm affectionately around his lanky shoulders. Together they turned to face Arthur.

"Arthur Ryan, meet my father, Abel." She smiled nervously.

The man walked over to the side of the bed. He looked down at Arthur, his familiar eyes crinkled with a warm smile.

"It is a pleasure to finally meet you, Mr. Ryan. I've been watching you for a long time, from afar. Oh, and my daughter has told me all about you."

"Dad!" Bay said mortified, blushing.

"You…you're Bay's father?" Arthur knew his expression must look ridiculous. How had he not known this? Bay was the rebel leader's daughter.

"Arthur! You're staring." Bay kicked him gently.

"That's all right, Bay," Abel said with a laugh. "I'm used to it. I have this effect on people the first time. Allow me to introduce myself, properly. I am indeed Abel, leader of the Red Rebels and most wanted man in the UZA. I am also the father of this lovely young lady." He nodded affectionately at Bay.

Arthur stared at him, his eyes studying Abel's unusual face intently. There was something about him, not just his likeness to Bay. He looked so familiar.

"You're Cain's bro…" He was going to say brother, but he knew that was the wrong word. He struggled to find a better term.

"Nemesis? Archenemy?" Abel said, smiling.

"Dad! Please!" Bay was crawling with embarrassment.

"You are quite right, Arthur. I am indeed Cain's clone twin, Abel, or to be precise…Abe L."

"No way!" Arthur's mouth dropped open so wide, he was probably drooling. "Abraham Lincoln. I knew it! I knew I recognized you." Despite himself, Arthur grinned.

"Indeed. So here we are Lincoln and Washington. Nice to finally meet you." The two of them stared at each other. The reincarnations of two great men, here in a scrappy tent in the Outside, in the midst of a new war. Arthur smiled.

"You're Abraham Lincoln's daughter. I should have guessed," he said to Bay.

She rolled her eyes, playfully.

"You know what they say. You can't choose your family." She grinned at her dad.

"Guys." Martin's voice sounded urgent, strained. Instantly the three of them were alert, turning to him. Martin swiped his hand in front of the VT, the screen expanding across the wall, the volume turned up. It was the news. Hope's voice sounded unnaturally excited for an operating system.

"This is it. The moment we have all been waiting for."

The White House appeared, floating austerely in the middle of the tent wall. An entourage of Secret Service agents stepped out onto the balcony, standing back in the shadows on both sides. Waiting. Arthur scanned their faces quickly, hoping to see Evan. But he wasn't among them.

The words INAUGURATION DAY flashed across the bottom of the image.

Arthur sat up, confused.

"This is it. Here they come."

The camera zoomed in closer as Kennedy walked onto the balcony, smiling and waving. Following close behind was Harry. She looked subdued, her eyes uncharacteristically blank. She stood directly behind Kennedy, smiling and waving blandly. There was nothing about her that seemed like the Harry he knew.

"Harry…" Martin's voice sounded choked. He recoiled from the VT, his face pale, as he turned and almost ran out of the tent.

A slight figure in pale blue had stepped out of the balcony shadows. The crowd went wild.

"There she is. The first lady!"

Arthur stared at her. She looked radiant. Gloriously happy and self-possessed. Nothing like the last time he had seen her. Arthur couldn't believe it was her. He wouldn't believe it. How could she smile like that?

Finally, after a long pause, a man stepped onto the balcony, walking forward into the sunlight. He was tall, handsome, and very much alive. Arthur gasped in shock. He was staring at himself. George Washington. The crowd went crazy, cheering and screaming with excitement, as he walked up next to Claire, his arm slipping around her waist, as they turned together to face the cameras. George raised his hand to his people and smiled.

Arthur gasped. "That's not possible."

"Look at us, Arthur," Abel said softly. "Anything's possible."

The camera zoomed in closer on their faces. Claire and George. Their perfect, happy faces. His face.

"People of the United Zones of America. I present to you, the first...and the fifty-seventh president...George Washington!"

Acknowledgments

I would like to thank the following amazing people for helping resurrect the once and future presidents. Extra special thanks to Susanna Francis, Aidan Healy and Iona Delander for your patient support and excellent feedback. For much-appreciated encouragement, a huge thank you to Frisco, Jane, John, Bob, Lindy and Marilee. And of course, to Natalie, Jack and Gemma—I couldn't have done this without you.

57404588R10168

Made in the USA
San Bernardino, CA
21 November 2017